P9-CRL-232

TALES OF THE SOUTHWEST

Also by Benjamin Capps

HANGING AT COMANCHE WELLS
THE TRAIL TO OGALLALA
SAM CHANCE
A WOMAN OF THE PEOPLE
THE BROTHERS OF UTERICA
THE WHITE MAN'S ROAD
THE TRUE MEMOIRS OF CHARLEY BLANKENSHIP
THE WARREN WAGONTRAIN RAID
WOMAN CHIEF
THE INDIANS
THE GREAT CHIEFS
THE HEIRS OF FRANKLIN WOODSTOCK

BENJAMIN CAPPS

Tales

of the Southwest

DD

A DOUBLE D WESTERN
DOUBLEDAY
New York London Toronto Sydney Auckland

A DOUBLE D WESTERN
PUBLISHED BY DOUBLEDAY
a division of Bantam Doubleday Dell Publishing Group, Inc.
666 Fifth Avenue, New York, New York 10103

DOUBLE D WESTERN, DOUBLEDAY,
and the portrayal of the letters DD
are trademarks of Doubleday, a division of
Bantam Doubleday Dell Publishing Group, Inc.

All of the characters in this book are fictitious
and any resemblance to actual persons, living or
dead, is purely coincidental.

Library of Congress Cataloging-in-Publication Data

Capps, Benjamin, 1922–
    Tales of the Southwest / Benjamin Capps.—1st ed.
    p.   cm.—(A Double D western)
    1. Southwestern States—Fiction. 2. Western stories. I. Title.
II. Series.
PS3553.A59T35   1990
913′.54—dc20   90-3574
CIP

ISBN 0-385-41444-7
Copyright © 1990 by Benjamin Capps
All Rights Reserved
Printed in the United States of America
January 1991
First Edition
BVG

10   9   8   7   6   5   4   3   2   1

To my grandson
Joseph Benjamin Capps

Contents

Introduction

When Daddy died in 1926, Mama was left with three small boys to support, ages two, four, and six. I was the one in the middle. Mama had been a schoolteacher before and during the war, so she rented out our house in the small town of Dundee and got a teaching job at Anarene, a still smaller town about thirty miles away. We lived in the schoolhouse; a fairly accurate picture of the situation can be found in the story "The Night Old Santa Claus Came."

I have been greatly influenced by Mama and much of it came from those four years we lived in the schoolhouse. She told us stories and recited poems she had memorized as a girl. Above all she helped me with reading, even in that year before I started to school, being always ready to help me with a hard word and to understand its meaning. I started to school at the age of five. Lest I be thought a mama's boy, I should mention that later on, working as a surveyor or in a machine shop, I always turned out to be low-level boss. For she had taught us by example always to do our best, to be dependable, and to meet our responsibilities.

About 1930 Mama married a rancher whose place was about three miles from the Anarene schoolhouse. Mama took us to school in her Model-A Ford the first year, then we rode horseback a couple of years, then we walked. We had chores to do around the place every day: chopping wood for heating and cooking, shucking corn, feeding the pigs, milking the cows twice a day, hoeing the garden and orchard in spring and summer. Because we were in the Great Depression and lived in an underdeveloped part of the country, we lived much like our ancestors may have lived a hundred years earlier.

But even though we had regular chores, we had spare time in the summer, on weekends, and on holidays. We had about fifty books—from the writings of Theodore Roosevelt to those of Horatio Alger, Jr., to those of William Shakespeare. I devoured them all once or twice and if some part was unclear, made up my own explanation to fill the gap. So while I lived part of the time on a small ranch in the Dust Bowl country of semi-arid West Texas, I lived another part rafting down the Mississippi with Mark Twain or watching some ancient Roman court with the Bard.

There was one long room upstairs, where we three boys slept. Sometimes when we were in bed and had blown out the kerosene lantern, I would tell my brothers stories, making them up as I went along. I remember one I called "The Search for the Great White Ape." (I had read *Tarzan of the Apes*.) I would carry my listeners along with the expedition while they escaped from the cannibals and crossed a crocodile-infested river; then, growing sleepy, I would say, "The captain held up his hand and made them be quiet. They could hear a distant moaning, like a poor woman in distress. To be continued . . ."

"What happened next, Ben?" "To be continued . . ." "What did they hear?" "To be continued . . ."

My younger brother Roy was actually a good poet for his age. The *Archer County News* printed one of his poems, "The Pirates." It probably is just as well that he gave it up. It's probably even harder to make a living with poetry than with fiction.

Anarene school was graduating pupils at this time after the eighth grade and sending them in a school bus to nearby towns. I went to Olney High School and then to Archer City High School. I did well in English and even better in geometry. In plane geometry I knew the answer to most problems at once and only needed to learn the steps the teacher wanted us to go through to work them. This aptitude would prove valuable to me in the future. In 1938, just a few days before my sixteenth birthday I graduated at Archer City. (There were only eleven grades in Texas public schools then.)

About June of '38 I went out to Lubbock, planning to enter Texas Tech that fall. I worked on a Double Cola route as a helper in delivering soda pop to a dozen small towns. Sometimes I got to drive the truck. The job paid me a dollar a day and board and room. The room was a cot in the rear of a small factory. As for college, I did not consider my dearest dream, creative writing. It seemed to me you had to be from New England or at least from a big city. I did consider studying the law. But Mama and other older advisers said that I was a country boy and Tech was a great agricultural school and that scientific agriculture was the wave of the future. So that was it; I enrolled in classes like Animal Husbandry and Dairy Manufacturing, but also some that would fit into another degree plan later, like freshman English, chemistry, and botany.

Between classes I worked for NYA, a federal program to help young people get the money to attend college. My work was sweeping classrooms with a push broom, a clumsy tool for getting around the legs of a desk, and sometimes I did odd jobs in the office of the Dean of Agriculture. Incidentally, if memory serves, the man in charge of NYA in Washington was a young fellow named Lyndon Baines Johnson, who would go on to other jobs later. I made thirty-five cents an hour and worked about ten hours a week. Mama sent me ten dollars or so two or three times. My room near the campus cost five dollars a month and was located in a basement. I was getting pretty hungry, so I took an additional job as a waiter and kitchen helper. The pay was all I could eat. But then, with studying and sweeping and working for meals, I was putting in some fourteen hours a day. I began to wonder if it was worth it to learn two dozen kinds of chicken diseases, their symptoms and prevention.

In the middle of the summer of '39 I quit school, hitchhiked back to Anarene, and, after catching up on sleep, joined the Civilian Conservation Corps. I was sent to Grand Junction, Colorado, on the western slope of the Rockies. Our camp, made up of several barracks, a mess hall, and headquarters building, was on the edge of town. We worked for the Grazier's Service of the Department of Interior. There is much public land in Colorado; there are national forests and national parks, but much of the public land is leased out to cattlemen. I found myself assigned to the surveying crew.

We did the surveying for a couple of stock tanks, which they called "ponds," for roads, for a telephone line across Douglas Pass out toward Utah, but mostly for locating things on the public domain, like an ice cutting and storing house on the Gunnison River. One boy went out with the camp engineer to make general plans for each project, and four or five of us went out in another truck to handle all the details. I progressed in the work from stake boy to rear chainman to head chainman. About my eighteenth birthday the boss of our crew was discharged, and I became boss, truck driver, instrument man, note taker.

The regular pay was thirty dollars a month plus board, room, and clothing. Twenty-two was sent home to the supposedly needy family, and the boy spent eight for tobacco, candy, shooting pool in the rec hall, going into town to the picture show. As boss surveyor I made thirty-six bucks, so I had fourteen to waste. I started going in to the roller skating rink and there met Marie Thompson. We became sweet on each other.

Mama had saved for me the money they had sent home. I sent for it and bought a '28 Model-A Ford for eighty-five dollars. Marie and I had a way to run around. We agreed to get married when I could settle down and support a wife.

I must skip over working in the District Grazier's office a couple of months, getting out of the CCC's, and surveying for the U.S. Corp of Engineers on a military airfield at Grand Junction, and briefly going into an unsuccessful chicken business with two buddies, one of which wrecked my car. Down at Denison, Texas, my two brothers were making big money working on a dam across Red River. I went home briefly to see Mama and my two little stepsisters, then to the dam site, a few miles north of Denison.

I immediately hired on as an assistant engineer for the principal dirt contractor. We were building what would be named "Texoma," one of the biggest man-made lakes in the world. I soon was detached from the main crew and assigned to the graveyard shift with a couple of rodmen to check grades in the large spillway and on the main dam and other fill areas. I was making about half as much as a truck driver, so I took the driving test and passed. These trucks were Sterlings and Westerns, huge snarling monsters that hauled twenty tons of dirt and rock per load.

We had a temporary layoff of drivers, so I went down to Greenville and surveyed a couple of months for a new army airfield. It was 1941, and it looked like we would be in a war with Germany. I was already registered for the draft. On a long shot I went over to Dallas and took the aviation cadet test. Somehow I passed and was sworn into the Army, but was told to wait and keep in touch because their training program was crowded.

I went back to Denison and started driving again. Marie and I were writing regularly, but our future seemed highly uncertain. In December the Japs plastered Pearl Harbor. I finally asked Marie to come on down and marry me. She was willing but, being pretty young, would have trouble getting her father's permission.

I remember clearly one night alone in Miller's Boarding House in Denison, looking out a second-story window. A strong feeling came over me, of frustration, of dissatisfaction with my life, mixed with a firm determination. I made a solemn promise to myself, one which I would never forget: if I lived through this war, I would become a writer some way or another.

Shortly afterward another problem came up. I wrecked a truck. I came down a steep grade toward the river and didn't make the sharp curve at the bottom. I went tumbling about a hundred yards down the hill, along with the truck and twenty tons of rock and dirt. I had a fractured skull, broken collarbone and shoulder blade, and cracks in my pelvic bone. I was in the hospital thirty-seven days, during which Marie came down from Colorado to cheer me up.

When I got out of the hospital, company insurance paid me a weekly wage while I was recuperating. We went up to Ardmore, Oklahoma, to get married, then out to Anarene so I could show off my bride. Shortly afterward the Army Air Corps wrote with orders to report for active duty.

The word was that in those hurried days they felt of you and if you were warm you passed the physical exam. That's about the physical they gave me. I felt the effects of my wreck in that year of 1943 while taking their rough physical training, and later when I got up around twenty thousand feet I felt a stinging sensation every place there was a broken bone.

I had intensive navigation training that year, as well as some meteorology, aerial gunnery, sending and receiving Morse code, optics, and military courtesy. I remember my first flight in an airplane; it was in the rear seat of an open-cockpit AT-6, facing backward with a .30-caliber machine gun practically in my lap.

In advanced navigation school we flew many training flights, four cadets and the instructor and pilot, day and night, in every direction from our field at Hondo, Texas. I remember landing at Meridian, Mississippi, and Las Vegas, Nevada. We practiced pilotage, dead reckoning, celestial, and using the radio compass.

Early in January 1944, they made me a second lieutenant, and I went to Anarene for a week or so to see my wife and folks and my new son, Ben Jr. Then I went to Tonapah, Nevada, to become part of a bombing crew. The ten crew members were all top notch, and our plane was a new B-24 Liberator. We shortly were on our way to Hickam Field, Hawaii.

On that flight I learned how big the Pacific Ocean is—two thousand miles just to Honolulu and Hickam and Pearl Harbor. After a few weeks there we were assigned to the 26th Squadron of the 11th Group of the Seventh Air Force and sent down across the International Date Line to Kwajalein in the Marshalls. Any combat veteran could write a book on his experiences, so it is necessary here to leave out most of the details. From Kwajalein we struck south to Jaluit and north to Wake and we staged through Eniwetok to strike west to Truk.

Then we moved northwest to Guam from which we struck back at Truk, east to Marcus, west to Yap, and north to Chichi Jima, Haha Jima, and Iwo Jima. We went over Iwo more than twenty times before any American marines or infantry saw it. Our old patched B-24 brought back a record number of bullet and flack holes one time—sixty-three. We saw some friends burn up four miles high over targets.

In the late spring of 1945 we had completed forty-one missions, and they sent us back to the States. Marie and I spent a couple of weeks at Miami Beach. Then I had hardly got started on another training program when the U.S. dropped the bombs and Japan gave up. I immediately put in for a discharge.

My determination about writing was as firm as ever. I entered the University of Texas at Austin in the fall of 1945. Besides the various courses such as Spanish and psychology required in a liberal arts plan, I took these writing courses: Exposition, Narration and Description, Creative Writing, Short Story Writing, Advanced Short Story Writing, Conference Course in Creative Writing, which I repeated twice for credit, and a thesis, which was a novel. In journalism I took these courses: Reporting, News Editing, Advanced Reporting and Ethics, Feature Writing, and Magazine Article Writing. By being one of the hardest-working students in school, I made Phi Beta Kappa.

We added another member to the family at Austin, a baby girl we named Kathleen Marie. I had sold four articles to magazines for forty dollars or less each and one short story for sixty dollars. It was obvious that the magazines were not ready for me.

I applied for and got a job as instructor at Northeastern State College of Oklahoma at Tahlequah, starting in the fall semester, 1949. I taught two sections of freshman English and all the journalism required for a minor, as well as sponsoring the school newspaper. Tahlequah had been the western capital of the Cherokee Nation, and that tribe founded the school. We had mostly non-Indian students. It was interesting work, but, especially because of the weekly school paper, I had hardly any free time to get any writing done.

They advanced me to assistant professor in 1951, but I quit anyway and we moved to Paris, Texas, where I spent full time writing. I didn't sell a thing. After a few months, broke again, we moved to west Dallas, and I worked for Chance Vought Aircraft, first as a student machinist, then a milling machine operator, then as a tool and die maker. We added another son to the family, Mark Victor.

We moved to Grand Prairie to be close to my job, and, after some three years at Chance Vought, I quit them to work at various tooling job shops in the area, becoming lead man and sometimes foreman. During some nine years I wrote mostly short stories, not realizing that it was hopeless because of the decline in the market. Three great weekly family magazines, *Saturday Evening Post, Collier's*, and *Liberty*, all using short stories, folded during the postwar years. Others either folded or quit using short stories. By 1961 I had written about sixty short stories, of which one had been published. In fact, most of them had been lost or thrown away.

We had saved enough money, so I quit my job again, concentrating this time on novels. Late in 1962 I published a soft-cover Western with Ballantine. Since then awards and recognition have come my way, but not much money, for both book-length fiction and nonfiction books.

I still have a real fondness for the short story. It's somewhere between the novel and lyric poetry. It's more concentrated than longer fiction and should have a single theme or impression or revelation about human life.

It is plain that a knowledge of human nature, of what a person might do when faced with certain circumstances, is extremely important to a writer of any kind of fiction. One can see from the brief biography here that I have seen various aspects of life. I have lounged on the beaches at Miami and Waikiki and also waded in a muddy stock tank on a ranch. I met Lady Bird Johnson one time at Austin and Joe Louis, the "Brown Bomber," one time in Chicago; and I lived with young men from the poorest families in the CCC's. I have flown many thousands of miles in an airplane and also ridden horseback to school.

But one has a great head start on life experiences through reading during the younger years. It seems to help in understanding motivation and in seeing what kind of events might make a story.

My courses in creative writing have helped me, but it does not take long to learn the general idea of abstractions such as "situation" and "conflict" and "development" and "resolution." The real help comes from being required to write a certain quantity of material, to hear and see it criticized, and to take part in the criticizing of the efforts of others. In the process one sees whether an idea is dressed in effective specifics so that it affects the reader.

One possibility in the technique of fiction is sometimes overlooked: irony, which is the effect of having two views of the same thing. Simple irony, such as calling a chubby guy "slim" may be slightly humorous, but the powerful irony is a matter of conditions or events. One may see irony in some stories in this volume. "A Secret of Military Significance" has the same idea as Walt Whitman's "O Captain! My Captain!" "Cimarron, the Killer" has irony in the very title when the reader understands the situation.

It was natural that I might turn toward the "Western" in my writing, as I have done in the case of nine published novels. My grandfather Capps was a mustanger who went out into West Texas with a gang of young men in the 1870s to capture wild horses, then bring them back east to break to the saddle or harness. My father in the early years of this century had a contract breaking and training horses for the huge Waggoner Ranch, the DDD's. That ranch is the setting I had in mind in the story "The Meanest Horses in the Country." But I have not been much interested in the standard, or formula, Western; it seems too simple and repetitious. More interesting is the mental or emotional conflict between people or inside one person. Some good short stories merely reveal some aspect of universal human nature in a unique setting or situation.

Generally a story has more sense of unity if it has a single narrator to tell the story, either a person in the story or an invisible observer. The writer may get around this by presenting fictional documents or letters, which may be written by different people. This handling of point-of-view may be seen in three of the stories here.

I have a tendency toward humor in writing, and that can be seen in two stories here. Perhaps it is a defense against getting old. That idea reminds me of my good friend Dorothy Marie Johnson, who lived in Missoula, Montana. She wrote such serious stories as "The Man Who Shot Liberty Valance" and "A Man Called Horse" but in her private life teased and laughed a lot. She believed that life always brings some difficulties and pain and frustration; one can cry about them or laugh about them. But it's better to laugh. She called herself the "Wicked Witch of the West." She became a semi-invalid and hired a girl to live with her; she called this helper "my seeing-eye girl." She said that after reading my story "Crime and Punishment" she and her seeing-eye girl went right out to the grocery store and bought a bunch of grapes. I took it as a considerable compliment.

The reader will notice several uses of children and animals in these stories. It is impossible to say exactly why certain things crop up in the imagination of a fiction writer, but we can say that the motivation of these kinds of characters is relatively simple. Sometimes it presents a little puzzle to the reader as to just what that motivation is, as in "Cimarron, the Killer."

Several stories, such as "Ruthy," are reminiscent of those of Hamlin Garland in settings and characters. The influence undoubtedly came through Mody Boatright, a great folklorist and teacher who insisted on the validity of a country setting or any other setting which the young writer might know about. In fact I believe the fiction writer serves an important moral function in showing the basic humanity in strange or unfamiliar human beings.

A Secret
of Military Significance

Note by Censor
Henry Smith
1st Lieutenant

I am unable to read this letter. Some questioning of personnel who appear, and/or claim, to have American Indian blood, indicates that it may be written in the syllabary symbols developed by a Cherokee Indian named Sequoya. It appears certain that Private Tso-o-wa knows no military secrets of significance. This question—whether a private knows any appreciable military secrets—is the reason for this note, or explanation to the proper authorities, in regards to my action in passing this letter.

I have had severe instructions from my superior, Captain L. D. Banks, in regards to passing anything suspicious, and understand his instructions and orders concerning censorship to relate primarily to the question: Does the enlisted man in question know any secrets of military significance? Having consulted the cryptographic officer at Battalion Headquarters, an officer who was a lawyer in private life, he said that the strange marks or writing do not seem to be any code and maybe might be considered harmless. He agreed informally that the issue is paramount if a private enlisted man could possibly know and pass on any information of military significance.

Regulation number 2306, dated January 14, 1918, specifically states that letters which are doubtful should not be passed, but this refers to illiterate or semi-literate writings which might inadvertently betray information. And in regards to writings which cannot be understood by the censor in question, it implies that it is a possible exception if the enlisted man in question could not possibly know any significant information of military significance and this letter may be completely harmless. I cannot determine if this letter is illiterate or semi-literate. Furthermore, Regulation 4139, paragraph 7, of July 7, 1918, further confirms the principle of the ignorance of letter writers being a factor for consideration, as the case may be, and rests by implication on the best sincere judgment of the officer performing censor duty.

The above-cited regulation, paragraph 14, states clearly that rumors of peace or expectations of peace shall in no case be a cause for relaxing military discipline or procedures. There are strong rumors of peace today, however, I wish to state categorically that I do not claim any defense which might be required from me in this matter on rumors of peace.

I have applied seven times in writing to be transferred out of censorship duty, especially in hospitals, as well as many times I have applied informally to my superiors and others, as they would testify in the advent that a Court of Inquiry or court-martial would consider the question of my proper performance of duty, according to rules and regulations. I could serve as a mess officer or as adjutant of an infantry company, because of my educational background, and would work extra hours to learn my duties if I could only be transferred from censor duty. As I have stated in my seven applications, the men write private things and it is difficult to ignore these things in question. As I have stated informally in conversations with senior officers, I cannot see everything in a letter, so I can ink out or cut out what must be censored, and at the same time not even read what is shameful for me to see. It is shameful because it is not addressed to the censorship officer in question.

In addition, should my actions be called in question by proper authority, I wish to state that a nurse has called a superior officer an "idiot" if I did not pass the letter as she demanded (she being a second lieutenant and the officer in question being a first lieutenant). She has also threatened to use physical violence against me, and even against general officers at higher headquarters, if the letter does not go to the address in Oklahoma. I suspect that she has signed the letter for the private in question and addressed it, though she does not admit to having any Indian or Negro or Mexican blood. The surgeon has stated to me, in the presence of witnesses, that the nurse is an excellent nurse and is suffering from the experiences of her position.

I would like to state categorically that her pleadings and threats have not influenced me in the proper performance of my duties. Nor have rumors of peace. I have taken into consideration certain aspects not in the regulations of the Army of the United States, namely the possible value of a private message from a soldier to a private citizen of America, i.e., merely the value to the soldier himself and to the recipient of the letter, but I rest my case on the fact that this enlisted man in question could not know any secrets of military significance. I therefore order that the accompanying letter be posted by regular military mail.

I hereby order to pass this letter, and take my consequences. In the name of God, I request to be relieved of censorship duty. I heard stories about what he did up there in the mud, as did all those young men his age. I heard he is nineteen, which I am older by nearly four years, and well educated. I am from Gutherie with kin in Louisiana and Texas both, but hereby certify that I do not ask any special privileges from my region of the country. But I do my duty as an officer and a gentleman with a commission stamped by President Woodrow Wilson. I order this letter to go through. It is a mystery to me what the marks mean, however I certify and order that it does not mean any military secrets of any significance. Sincerely yours,
HENRY SMITH, 1st. Lieutenant

Somewhere in France
November 9, 1918

From Tso-o-wa, gone to be a soldier, to my father and mother and little brother and sister. And to some man who holds a grudge against me among the Cherokees, and others, and to anyone who thought about me.

Now. I am writing this letter to you. The preacher, he will read it to you. Or Miss Dodson at Echota that was my teacher. She will read to you. To all the people I said.

Now. My father, you said I would write what I saw and what I did, but I did not have time. I was busy. Now I have time in this last place.

Three preachers come here to help. One wears a black dress, and they give me paper and a pen because I can write.

Now. The ocean is larger than we understand. It is more than the Carolina People all the way to the Oklahoma People. It is empty water, full of mystery. I cannot tell how big it is. We crowded side by side in the big boat. The people here cannot speak English. They want us here. They cheer and smile. When they talk it sounds like they have a cold in the nose. Ha! Ha! It is for Big Joe to laugh about.

Now. It rained all the time up there and too much mud. We ran toward them the first time. They shot me in the arm that time. Some men try to help you every time you get shot.

I have thought in these months about the old Cherokee warriors in the past. What they did to serve and protect the People and how they acted and what they had in mind. I know they were brave heroes, but it is hard to understand things which happened a long time ago. When I think in their same kind of thoughts, it makes me feel proud.

Now. The second time we ran toward them they shot me in the jaw. They shot my face mask. The air smells sour and burns your mouth and throat and chest.

Now. I saw a Creek boy and we wanted to talk. They cut his arm off from poison. He could not speak Cherokee and I could not speak Muskogee. We use English to say the white man is crazy and his war is too big. Ha! Ha! It is for Big Joe to laugh about.

Now. It always rains up there. The last time we ran toward them they did not fire till we got to the gap in the barbed wire. They do not shoot only one bullet. It is like bees. They shot me in the stomach. I went on. They shot me from the front, not the back. Tell my littler brother all my times I got shot it was all three times from the front and never from the back.

Now. This last place is a bad place. The men die on the beds here. I do not like to hear the ones who make noise when they die. A nurse calls me Chief. She talks to me because she is from Tulsa, and she goes out alone to weep when the men die.

Now. Go to the young man in Tahlequah I had the fight with over the girl and read him part of this. Tell him I forgive him and I want him to forgive me. Then go to the store where the trader said I owe still four dollars. Pay him. Every person you think I argued with, tell them I forgive them and ask them if they will forgive me.

Now. A night went by and it is November 10, this year. I am too tired to write. They told me something. If they give me a medal for the

German machine gun, they will send it. I want my mother to keep it till she is ready to turn it loose, then give it to my little sister. I want to finish this letter.

Now. November 11, this year. I can write some more to you. It is late morning and they ring bells in the tall churches over in town.

But the eyes in my heart see the time of year and the colored hills of that country where you are. The sugar maples are yellow, the holly and sumac are red as blood, the cedar are deep green. They stretch away many miles to misty distance. Please use your eyes to look sometime at the colored hills for me.

Now. I want my father and little brother to shake hands for me and kiss both my mother and little sister. I hope in years coming you laugh a lot and cry only a little, and get along all right.

Thank you.

From Tso-o-wa.

Ruthy

The little girl, not more than two years old, peered intently into a five-gallon can which sat on the smoke house step. The can was half full of lye soap cut in great brown chunks, and the child could barely touch the soap with one stubby finger. She strained. She pushed up on one toe to reach farther into the can. Her little, round body looked short because of the baggy sunsuit. Her hair was yellow and curly, bright in the morning sun. Beside the weathered boxing planks of the smokehouse wall and the hard-packed dirt of the backyard, her hair was a halo of fine-spun gold.

The old woman continued to look into the washtub as she spoke, half to herself, half to the girl, pretending that she was old enough to understand. "I'll be glad when your ma gets here. I'm getting shed of you this evening." Her voice was monotonous, her words accented by her regular, slow labor on the rub board. "I'll be glad when she comes to get you. Other people gad around, and I get to raise their kids." The old woman looked skinny with her back bent and her sharp elbows jerking out behind as she rubbed.

It had been shady by the smokehouse when she started washing. Now the sun was on her. Sweat fell from her chin into the gray soap suds. She wrung the water from a pair of faded blue denim overalls, clumsily, her bony fingers straining at the heavy twist of cloth, then dropped it into another tub on the wash bench. She picked up the bottom of her dress, wiped the sweat from her face, squinted at the girl, who had tilted the can over to reach down inside.

"Get outa that soap."

The little girl might not have heard. The woman repeated, louder, more insistently, "Get outa that soap!"

The little girl turned her head up slowly, looking at the old woman with large, innocent eyes, still digging her tiny square hands into the can.

The old woman made her voice harsh. "I said for you to get outa that soap!"

The little hands stayed in the can, fumbling. The little head again turned up, her face responding to the repeated words as if it were all a game. Her artless bud of a mouth, her impudent nose, and her crinkling eyes seemed to ask devilishly, "What will you do if I don't?"

"You little rascal! You ain't as dumb as you make out." She picked the child up, with a tenderness that contrasted with her harsh words, and swished the small hands back and forth in the blueing water to wash off the greasy brown soap. The little girl laughed and splashed at the blueing water.

"As if you wasn't enough bother to your old granny already without just *trying* yourself." She dried the child's hands on her own dress bottom and went back to her rub board. (She had done the child's things first, before the water got dirty: dresses, panties, rompers, sunsuits, the new bonnet with green polka dots and lace on front. She had already starched them and hung them out, so they would have plenty of time to get the sun.) She rubbed the heavy pieces one by one and plopped them into the rinse water, whining to the child and to herself without interrupting her work.

"Raise all my own kids; now I got to raise other people's kids. Other people gad around, and I got to raise their kids. I got to clean up after ther brats. And me a old lady, worked hard all my life, and now I got to wash and arn and clean up after somebody else's kid. I got to take keer of ther kid and me a old lady. Raised seven of my own; now I got to do for other people's kids."

She was hanging clothes on the line when the old man came up from the barn at noon. He came out through the broom weeds toward the clothesline without her hearing him, because she was still complaining, and she saw him only when the little girl ran toward him. He was a tall, stooped man with a weather-red face. His chin was small and his Adam's apple stuck out prominently below it. On his mouth was a pleasant, naive grin.

"I hope a stranger don't never slip up behind you and you talking to yourself like that," he said. "He would think you was crazy."

"Get out of here and leave me be," she said. "I want to get this washing out."

"You don't know what you want," the old man told her. "I believe I know more about what you want than you do yourself." The foolish grin never left his face.

(He was a good poker player and it was partly because of his looks. He played with the boys over in Hooker; he would sit there looking at his hand and grinning. The boys would put on their poker faces and bet the limit; then when the betting was over, the old man would drag the pot. It took years for some of them to learn that his winning wasn't just fool's luck, but was a kind of natural shrewdness about people; and it took them years more to find that his grin wasn't put-on, that he looked exactly the same whether he had a straight flush or a pair of treys. He never went home without two or three dollars more than he came with. Now that all the kids were grown and gone from home, he hated to leave the old woman alone at night, so he played only once a month, on the first Saturday. If that day came and he said nothing about it, she would remind him, "Ain't this your poker night?" Then she would fuss at him: "All you think about is yourself. You lay out half the night over there in Hooker, and me here at home without nobody." So he would grin at her and say, "I'll stay home. I better be here in case you think of something new to fuss about." But she would have none of it. "No, you go on. I'm lucky to be shed of you once in a while.")

Out under the clothesline were a few grass burs and the little girl stepped on one. She stood still, looking solemn but not crying, with one tiny bare foot cocked up in front. The old man picked her up and removed the sticker. Then he set her to laughing by pitching her into the air over his head. Her scream turned into bubbling laughter each time when he caught her. Her yellow hair tumbled in shining disarray.

"Is dinner ready?" he asked the old woman.

"I never figured to fix anything. We can snack. Myrt and Lester will stay for supper, and I'll have to fix special for them, so it ain't no use to fix a big dinner."

"Reckon they'll come in this evening?"

"They better come in. I'm getting tired of working my fingers to the bone taking keer of her kid, and them off gadding around."

The old man was standing behind her, holding the little girl on his arm and grinning his little grin. "You never raised no objections when they left her here."

"I never knowed she was going to be so much trouble."

"Naw," the old man said, "you don't know nothing about how much trouble kids is, do you?"

The old woman snorted. She accented her speech by whipping the blue denims in the air to straighten them before hanging them on the line. "I don't see where Myrt had no honeymoon due her, no ways. She had one honeymoon. All this divorcing business! A woman can't live with one man, I don't see she's got another honeymoon due her."

He spoke to the little girl. "You hungry, Ruthy? Let's go in and see if we can find something to eat."

"She's so sleepy she can't hold her eyes open," the old woman said. "I been trying to get all her clothes dry so's I could arn 'em this evening."

The old man took the little girl into the house and set her on a box at the square oilcloth-covered dining table. He spread the halves of a biscuit with butter and apple jelly and poured a glass of sweet milk. The little girl ate eagerly. She stuffed her mouth and kicked her tiny heels against the box as she ate. The old man went into the kitchen to fry himself an egg. He heard the heels kick slower and slower. When he came back in, she was asleep with her head over on a piece of the jelly and bread. He picked her up clumsily.

The old woman came in. "Law," she said. "Look at that face. Ain't you got no more sense than to put her to bed and her face dirty? You'll have the flies just swarming after her."

He carried her in and put her on the bed in the front room, and the old woman followed with a wet washcloth. She wiped off the little girl's face and sticky hands. The child's chunky body was completely limp, her mouth slightly open and her eyes not quite closed, though she slept. Against the cotton of the quilt her skin was fine in texture. Her hair, flung out against the faded colors, was living gold.

(It was the old woman's wedding-ring quilt that the child lay on. The old woman had dug it out of the quilt trunk in the big closet, where it

had been packed away with a dozen others, unused for years. It had
been on the bottom, but the old woman dug it out. "It don't matter,"
she told herself. "She'll wet it, but it don't matter. I ain't got no use for
anything nice nowadays anyway." The fancy pattern and the tedious
quilting stitches were as good as they had always been, but the colors
were pretty near gone. It had been thirty-five . . . nigh forty years.
She had made it before the twins were born, between Lettie and the
twins.) The old woman brushed a strand of hair back out of the sleeping child's face.

"Don't she put you in mind of Myrt, lying there?" the old man said.
"I mean when Myrt was about that size."

"No, she don't."

"She's got hair like Myrt had, seems to me."

"No, she ain't. Myrt's wasn't that way."

"It was about that color, and pretty that way."

"A lot you know about it," the old woman said. "You had to brush it
and get the tangles out, you wouldn't think it was so pretty."

They went back into the kitchen to eat, and he asked, "You reckon
Myrt and Lester will make a go of it?"

"They ought to. Ther two of a kind, if you ask me."

"Ain't that fine way to talk about your own daughter."

"I never said a thing."

"You said they was two of a kind, her and Lester."

"That ain't nothing. I *could* say plenty. Leaving her kid here for me,
and her off gadding around in Oklahoma. She's done been to California and I don't know where all, and always leaving her rightful work on
somebody else."

(He started to say, "You sound like a jealous woman, instead of a
woman talking about her daughter. You sound like a poker player trying to run a bluff by bragging about your own hand and running down
the other feller's hand, all the time knowing you haven't got a chance
of winning, and that ain't the way to play poker." But he didn't say
anything.)

After they had eaten their snack, she set up her ironing board across
the backs of two cane-bottom chairs. While she ironed, they talked
about Myrt and Lester. They wondered if Lester would make a good
stepdaddy. Every time the old man said anything, she would disagree.
She was ironing the new sunbonnet she had made for Ruthy.

"That won't keep no sun out of her eyes," the old man said, "not
with all that lace on there, it won't."

"Why, I reckon it will," she said. She stopped ironing a minute and looked at him without blinking an eye. "I reckon it will."

"Not with all them little holes in there, it won't. How come you didn't use some chambray or something that would keep the sun out of her eyes?"

"A lot you know about it," she said. "You ain't never made any bonnets."

The old man grinned. "When Myrt gets here I aim to ask her if we can keep Ruthy for good; you like to make things for her so much."

The old woman didn't answer.

"You think I'm joshing you but I ain't," he said.

She didn't speak to him again until Myrt and Lester came, about the middle of the afternoon. They stopped in front of the house and honked the fancy, two-note horn on Lester's car and then came in talking loudly, greeting the old man and the old woman and telling about their trip. "If we never had a time," Myrt said. "Tell 'em what a time we had, honey."

"You said it, Myrt. We had a time. If we never painted that old town red, I don't know what we done."

"Where all did you all go?" the old man asked.

"Oh, we never went any place else, Pa," Myrt said. "We stayed right in Oklahoma City. But we had a time, I tell you."

"None of that coming back around Hooker here where they know us," Lester said. "We knew better than to come around here and get shivereed. Old hands at this marrying like Myrt and me knows better than to get caught in any of these shiveree parties."

Myrt giggled. "Ain't he a card. He ain't bashful a bit, Lester ain't."

They sat in the dining room, because the old woman said it was cooler, and talked. The old man said, "Myrt, did you leave anything here when you was here before? Did you miss anything?"

"Why, I don't think so, Pa. I left my black purse at Lettie's, but I meant she should have it; it was about worn out. Did you all find something of mine?"

"No," he said. "I just wondered if you missed anything."

"Now, Pa, if you found anything of mine, I want it."

"No, I was only kidding you, Myrt." He turned to the old woman. "Hadn't we ought to wake Ruthy up, Ma? She's slept over two hours."

"I 'spect so."

"Why, how is Ruthy?" Myrt asked. "Is she all right? Has she been good?"

"Yes," the old woman said. "But she's a handful for a old lady like me to take keer of." She went in and picked the little girl up and brought her into the dining room.

The little girl was rubbing her eyes. She clung with one hand to the front of her grandmother's dress as Myrt took her.

"Come here," Myrt demanded. "If you ain't a sleepy head. Look, there's your new daddy." Myrt laughed. "I don't believe she likes you, honey. She sure ain't smiling at you."

"Aw, she'll learn to like me," Lester said. "All the ladies like me."

"If you ain't a card," Myrt said. She slapped herself on the hip.

The old woman finished her ironing and began supper. She listened as Lester told the old man about his job in Dallas selling used cars.

"It's all in knowing your business," he said. "You got to be a real operator, see? It ain't like selling something that's got a certain price. You got to get the top dollar when you sell and the same way when you buy; you got to get it for the least dollar you can. You might make a deal one way for one feller and higher or lower for some other feller. It's all in being a real operator, see? If you know what you're doing, you can make some money. I'm going to have a car lot of my own inside of no time; that's what I'm going to do. If a man is a real operator, he can do good."

"Lester's going to have a lot of his own inside of no time," Myrt put in.

"And you got to understand class, too," Lester went on. "Sometimes you can put a lot of class on an old wreck just by putting on a few shiny doodads. You might jazz a car up where you could get fifty dollars more just by painting the wheels yellow. It's all in knowing class when you see it and being a real operator."

"Lester's one guy that knows class when he sees it," Myrt said.

The old man grinned at Lester all the time but made no sign of agreeing or disagreeing.

Myrt wanted to get away before dark, so the old woman laid supper early. She put her good white tablecloth on the table. Ruthy wanted her box moved over by her grandmother. "You little rascal," the old woman said, "you needn't be making up so to your old granny. I'm getting shed of you tonight. Here, you want a drumstick?"

There was fried chicken and gravy, hot biscuits and butter, black-eyed peas, fried potatoes, candied sweet potatoes, buttermilk, blackberry cobbler. (The old woman was a good cook. She still remembered how to cook for a large family.)

"Ma," Myrt said, "I got a proposition to put to you."

"How's that?"

"Well, me and Lester was talking about it. We ain't got no house in Dallas and we don't want to rent right now because we might build and we ain't sure. What I'm getting at is we'll probably live in a hotel for a while. Would you want to keep Ruthy for a few weeks more, do you think?"

The old woman looked up, wide-eyed. Then she stared down at her plate. "Why . . . I don't know . . ."

"What it is," Myrt said, "we'd have to live in a tourist court instead of a hotel if we take her right now, and I just can't stand them tourist courts."

"How long would it be?" the old woman asked. She picked at the black-eyed peas in her plate with her fork.

"Well, a few weeks. Not over two months anyway, would it, honey? We just got to make up our minds what we're going to do, build or what."

"Well, I reckon we *could* . . ." She looked at the old man, abashed.

"Naw," he said. "We better not, Myrt. I think you ought to take her. We better not keep her anymore."

"Oh, good-*ness*, Pa," Myrt said. "You don't have nothing to do with it. Why don't you let Ma say?"

"Well, I don't know," the old woman said; she seemed to be appealing to the old man, but he only grinned at her. (He was the boss at that moment. You wouldn't have thought it if you had just met him, because he looked simple and harmless and weak. But the old woman knew better; she had lived with him forty-one years and she had come to be not less willful, but to have a faith in him, that he knew what she wanted and that he would get it for her. Their desires and purposes through the years had come to be fitted together like the fingers of two laced hands.) She went on, "I don't know, Myrt. I reckon we better not."

"Well, I can ask Lettie, I guess," Myrt said. "The way she griped last time I had her keep Ruthy, I hate to ask her. You'd of thought I was trying to borrow a bunch of money off of her."

"Well, she's done got the two of her own," the old woman said.

"Three ain't much more trouble than two, Ma. She could keep Ruthy awhile and not hardly notice the difference, looks like. Pa, why don't you write her and ask her if she would? Lettie'll do anything you ask her to."

The old man shook his head. "Naw, if I write Lettie, I'll tell her *not* to. You ought to keep Ruthy yourself. She's your'n."

"Oh, good-*ness,* Pa. You and your ideas about raising kids. If you ain't the stubbornest thing. What if you had a chance to live in a hotel and had to live in a tourist court instead?"

The old man grinned. "She's your'n. She ain't our kid."

"Why, it ain't that we don't want her, Pa! Good-*ness!* Lester just thinks the world of her already, don't you, honey?"

"Sure, I just think the world of her already."

"If you want her, you better keep her," the old man said, "and not be leaving her around places and coming to get her, and leaving her and coming to get her."

The old woman kept stirring the black-eyed peas in her plate.

"This sure is good chicken," Lester said, "good as you can get in Oklahoma City."

They were in a hurry to leave. The old woman went in to pack the little girl's bag. She folded the freshly ironed clothes carefully. Some of Ruthy's things were right pretty. She put the two fancy dresses and the bonnet on top so they wouldn't be messed all up. She was good at ironing little ruffles and things that had to be starched, and she hated to see it messed all up.

The old woman said good-bye to them and went on into the kitchen. The old man went out to the car. She would have gone out to the car with them—she usually did—but she didn't feel so pert tonight. She scraped the dishes up and cleaned off the table, then set a dishpan of water on the cookstove and began to wash dishes. Twenty minutes passed. She thought they had gone. Then she heard the car start and finally the front door screen slam as the old man came in.

He called to her: "Come see what I got."

She came out of the kitchen drying her hands on her apron.

"I called ther hand," he said, grinning, "and I taken the whole pot." On one arm he held the little girl; in the other hand, her bag of clothes. "I made 'em give her up definite, too. I made 'em both say it cler and plain; she's our'n. There ain't going to be no more of them coming back to get her."

The old woman might have been trying to think of something fussy to say. She stood there, neck straight, eyes wide, wrinkled cheeks motionless. She blinked her eyes once. Then she tried to swallow. The effort of it broke the stiffness of her face, and all at once she gave in. She turned from him and hid her face in her bony arms.

The old man stood there grinning and watching her back shake.

The little girl toddled across the floor, past her grandmother and into the kitchen, making a low humming baby noise. In a moment the old woman followed and gathered the little girl up and folded her tightly against her breast.

The Last Bearden

They stopped at the freeway and stood uncertainly, watching the heavy traffic zoom by and peering directly across it where the skyline of the city rose in the smog two miles away. The man was old, maybe seventy. A big, bony nose dominated his face. His shoulders were hunched, hawk-like, under a loose blue denim shirt. The right front pocket of his baggy overalls bulged and swung with his movement, as if it contained a piece of iron.

His companion was a young girl, maybe fourteen, dressed in a red cotton blouse tucked into blue jeans. Her hair was brown, short, and straight. She carried a paper sack in one hand, swinging it by its wadded top, and in the other hand a black patent leather purse. Her breasts were beginning to swell under the blouse, but the blue eyes she turned to the old man were those of a trusting child. "Grandpap," she said, "you think we should of taken the bus clear into town?"

He thought it over carefully before he answered. "No, Angie Baby, like I said, we don't know but what Amos Bearden might have a spy at the bus station. He probably don't, but we don't know."

"You don't think he knows we're coming, do you? How could he?"

"No, he don't know we're coming today, but he knows we're bound to come. An' you know how it is when you go into a place on a bus. Right away the news is all over town."

The freeway was like a savage barrier in front of them, and they studied it as they talked. The two wide concrete slabs swept in a great arc, the slabs separated and bordered by tailored strips of grass. The old man would pick up a roaring diesel truck with his eyes far to the left and follow it until it disappeared to the right.

The girl said, "I believe this is the damndest road I ever saw, Grandpap. Don't you think so?"

"Don't say 'damndest,' Angie Baby, even if you hear me say it." He dreamed a minute, then went on. "Here of late it seems like I keep remembering things that happened a long time ago. You know what this road puts me in mind of?"

"What, Grandpap?"

"Well, a time when I was littler than you. Maybe I was eight or ten. It was about the time they had that war when Teddy Roosevelt was in the newspaper. Anyway, it was the first long hunt I went on with my pap; that was your great-grandpap, Angie Baby. We came to Dead Squaw Crik and it was flooded away out of its banks and we couldn't cross over, but Pap said, 'We're in no hurry; we'll figure out some way to get across.' So he stuck a stick up in the mud at the edge of the water, and we watched it maybe three hours, and sure enough the water was falling. We camped there four days until the water went down, then we rolled up our britches and loaded our gear on our backs and waded on across."

"You think if we set down here and wait the cars might slow down?"

"They might. Anyway, we can see." He sat down carefully on the grass, with much grunting as he arranged his old bones. "Come set around on this side, Angie Baby. I'm going to load up my gun. We're running into lots of people, and we can't ever tell when we might meet Amos Bearden."

When she had sat down beside him, he took from his pocket a heavy single-action .45 revolver, hiding it down between them. The gun was pitted with rust on the outside, but the action clicked smoothly as he pulled the trigger twice, then swung out the cylinder. From another pocket he took a box of cartridges and shook six into his lap. The heavy shells looked small in his big bony hand. He slipped them one by one into the cylinder, clicked the gun shut, and put it back in his deep overalls pocket.

"Grandpap, you want me to carry that in my purse?"

"No, it's all right, Angie Baby."

"Well, you let me carry the bread and meat and the newspaper picture of Amos Bearden, and you let me carry ten dollars. Why don't you want me to carry the return bus tickets?"

"I'll carry them, Angie Baby. You want to carry some more money besides the ten dollars?"

"No, I don't guess so."

They sat in silence watching the traffic going sixty. The trucks snarled like animals. They could feel the wind whip from the big vans. "I believe one of them big trucks would run over you and never know it," he said. "If anybody was going to live in a town like this all the time, that's what he would need to go around in, one of them big trucks, or a bus."

"You wouldn't get run over," she agreed, "but you would have to learn to drive it."

He chuckled.

"I believe anybody would have to be nearly crazy even to live around a big town like this," she said.

"Well, me and you will get where we're going on foot. We've been over many a hill on foot, haven't we, Angie Baby?"

"Yes, and mountains too."

The traffic was less heavy. They rose and stood nearer the concrete slab. He bent down over her to be heard above the noise. "It's thinning out some, all right. Now, Angie Baby, when I say 'go' you run for that grass in the middle. Don't stop and don't look back at me." He judged the vehicles carefully, then just as a red truck whizzed in front of their noses, he yelled, "Go!"

She made it to the dividing strip and turned. The old man was barely missed by a blue sedan, the driver of which yelled something. They made it in the same manner across the other half of the freeway.

They came down the grassy bank and into an area spotted with big warehouses. They kept their direction by the skyline of the city rising dimly in the smog. Some of the streets were dirt and some paved.

"Grandpap," she said, "it's going to be hard to find Amos Bearden, there are so many people."

"We'll have to keep our eyes open."

"It may take us a week to find him, there are so many people and so many places to hide."

"We'll find him, Angie Baby, if it takes a month. Me and you are Tuckers, and we don't give up because something takes a month, or longer than that. I won't live forever, and me and you are going to finish it while we got the advantage. Then we can have peace of mind, and our folks that's sleeping, they can rest in peace. I don't aim to pass away and leave you alone with a Bearden still alive in the world."

They came to a street that led in nearly the right direction. Along it were tourist courts, filling stations, garages, and stores, with signs of all kinds, wooden and tin, and flashing red and green and yellow neon.

The cars did not go so fast but there was more honking of horns and screeching of brakes.

"Angie Baby," he said, "would you like to stop some place and drink a glass of milk?"

"We still got plenty of bread and meat," she said, holding up the paper sack.

"Well, we got money if you want milk. I'd like to go in some place, anyway. I aim to ask around about Amos Bearden if I get a good chance."

"All right, I would like to have some milk."

They went into a small café. There were three tables and a row of stools along a counter. The man behind the counter looked pleasant. He had no other customers. When they sat down on two stools, he wiped the counter with a large towel and gave them two glasses of water. The girl put her purse and sack in her lap.

The old man took a cup of coffee, and after they were served he looked around carefully again to make sure no one else had come in before he spoke. "Mister, do you know Amos Bearden?"

"Bearden. Bearden. No, can't say I do, old-timer. Wait, what you say that first name was?"

"Amos. Amos Bearden."

"Amos Bearden! You don't mean him! You must be thinking about somebody else from who I am."

"Show him the newspaper, Angie Baby."

She opened her purse and unfolded the top half of a newspaper front page. There was a two-column picture of a man and under it the caption "Indicted." "We found it on the railroad track a week ago," she said. "Grandpap thinks it probably blew out of a train."

The café man frowned and asked the old man, "You know him, do you?"

"We know him."

"Well, he's not indicted anymore. He beat that rap like he did all the others."

"Whereabouts does he live?"

The café man frowned and looked from one to the other. "Look, I don't know anything about him. I just don't want any trouble." He began to wipe the counter with the towel, then he moved down to the end and began washing glasses.

The old man asked with irritation, "How can anybody find their way around in this town if people won't answer a plain question?"

Without looking up, the café man said, "I got city maps up in the rack. Twenty-five cents."

The girl went up and found the folded map and brought it to the old man. He put it in the top front pocket of his overalls.

The café man frowned and studied them when they paid him. As they opened the door he said, "Look, old-timer, I didn't mean to be impolite. But if you want some good advice, stay away from Amos Bearden."

"How come?"

"He runs the rackets in this town. He won't cause you nothing but grief."

"How come?"

"If you don't know 'how come' you sure better stay away from him. He's got nothing around him but hoods and bodyguards."

They went on down the street and the old man snorted in disgust. "Stay away from him! I aim to stay away from him, about six feet! I knew his pappy and his grandpappy! They made the rottenest whiskey for twenty miles, and all of them was cowards, uncles and cousins and all!"

The busy street was angling away from the direction they wanted to go, so they turned off. On a quiet street they sat on the curb and unfolded the map. It was just a maze of lines. She read some of the street names off to him, but they did not find their own location.

They walked on toward the city skyline and she asked, "Grandpap, how come it all to start in the first place?"

"How come what to start, Angie Baby?"

"The feud."

"Oh, it was just them Beardens, Angie Baby."

"I mean, was there any certain thing that happened right at the first?"

He rubbed his chin. "Let me see. I did know, Angie Baby, but seems like it's slipped my mind. I guess it was just because them Beardens was always like they was."

They came to an area where the streets were not paved but were covered with lumps and mud holes. The small unpainted houses crowded against each other and left no room for sidewalks, so they walked in the sorry street. Small children with bare feet ran among the houses and fought with each other and cried, and women stuck their heads out of the windows and screamed orders at the children: "Shut up that crying!" "Get in this house!" "Stay out of that mud!"

On a bench at a city bus stop, a woman sat with folded arms. The old man approached her. "Ma'am, me and Angie here are strangers in town and we're looking for a man, but we don't know where he lives. What would be the best way to find him?"

"Look him up in a phone book."

The old man and his granddaughter looked at each other. "We don't have a phone book, ma'am."

The woman shrugged. "You don't think I've got one, do you? Go to a drugstore or some place there's a public telephone."

They thanked her and went on. The crowded houses gave way to factories; at first the buildings were of corrugated sheet iron, then they were of brick with green-painted windows. The stacks spouted black smoke.

"Grandpap," she said, "don't you think it smells awful in this town?"

"Smells like a coal-oil stove turned up too high and not drawing enough air," he said.

They went through the open gate of a chain-link fence and passed beside a long brick building. On the other side of them was half a block full of automobiles, lined up waiting. When they had come to about the middle of the factory, without warning the doors burst open and men poured out, coming fast.

She took hold of the old man's left hand and they stopped. Back the way they had come was no retreat, for the whole side of the building had erupted with hurrying men. They stood close together, and the old man's hand hovered over the deep overalls pocket where the .45 revolver lay. The crowd came around them as water around a stone in a stream. The automobiles began to start and move. One came directly toward them, honking. They took refuge by a telephone pole and waited.

The rush of men and cars was over as suddenly as it had come. "Let's get out of this place, Angie Baby," he said.

They went on past the long building and out through a gate in the chain-link fence. Then they turned down a street with sidewalks. The skyline of the city was spreading out as they drew near it. On the corner they found a public telephone booth.

The old man could not read, but the girl was sure that she could find the name. She spread out the thick book on the little shelf and leafed through it. When she found it, her heart became like a weight in her chest. He was wrong. There were many Beardens. Bearden, A. C.;

Bearden, Amos; Bearden Beauty Salon . . . She looked up to see that he was not watching and then counted them: sixty-three Beardens.

"Can you find him, Angie Baby? Does it say where he lives?"

She looked back at Bearden, Amos. "Yes, Grandpap—2217 Hickory Avenue."

He repeated the address two or three times. They opened the map and she found Hickory Avenue, but they did not know their own location.

As they walked on, she carried a burden such as she had never felt before. If she told him about the sixty-three Beardens, what could he do? He could only feel the same disappointment. He had always before known what they should do and he had always been right. Now he was so sure—and so wrong. For the first time she saw that he was old and she couldn't share a burden with him. It wouldn't make it less for her but would double it, because he had to bear it too.

"Grandpap," she said, "I don't like it around this big town very well, do you?"

"No, I don't, Angie Baby. Don't like it at all. When we get our business took care of, we'll get on that bus and go back to the hills where we belong."

"Well, Grandpap, how do you think it would be if we just let Amos Bearden stay here? It would be good enough for him."

He thought it over carefully. "No, he may be used to it and like it. He may have him a big truck to go around in."

They came to a place where the streets met to make a large circle. The cars went around it, then turned off. She remembered the circle on the map and they spread it out. They were four blocks from Hickory Avenue.

As they turned down the avenue, checking by the numbers to see that they were going in the right direction, the sun dropped behind the houses. It had been a dim sun all day, like one seen through a thin cloud. They found the number. The house at 2217 was two-story stone like the others. In front of it sat a low, shiny black car. In the garage were two more long black cars. They walked past the house. Across the street and past three more houses was a drugstore on the corner; here the old man took the girl.

"Now you stay right here, Angie Baby," he cautioned, with more authority than usual. "Here. You better hold my pocketbook." He fished it out of his hip pocket. It was of worn leather, curved from long contact with the curve of his buttocks. "Now, you wait right here, and your grandpap will take care of it."

She stood in the door of the drugstore clutching the pocketbook in the same hand with her patent-leather purse, watching him go back to the house. He was on the porch a minute, then he went inside with his right hand in his big overalls pocket.

It was two or three minutes before the first shot, a loud BAM that could have come from no gun except the heavy old .45 revolver. It was followed by a second shot from the same gun, then by the crack and spit of other guns interspersed with the unmistakable BAM of the big revolver. More shots altogether than she could count. People began to run out of the house and out of other houses.

She felt that she might cry without meaning to, and the idea "I am a Tucker" ran through her mind. She went into the public telephone booth in the corner and closed the door to hide herself from the eyes of the people on the stools and the man in the white cap. She put her things on the floor and opened the thick book thinking, "Maybe it's not true. Maybe I made a mistake before." But it was true. There they were still: Bearden, A. C.; Bearden, Amos; Bearden Beauty Salon; all sixty-three of them. She was not really hunting as she turned further in the book, but only keeping her hands busy. There were so many people. Then she came to the place where her name would have been if it were in the book, and it seemed for a moment that she must have forgotten how to spell it. She said the letters softly to check, "T,U,C,K,E,R."

The pages were large and the names small, and there were more than two whole columns of Tuckers. She counted three hundred and twenty-seven and dwelt lovingly on the first names: Albert Tucker, Amy Tucker, Charles, Emma, Jesse K., Lloyd, Melvin, Mary Lee. When she came out, feeling less alone than before, the policemen were there. They talked to her in a friendly manner and were very kind.

At the police station they took the pocketbook from her and examined the contents in front of her. They found a dozen old pictures, some of people she knew, some of people she didn't. One showed Grandpap in the woods standing behind a dead bear, and holding a long-barrel gun in the crook of his arm. They found a flour ration stamp issued in 1918 and a dollar bill, folded in creases that seemed to have been in it a half century, issued by the Confederate States of America, with writing across its face in ink that was faded brown and illegible.

In the main pouch of the pocketbook they found twenty-eight dollars in good money and the return half of one round-trip bus ticket.

"Is there another ticket?" she asked the sergeant.

He looked again, then smiled at her serious face. "No, miss. But one is all you'll need."

Caught
in a Dying Situation

The waitress lounged in front of Teddy, pressing her shapely belly against the edge of the counter. Friendly, he thought. Deedie—that was what they had called her. Deedie Something-or-other.

"How you and Jimmy getting along these days?" he asked.

"That damn ape!" she whispered huskily, low enough not to be heard by the customer four seats down. "I haven't gone out with him in six months."

He remembered her now, all but her last name. She had been in that wild party out at the Vino Negro.

"Come go on a little trip with me this afternoon," he said, not meaning it, just feeling her out. She was a good-looking black-headed girl. Been married once, he thought he remembered. Lots of fun, one who didn't mind cutting loose.

"Where you going on your little trip? Up to the lake?"

"No, East Texas."

"I might just go with you if you went up to the lake. What's in East Texas?"

"Well, it's this way," he said. He was wanting to say something smart and humorous and impressive to her. "I've got this old uncle, see. He's going to leave me a big inheritance someday, and I have to keep going to see him to check on the state of his health."

"Bull," she said with a big smile. She looked better when she didn't smile big enough to show her teeth.

"No, it's a fact. He owns half the real estate in this town where he lives, and I'm the only heir he's got young enough to enjoy it."

"That's a cute line," she said. "How big is this big inheritance?"

"Big enough to have a ball on for about fifty years." Suddenly Teddy had an impulse. (It was studied philosophy with him to follow impulses. You missed a lot if you didn't.) "Come go over there with me a couple of days. I'll put you up at a swanky motel that's got a swimming pool."

"You're kidding."

"No. It's a hick town, you know, but there's this fancy motel out on the highway that's got a swimming pool and television."

She was interested. "I can't get off," she said.

"Tell the boss you're sick or your grandma died. Look at me; I'm supposed to be working, but I took off."

"Oh, I don't know. I'd have to get a bunch of clothes and everything."

"Clothes!" He laughed at her. "You won't need any clothes. Well, maybe a bathing suit. We could go by your place. Look, I've got to go down to the drugstore, and I'll meet you out front in fifteen minutes." He gave her an exaggerated wink, turned his back while she was still trying to make some weak protest, and went to pay his check.

A quarter of an hour later he came down the sidewalk in front of the place without any idea whether she would come out, not caring much one way or the other; he had given impulse its chance. She came out five steps ahead of him, as if on cue, but did not look at him until they were nearly to the corner.

"Did your grandma die?" he asked. "Poor woman."

"No, I got sick."

"You don't look sick."

"And I don't feel sick."

"But you're sick."

"Boy, am I sick! Where's your car?"

He headed the red Buick east out of Dallas and stopped at a package store to pick up a fifth of bourbon. His destination was a dry town. One of the dignified town fathers who kept it, and the county, that way was his Uncle Alvin. And yet no one would welcome more heartily than Uncle Alvin a nip of whiskey on the sneak.

"For Uncle Alvin," he explained as he wedged the bottle into the whiskey hole.

"Yeah, I'll bet," Deedie said. "What's he, the town drunk? I thought he was going to leave you a big inheritance."

"Honey, it's a fact. But guys like Uncle Alvin, you got to understand them. He's against everyone drinking except me and him, as long as Aunt Abigale doesn't know anything about it, and he doesn't care for you drinking as long as *he* doesn't know anything about it."

"He's cute," she said.

They couldn't talk for the wind as he lined the red Buick out on the broad new concrete highway; effortlessly it climbed to ninety, then one hundred, the needle gently rocking across the zeroes as he let her sway a little like a boat from side to side. The "plump—plump—plump" of the tires on the tarred cracks was a rhythmic background music to his thoughts. It was like a hep cat who is gone way out, the way he drove; he gloried in it and less consciously he gloried in his healthy young body and his checkered sports coat and his lack of a tie and his lack of inhibitions, and Deedie. She was a damn good companion with whom to go roaring down the highway in a good car.

In a languid manner he thought about his own motives for visiting his uncle. All of that—the one-horse town, their petty affections, their hypocritical old-fogy morals—what did he have to do with all that? His own life was light-years removed from that of his uncle.

Well, there was some sentiment. They had been somewhat like parents, the old uncle and aunt, childless in their own union, too old to be father and mother from as early as he could remember. He had been tolerant, during those few years he had stayed with them, of their old-fashioned kinfolk manner of making over him; and probably they had been tolerant too—how could they have understood his young desires and passions, the necessity for his living in the world as it is, instead of as it used to be in the Middle Ages. They must have tolerated much in him.

But their time was over and gone. Uncle Alvin had done nothing with his money for years but meanly preserve it, fight off the younger businessmen as a bull animal fights off from his cows the young bulls by his weight and reputation even when his breeding days are gone. And Aunt Abigale, childishly like her spouse in their home, was nothing in town. They had both been dead fifteen years without knowing it.

It was as if the sentiment in Teddy's mind was partitioned off in a small area of its own, not trying to escape into or influence that larger area of his thoughts wherein he realistically considered himself and his old uncle. Hell, he didn't need to feel any guilt about his motives. He *would* find out what his inheritance would be. He would make that the purpose of his visit. Nothing so dumb as "What are you going to leave me in your will, Uncle Alvin?" They didn't allow any such honest and straightforward questions. But he would find out from the sly old devil some way. Maybe the liquor would do it.

Deedie had found some music on the radio that pleased her and she lay sprawled back dreaming. As Teddy drove he strangely anticipated little things that would surprise him at their destination, things he knew there in their world and in their way of life, which, however, if you got away from them awhile, you would cease to believe existed. The first of these he met was the narrow street paved with brick onto which he turned from the highway as he entered the town. Brick! My God! Imagine what pains and care they had taken setting these little red chunks into this narrow, bumpy street.

Another thing, it was nearly four by the courthouse clock, which reminded him that the three old-maid aunts, Aunt Vicky, Aunt Cora, and Aunt Nan, in their decayed old house on the other side of town, would be sitting down to tea. Tea! My God! Think of that! Three ancient old ladies, alone, sitting drinking hot tea.

He drove through town out to the Texarkana highway to the Sky-View Motor Lodge, where he registered as Mr. and Mrs. Percy Peyton Northcliff, out of which Deedie got a good laugh, and he paid a night's lodgings. She wanted to go with him, but was not hard to persuade to stay near the swimming pool, after he agreed to come back and take her to supper. If she got hungry before he made it back, she could have something at the Sky-View Cafeteria.

A few minutes later Teddy was completely away from the highway and motor court part of town and pulling into the rock-lined drive and up under the mulberry trees at Uncle Alvin's house. He leaned on the horn, not thinking to be rude but as a hearty greeting. He could hear commotion, doors opening and closing. A spry little lady bounced toward him before he could get out of the car. She squinted and came within a few steps before she recognized him.

"Lord bless," she said. "Teddy, it's been ages. Lord bless! You naughty, naughty boy." She hugged him, and he could feel that the dear little woman was made up almost entirely of bones.

Uncle Alvin came hobbling out of the house. Teddy could never have foreseen his appearance, for he had failed; his shoulders had pinched in and his gait was halting. As he came near, Teddy was horrified to see that his face, behind his white handlebar mustache, was dark red and splotchy.

"Uncle Alvin!" he cried, again not thinking to be rude, "have you been sick?"

"He's faking," Aunt Abigale said. "Alvin, you get back in that house! He pretends to be sick and then he won't mind the doctor. Lord bless! If you only knew. He moans and carries on like he was dying and he won't stay in his bed and he won't stay on the divan and he won't take his medicine. He just wants to be petted. Alvin, you get back in that house right now."

"Well, so you finally decided to honor us," Uncle Alvin said, with a gruff, wry humor. His handshake was weak and uncontrolled.

Teddy laughed at the way she ordered the old man as if he were a child and at the way he disregarded her as if she might have been a cackling hen walking about. Inside in the front room she said, "You lie down on that divan and keep still," and he sat down in a straight-backed chair, breathing so hard through his big nose that he could not speak.

Teddy did not know what to make of it. One minute he thought of enticing the old man out behind the stables to have a drink that would maybe cheer him up; the next minute he was thinking, Maybe a drink would kill him. My God, can Uncle Alvin be actually as sick as he looks?

He decided not to take him out behind the stables today. Maybe tomorrow. (The stables consisted of a lot and stalls and a big bin for grain and a loft for hay, all still there thirty years after any horses were used. "I may get me some horses again," Uncle Alvin would say. "One thing, you don't have to trust any crooked mechanics when you drive horses." In those four years when Teddy had lived with them, after his own parents had died, it had been one of his chores to keep the stables painted and clean of weeds; now they were grown up thickly with all manner of vines and brambles and Johnson grass.)

Aunt Abigale was in the kitchen preparing an enormous supper, a homecoming feast for Teddy. He realized now that he could not possibly skip eating supper here. Deedie would have to make out on her own; he would call her.

"Yeah, I been stove up here lately," Uncle Alvin told him. "I got to get back on my feet. Got to get back down to that bank. They'll steal me blind. Here I been working six years to get Ransome off the board of directors, and I no sooner get him off, and I get laid up this way.

They'll steal every cent I got." The old man had regained his calm after the exertion of going out to meet Teddy; now he was becoming excited again. His heavy breathing made his speech difficult.

"They'll have every loan . . . uh . . . every loan . . . tied in with that damn Ransome's insurance business . . . uh . . . or his real estate business. I no sooner turn my back . . . uh . . . I turn my back and they'll rob me." Uncle Alvin was half risen from his chair. His face was again dark red and splotchy; his mustache quivered. Obviously he was so carried away by his own emotion at the poor treatment he suspected from his business associate that he did not notice his own physical distress.

"Uncle Alvin, that's all right. Everything will be all right," Teddy said.

"Go to . . . uh . . . get back. Uh . . . uh . . . I want . . . uh . . . I want an audit. No . . . They'll steal . . . uh . . ."

"Don't excite yourself, Uncle Alvin," Teddy said, but the old man had already excited himself into some sort of a halfway-down, gasping, struggling heap. Teddy began to try to lift him by his arms, which were too limber and uncontrolled, trying to get him back into the chair. The old man presented nothing to hold on to. Teddy called, "Aunt Abigale! Aunt Abigale!" and was greatly relieved when she came, not only because of her help but because she seemed not too much concerned.

The little woman displayed more strength than one would guess was possible from her appearance, and together they deposited the broken old man into his bed. She arranged him and his bedclothes into some order, and during this procedure he made no rational movements of his body or eyes, but only gasped some short animal noises in his throat.

"I'll call the doctor," Teddy said. "You want me to call the doctor, Aunt Abigale?"

"No, it won't do any good," she said, surveying her handiwork with no regard for the fact that her husband might be unconscious or in a fit. "He won't mind the doctor. I know him. He's faking. Most of it he's faking. Lord bless! Teddy, he probably just wants to be petted. Alvin's always been that way. Come on, now eat your supper."

During supper, she assured him that his Uncle Alvin would get hungry smelling the fried chicken, and would be in the dining room to eat with them before they finished; but he did not come. This made Teddy suspicious of her lack of anxiety. Maybe Uncle Alvin was about to die and she just couldn't see it. Maybe she was so familiar with his crotchety ways and so used to opposing his petty whims that now she couldn't accept his serious illness. But after all, from what she had said, Uncle Alvin must be under a doctor's care; maybe he *was* about halfway faking. Old people will do funny things.

After supper, Aunt Abigale said he must plan to go over to Aunt Vicky's tomorrow. "They think so much of you. Law! I don't see them but what they ask about you. And Aunt Nan is getting old; she'll be hurt if you don't go to see them." By "Aunt Vicky's" she meant the huge old house where the three deaf old maids lived, under the direction of the youngest, Aunt Vicky, and in the manner, in so far as their proverty permitted, of genteel people a half century earlier. What she meant by "Aunt Nan is getting old" he did not know. Getting old! God! For as long as he could remember, for at least twenty years, Aunt Nan had been so old and shrunken and frail as to seem ready to blow away in the wind.

He didn't know what to do about Deedie. He had meant to go back out there tonight, but now, for no reason that he could give himself, it didn't seem the thing to do. He got on the phone while Aunt Abigale was in the kitchen. For one ridiculous instant he thought, I don't know her last name! then remembered and was still laughing at himself when Deedie got on the phone.

"Is this Mrs. Northcliff?"

"Yes, is this Percy Peyton Northcliff?"

"I'm guilty," he said. "Look, Deedie, can you get something to eat by yourself? You know how these old aunts are; she's fixed a bunch of stuff special for me, and I wouldn't want to offend her. Did you have a good swim?"

"Hell, I'm waterlogged. When will you be over?"

"Well, look, honey, I wanted to talk to you about that. My Uncle Alvin is pretty sick, and maybe I ought to stick around here tonight. I wouldn't want to worry them."

"My God!" she said. "I thought we were going to have a party tonight. Did you run into some old girlfriend?"

"No, I'm serious, Deedie. I'll explain all about it tomorrow. You're not sore?"

"Why should I be sore? You bring me out to this godforsaken hole and tell me we'll have a ball, but you run off with all the liquor, and now you come up with this story about your uncle is sick. Goddamn! We've already used that one today; why don't you say your grandma died."

"Aw, come off of it, honey," he begged. "Would I have brought you along if I wasn't crazy about you. I'll make it up to you. I guarantee. Don't be sore."

"Okay, this once. I'll watch Roy Rogers on the TV. I always thought he was better looking than you anyway."

"You're a peach, Mrs. Northcliff."

"I'm a frustrated peach," she said. Her tone was such that he decided that she really wasn't angry. Maybe she had a right to be a little miffed.

That night Teddy drove over to the home of a boy with whom he had gone to school, mainly to show off his red Buick; the car was new since he had been last in town. He chatted later than he meant to. It was near midnight when he drove back to Uncle Alvin's house. His aunt had waited up, as if he didn't know where to find his room and bed. He wondered how Uncle Alvin was feeling, but realized that she would probably say only what she had said before—that he was faking.

Teddy lay in bed some two hours before the commotion started. He had been lying wide awake thinking about the curious paradox: how little he belonged under this roof with these people, how little he had in common with them, and yet how, some way, there was a tie to them that he could not deny nor explain. Then he started and sat up upon hearing a moan and bare feet stumbling against the floor.

He sat up a minute before he thought, Uncle Alvin! As he slipped on his pants he heard more moans and the quick sharp steps of Aunt Abigale. He ran into the kitchen and turned on the light.

She was struggling with Uncle Alvin, trying to pull him back; and the old man, grotesque in his long-handled underwear, was struggling weakly but viciously against her and against the door to the back porch and also evidently against something in his own chest. "Let me out!" he said. "I can't breathe! Help me!" She pulled him, but he clung to the doorknob, and there he sank to the floor.

Teddy helped break his fall, and heard the old man beg again, in a curiously weak voice as if he had no air with which to speak, "Help me!" His face was distorted, but it was the color of it that shocked Teddy; it was so dark red as to be almost black.

"How can I nurse him if he won't stay in bed?" Aunt Abigale pleaded. They lugged him back again, as they had in the afternoon. But Teddy could tell that there was a difference. The old man had his own chest and throat in a hard solid grip with motionless hands, and he was not making any noises. Teddy found the phone number of Dr. Small, the doctor they had always used, and called him without waiting to ask Aunt Abigale.

"Yes, sir, it's absolutely necessary," he told the doctor on the phone. "I think he's dying." Actually, Teddy felt certain that his uncle was already gone, and he thought, Is that the way it is? Your chest hurts and you can't breathe and you go and fall on the kitchen floor and die? It seemed inconceivable that the awful and final act of death should be thus connected with such simple, crude events.

Aunt Abigale was more concerned now, but not so much that she forgot to tidy the room for the doctor and place the old man's medicine on a clean lace cloth on the table beside his bed.

Dr. Small came in with a grunt for greeting, and Aunt Abigale nervously chattered at him as he began his examination. "He's only faking, Doctor. Oh! I know he's sick, but he likes to get attention. You'll never know the trouble I've had. He wants to be petted. He won't stay in bed and he won't take his medicine. I said to his sister just the other day— that's Miss Victoria Basset—I said I just don't know how I'm going to keep on nursing him and never know how much he's faking and wanting to be babied. Just like a child. And I can't just let him go, because I know he's sick. I said sometimes I just don't know how I'm going to carry on . . ."

Teddy could hear anxiety in her voice that was deeper than her words. She might have been trying to convince herself of something. She had become aware that the doctor was looking up at her, waiting, and she paused.

The doctor said simply, "This man is dead."

Aunt Abigale stood still for a full minute, then put her hands to her face. She mumbled, "I can't believe it," and turned and went into the front room.

Teddy followed her. She raised her head, and he saw that her face had become older and softer. She said quietly, "You must go tell Aunt Vicky, Teddy. They would want to know as soon as possible." As he went out the door she said brokenly, but not to him, "I don't believe it!"

He started to back his car out of the driveway and all at once the enormity and impossibility of the task before him became clear. How could he possibly break this news to them? Here at two o'clock in the morning! How easy it would be to head the red Buick out to the highway fast and get the hell out of this place! Well, of course he couldn't do it. It would be shameful. There was his Uncle Alvin lying dead, a man who had been like a father to him. But why couldn't he just be sorry, sincerely and naturally, and not have to be mixed up with all these old women. Goddamn it all to hell! Suppose he was too clumsy about breaking the news and caused Aunt Nan to have a stroke from the excitement. All these goddamn peculiar old people and old customs and old ideas. Where it's like walking around on light bulbs, trying to keep from breaking any!

He might have sat there forever, procrastinating, if he hadn't remembered the bottle of artificial fortitude. Taking a long, throat-searing drink, he thought, I bought this for Uncle Alvin. Well, that's who it's for. Here's to you, Uncle Alvin!

"Aunt Vicky's" was the house that had been the original family home. It sat far back behind a picket fence and hickory, walnut, and pecan trees, a tall house, gray in the moonlight, with a wide porch. There was a driveway, blocked by a locked gate.

Teddy thought as he climbed over the fence and made his way up the ill-kept lawn that he would be lucky if he were not taken for a peeping Tom. He cleared his throat as he stepped on the porch and knocked decorously on the door facing. He waited a minute but, hearing no movement from within, knocked a bit louder. Thus he knocked and waited again and again for fifteen minutes, thinking for one moment he heard someone stirring, then deciding it was the old house creaking. At last he pounded impatiently, so fast and hard that he had bruised his knuckles before he could stop himself. I guess they heard that! he thought. Surely everyone for two blocks must have heard it.

But he was becoming too rough and ill mannered. At such an hour, on such a mission, and dealing with three timid old ladies, was that any way to act? He just hoped he hadn't frightened them into never answering the door. He backed up to the edge of the porch thinking, At least they won't open the door and find me standing right in front of them, like I was going to attack them or something.

A light over the door came on. After what seemed like an hour's wait, during which he imagined he could see something behind the door glass, the door opened. He still could see no one clearly.

"I'm Teddy," he said. "Teddy Basset. I've just come from Uncle Alvins." He had already strictly resolved that he wouldn't mess around about breaking the news. There was no way to break it gently.

"Who is it?" called a voice behind the screen.

"I'm Teddy Basset. Don't you know me? Is that you, Aunt Vicky? I've just come from Uncle Alvin's. I'm afraid I'm bringing bad news."

"Who is it?" came the voice. It was Aunt Vicky, all right. "Come under the light, young man! What in the world do you want?"

"It's Teddy, Aunt Vicky. I've just come from Uncle Alvin's. I'm afraid . . ."

"Why, it's Teddy! Why didn't you say so at first? What in the world are you doing out in the night air at this hour?" She still didn't open the screen.

"Uncle Alvin's dead!" he yelled. "Dead! Uncle Alvin!"

"You've been drinking, young man," she said.

My God! Hadn't she heard him? Or did she think he was pulling some kind of drunken joke? Why hadn't he remembered the liquor and not yelled in her face. Damn a woman who couldn't hear a train wreck but could smell the faintest breath of whiskey! "It's true, Aunt Vicky! I'm sorry to have to tell you. But Uncle Alvin is . . . uh . . . passed away. I'm giving you the straight . . . uh . . . it's true."

"Oh, dear! Oh!" she moaned.

He saw a movement behind the screen but heard nothing else. He knew a moment later that she had gone, for another moan came from the far end of the front room. Another voice; it would be Aunt Cora's. Another minute and another moan. He tried the screen; it was hooked. Well, it looked as if he were going to be expected to stay out here on the porch and wait for whatever they planned to do.

It seemed hours. From the recesses of the house came muffled moans and faint scurrying noises. He felt sorry for them, so old and upset, in such a big house, like three scared cockroaches rattling around in a big pasteboard box. He cursed himself for a callous fool—stirring them up this way after midnight, shouting at their door in a drunken voice. But the pity and self-accusation could last only so long. After all he was not in this awkward place, locked out here on this front porch, by his own choice. If they were upset, it was the fault of the situation. He hadn't caused his Uncle Alvin's death. Indeed, he thought philosophically, death is just the penalty they must face for being old.

Finally a car with taxi lights pulled up out front behind his own; then the three little women, almost entirely covered by coats and shawls, came waddling out, helping one another.

"Why, I have my car, Aunt Vicky," he said. "You all could ride with me!"

"No, we have the taxi. We'll go in the taxi," she said. Then out front, she instructed him, "You go with us, Teddy. Get in the front seat with the driver."

No explanations, nor further talk about it. He got in the front of the taxi. At first he thought it must be custom or some propriety that he go with them—maybe something simple, such as that he was needed to give the driver directions so that the grief-bearing ladies would be preserved from contact with the uncouth driver. Or some old-fashioned custom connected with death. Then into his head came a suspicion, that grew to a certainty, that he was considered irresponsibly drunk, unfit to drive. And now he would have to get back some way to get his car. Damn this poor little woman and her kind, protective ideas!

Back at Uncle Alvin's people had begun to gather: a neighbor man and woman, a nephew who was the son of old Uncle Ben, the oldest of the Bassets, and a niece who was the daughter of this same Uncle Ben, along with her husband and two sleepy children. By the time Aunt Vicky, Aunt Cora, and Aunt Nan became a part of the gathering it seemed to Teddy a confused babble of solemnity and activity, hushed tones, and an occasional shriek when someone tried to convey a message to deaf Aunt Nan.

He slipped away and made the long walk back to Aunt Vicky's for his car, cursing all the way. The goddamned ironic thing about it was that in paying for Aunt Vicky's taxi he had realized he might run short on money, so that now he couldn't afford to take a taxi but must walk. He had been too childish to know that he was unfit to drive, but he hadn't been too childish to pay the fare. That fine bitch of an old maid had not even tried to outfumble him on paying the fare but had counted on his gallantry, as if he were a gentleman and she a helpless female. But she hadn't hesitated to blithely order him to get in the taxi, for no reason on God's green earth. He would be damned if he would cater to her anymore. But, oh, what the hell! What can you do?

He had another drink when he got to his car. He drove back through the empty streets as the light of day first broke, and the loneliness of the streets made him thoughtful; he knew the force of the death that had happened that night and how one man's time on earth had come irretrievably to an end.

Confusion reigned at Uncle Alvin's house. Teddy thought that surely there must be enough people to do, and better than he could do, whatever might need being done. He brought his car around to the alley by the stables, stretched out as well as he could in the seat, and went into a fitful sleep.

He was awakened at midday by Aunt Abigale's light hand on his shoulder. "Don't you want to eat something, Teddy? You missed your breakfast. There's so much food. All the neighbors have brought food." He followed her small figure to the house. She said, "Everyone is being so nice to me," and the idea made her voice break.

After potato salad and pie in the kitchen, he learned from a cousin that his Uncle Alvin's body had already been taken to a funeral home and that the funeral was planned for the following day, a Sunday. He was beginning to wonder what he would do with himself during all that time when suddenly he remembered Deedie. She would be furious. It seemed a year since he had left her at the tourist court. He would have to go out there; she might do something foolish such as try to look him up.

He felt that he should hang around long enough to speak to the kinfolk and make some excuse to Aunt Abigale for leaving. Then he fell into conversation with the fantastic old Uncle Ben out on the front porch. Or conversation was not exactly the word for it.

"Set down, boy," the old man said. "You're Alvin's boy."

"No, I'm . . ." Teddy began.

"You're a good boy," Uncle Ben said. "I want to tell you something." He had a peculiar nervous mannerism of nodding his head and preceptively his shoulders, not in a jerky manner, but deliberately, as if he nodded each time his heart beat.

"It's this city life, boy. I told Alvin it would get him. Told him fifty years ago. He was always a stubborn kid."

The old man was tall and spare and well preserved for his great weight of years. His face was the texture of faded bond paper and he wore a handlebar mustache, as had Uncle Alvin, except that it had passed being white and was now an unnatural yellow. My God, Teddy thought, this man is older than them all, even older than Aunt Nan.

"Look at me, boy. I was a full-grown man when Alvin was still in didies." His nod gave a solemnity to his slow words. "I see 'em come, boy, and I see 'em go."

The old man was staring out across the myriad rooftops of the town with his eyes half closed. He mumbled something like, "You're a good boy . . ." and became silent. Teddy did not know whether he was looking at something or was asleep.

He couldn't find Aunt Abigale so he slipped out to his car and headed for the Sky-View Motor Lodge. He didn't know what he was going to do with that girl; maybe he should send her on back to Dallas.

She was lying across an unmade bed in a rumpled dress and with uncombed hair, her head propped up in two cupped hands.

"Hello, Mrs. Northcliff," he said gaily. "Your hair looks like you slept in it." She didn't smile.

"Have you had a big time in the swimming pool?"

"I had a ball in the swimming pool."

"I thought you'd have a good time," he said. "You've got a good figure for wearing a bathing suit."

"I had a ball in my bathing suit."

"You're not sore?"

"You're not sore?" she mimicked. "Where in the hell have you been?"

"My Uncle Alvin died last night about two o'clock."

She didn't bat an eye. "This precious 'swimming pool' you're always talking about hasn't got a drop of water in it, and I think you knew it."

"Why not?"

"Why, this hick town has got a water shortage or something! If you came around once in a while you'd know there was no water in the swimming pool."

"Well, like I said, Deedie, my Uncle Alvin died last night and I've been busy."

"I don't know what kind of girls you go out with, but I'm not used to being treated this way!"

"Can't you hear me?" he insisted. "I said I was busy. My Uncle Alvin died last night!"

"I thought it was your grandma that died."

"You don't have to be that way," he said. "Look, honey, you want to take the bus and go on back to Dallas? I've got to stay for the funeral tomorrow, and you could take the bus . . ."

"I didn't come on the bus, and I'm not going back on the bus!"

"Well, it was just a thought. I'll pay the man for another night, and we'll go back tomorrow."

"What time is this funeral you say they're having?"

"Two o'clock, I guess."

"I'll be there in my bathing suit." She rolled over and would say nothing else.

Well, he thought, if she were going to be angry, she would just have to be angry. He paid the man at the office for another night.

He had begun to worry about his clothes. They weren't suitable for a funeral. He had fourteen dollars left in his pocket. He thought about hitting up Uncle Ben for a loan, but the idea seemed farfetched. The old man probably wouldn't even understand what was wanted. Then Aunt Abigale solved the problem.

"Do you have a black suit, Teddy?"

"No," he said, and lamely continued, "I thought I might buy something."

"You can wear one of your uncle Alvin's. Come."

She fixed him up with a shiny black suit that was only a little tight across the shoulders, a dark blue tie, a pair of ancient black shoes, and a white shirt. He wore all of it that night when they went to sit up at the funeral parlor and felt as if he were like someone else.

Aunt Abigale sat there in the dim room full of flowers and the coffin, and the others came, by turns, to sit with her. Uncle Ben came out into the foyer where Teddy had come to smoke.

The old man gestured gravely toward the room where Aunt Abigale sat. "Say's she can't believe it. And she can't." He sat down carefully in one of the hard polished chairs, nodding all the while.

"She can't. That's how come they have the ceremony at the graveyard. She knows all those people are dead. When they put him in that hole out there . . ." The old man leaned over carefully, cleared his throat, and deliberately spit on the floor beside his chair. ". . . and cover him up with dirt, then she'll believe it."

Teddy was shocked at the spitting. The old man acted as unconcerned as if he were in a barn. Teddy had felt guilty about throwing a cigarette butt out the window onto the lawn.

The funeral was like funerals he had seen before. The red Buick he left out in the alley by the stables and found himself driving a big black rented car with Aunt Abigale, a cousin, and the three old-maid aunts. They all sat together near the front. There was much wearing of black and much silent weeping of old women. Teddy felt like someone else and also felt strangely as if he belonged.

At the end they filed in a shuffling slow line past the bier. Most of them paused silently a second and went on. Tiny, frail Aunt Nan, a few feet ahead of Teddy, said brokenly, "Alvie! Little Alvie!" and would have collapsed had not the cousin caught her.

Uncle Ben stopped a long moment and gazed into the waxlike, powdered, and dignified face of his dead brother. His nervous deliberate nod made it seem as if he were saying, "That's the way it is. Yes, that's the way it is."

At the cemetery it was the same, only hot and sunny and dusty. When they gently placed earth on the casket, Aunt Abigale fell against Teddy, and he put both arms around her and all but carried her back to the car.

Aunt Vicky would stay with Abigale a few days. Teddy went into her room where she was lying down. "Aunt Abigale," he said softly, wondering if she were asleep.

"Yes, Teddy."

"I'm supposed to go back in the morning, but I will call and tell them I won't be there if I can help you in any way."

"No, Teddy, you must go back to work. You keep that suit; you look nice in it. Come kiss me and then you go back to work and be a good boy."

For some goddamned incomprehensible reason the admonition to "be a good boy" brought tears to his eyes.

Teddy was in no mood to argue when he got to the Sky-View Motor Lodge. He thought it the best policy to just remain silent and not try to pacify Deedie.

She had combed her hair and was ready to go. "Will the top go up on this damned wreck of a car?" she asked.

"Sure."

"Well, I'm tired and dirty and disgusted and I don't want to get sunburned on top of everything else."

He put it up and swung out onto the highway.

"Where are we headed?"

"Big D."

"I'll believe it when I see it. You sure nobody else died?"

"Yep."

They drove for fifteen minutes in silence. He thought that it was working; by not trying to cheer her up, he didn't give her any chance for sarcastic remarks.

Then she said, "I really don't see why you don't want me to know what went on back there in that town."

"Why don't you try believing just what I told you. My Uncle Alvin died and I went to his funeral."

"Well, honey, that would be just fine, but you may as well know that I took a taxi this afternoon and went all over town, just to check on you, and there wasn't any funeral."

"Did you happen to go by the Baptist church?"

"I went all over town." She was lying, patently.

Suddenly the strain he had been under, the way Aunt Vicky had treated him, the uncertainties, and now the stubbornness of this girl caused him to lose his temper. "Listen, woman," he said, "why is it that you can't believe a simple thing like that? Didn't I tell you my uncle was old? Don't you know that old people die one time or another? God-damn it all to hell! Don't you know that someday *you* will get old and die?"

She didn't answer, but from the look on her face he knew that he had dealt her a dirty blow. They went on in silence; his mind was full of the events of the last two days.

Some of it was hard to grasp: Aunt Nan's words, "Alvie! Little Al-vie!" You could see how they might have come up with a ridiculous pet name like "Alvie," but why the "Little"? Uncle Alvin had never been little. Oh well, of course he had too, seventy years ago. My God! That would have been back in another century! For a moment he could visualize a bare-legged girl of twelve in pigtails, Nan, rocking her two-year-old baby brother and calling him "Little Alvie."

They had once, all of them, been children. And young people. Alvin and Abigale had been twenty once and lovers. Maybe they had sat in a buggy once as he and the girl Deedie sat here now. It was hard to imagine that they had ever done anything immoral, but Alvin had drank. Who could say?

He felt it unbearable to be with anyone now, whether it was a girl or man or child, and not be on good terms with them.

"Deedie," he said gently. "I'm sorry. I know you didn't have a good time, and I'm sorry. I'll make it up to you someway."

"Did you get your big inheritance?" she asked.

"Yeah, I've got it in a bag right behind the seat there."

He stopped at a filling station to buy two Cokes and he took out the bag and showed her the black suit. They got a laugh. Then he broke out what remained of the bourbon, and before they came into the city limits of Dallas, they were friends again.

The Shame
of Country Children

The three youngsters had come past the bend in the wagon road they followed and were out of sight of the house. The larger boy and girl looked back at the smaller boy impatiently.

"Come on here," Chester said. "You want to miss the bus?"

The younger boy, not intimidated, said, "I can't carry my lunch and reader and go so fast. You all don't have to go so fast. Every day we have to stand and stand and wait on the bus."

"Well, we're all going to get a whipping if we miss the bus."

Ella said, "Willie won't get a whipping. He'll get a spanking, because Mama will do it."

"And so will you," Chester said. "I'm the only one that will get a bad whipping from Papa. Come on. I'm supposed to take care of both of you."

"You are not supposed to take care of me," she asserted. "I'm nearly thirteen and in the sixth."

"Well, Miss Smarty-pants, I'm fifteen and in the eighth. Are you going to hide those silly brown cotton stockings today?"

"I sure am."

"Well, you just remember. If you ever tell on me for anything in your whole life, I'm going to tell Papa and Mama you don't wear those things to school; you hide them."

"Ches . . . ter," she pleaded, stretching out his name, "you know the town girls don't wear things like this. You want me to be a country hick?"

"Well, you just remember what I said."

They slowed enough so that Willie could keep up. It was a fair day in October, the sun only a quarter hour over the morning horizon. The grass was turning gray. Leaves on the post oaks were turning yellow and tan. Beans on the mesquites were ripening and falling. Indian blanket flowers bloomed in large patches. The fruit on prickly pear cactus stood in red rows on top of the thick leaves.

As if proving that he did indeed take care of the other two, Chester opened the wire gate into the next pasture and held the post while they went through. Each of the three youngsters carried one schoolbook and a small lunch wrapped in newspaper and tied with a string. The boys were dressed in overalls and blue chambray shirts, the girl in a faded print dress. All wore brogan shoes.

Willie asked, "Chester, why do country kids have to be so low-down?"

"They're not low-down," Ella said.

"Don't even say that," Chester ordered.

"Then why do we have to hide our lunches? And I just know the coyotes will get them again."

"Why? Why? Don't you have a lick of sense at all? Ellie, tell this dumbhead what's in the lunches."

"Don't call me 'Ellie.' My name is Ella."

"All right, but you tell him. You saw Mama make them."

"It's four biscuits split open and two have a spoonful of beans and one has a sausage and one has butter and jelly."

Chester took up the lecture. "And wrapped in one page of the *Semi-Weekly Farm News* and tied with a string. You want to eat that lunch right in front of the town kids? And them looking at you? When they have their lunches in a brown sack? And sliced bread and bologna and bought things? Is that what you want?"

"Chester, I don't want the coyotes to keep on getting my dinner. I get hungry. I'm going to eat it now."

"No, Willie," Ella said. "You just ate scrambled eggs and buttermilk and everything for breakfast."

"But I get hungry. The coyotes will get it."

Chester said, "Don't touch that lunch. I've got a plan. We'll see. Won't no coyote get it. They can't climb a tree."

"What you going to do, Ches?"

"Just wait and see."

Two hundred yards from the highway they stopped. Ella went over behind a chaparral bush and could be vaguely seen taking off her garters and stockings, then putting her shoes back on. She put the brown cotton stockings under a flat rock and came back bare-legged.

They had stopped by a large mesquite tree with a sloping trunk.

Chester produced from his pocket a folded-up length of baling wire. He wrapped the three lunches, which had now begun to show grease spots through the newspaper, securely with the wire, then climbed up the trunk. He hung the lunches on a limb a full ten feet above the ground.

They walked on. Chester instructed the smaller boy. "Willie, at noon, soon as the bell rings, we'll meet right where the bus turns into the school grounds. There's a fire plug and a stop sign. Not in the back. Right in the front. Don't mess around."

"I know where."

"Well, don't mess around."

They caught the school bus on the highway five minutes later.

They met as planned at noon. The school yard around the cluster of buildings was alive with children, yelling, laughing, talking, those who had not brought their lunches to eat in the gym or in their classrooms. Some two hundred youngsters of every age, dressed in every fashion, were exhuberant in their hour of freedom. Willie ran to join Chester and Ella.

Ella took Willie by the hand, and Chester led them down the sidewalk toward the center of town. After walking a block and after the crowd of youngsters had spread out, Chester spoke to his sister and brother in a low voice.

"Act like we are going to our house to eat dinner. Or like we have got money and we are going to the café or some place to buy something good to eat."

"Don't be looking around," Ella said. "Just act like we are going to a certain place to eat."

Willie protested, "I know how to act! Same as always. You're as bossy as Chester. But I sure am hungry."

The business part of town had three grocery stores, one bank, a dry goods store, four filling stations, a hardware store, a lumberyard, a post office, and other establishments. When they came near the business district, Chester said, "We turn down here and go around two blocks. Just act natural. Then we can go back to school. Don't go too fast."

Willie protested, "I know how to act."

They got back to school, pretending to be well fed and happy.

When the school bus let them off at the wagon road, Willie started running. The two older youngsters soon saw that their younger brother had disturbed a flock of crows, sending the birds cawing and circling in the air.

Willie was crying and staring at the scene with disbelief. Scattered around under the large mesquite tree lay pieces of torn newspaper, here and there a crumb of biscuit in the dirt. Chester's baling wire hung empty on the limb. The circling crows drifted away, complaining about the interruption.

Ella and Chester got the smaller boy and pulled him on down the road. Each of them told him, "It's all right. It's only two hours till supper."

Willie turned out of the road, picked a handful of yellow and red speckled mesquite beans, and started eating them.

"Stop that!" Ella said. "You know they will give you a stomachache."

"I'm just chewing them. I spit out the hard parts."

Chester said, "Willie, come on. We're going to get in trouble if we don't go on home and do our chores."

As if trying to take the smaller boy's mind off food, Chester launched into a lecture. "You have got to get in a bucket of chips, and you ought to get good ones. You know good and well I have to build a fire in the cookstove in the mornings, and I don't want clods of dirt or damp stuff. I want good chips."

About then Ella gasped and started running back toward the highway. She had forgotten her hidden stockings. In five minutes she returned, the cotton stockings looking not much worse from being under a flat rock. But she was aggravated. "I broke one of my garters and had to tie it back. It hurts my leg."

They moved on toward home, and Willie roamed out to the side again. Soon they noticed that he was eating one of the fruits from a prickly pear cactus.

Ella yelled, "Stop that, Willie, right now!"

"You nut," Chester said. "You'll have your hands and your mouth full of those little tiny stickers. Don't you have any sense?"

"I rubbed it in the dirt to get the stickers off," Willie said. He dropped the rest of the red fruit, came to them, and sat down between the tracks of the wagon road, crying again.

Ella told him, "We are all going to get a spanking if you don't come on."

"I don't care."

Chester said, "We get to eat supper at dark. Can't you wait that long?"

"I don't care if we eat or not."

Ella put her arm around the child's shoulder. "Please don't cry, honey. Why are you crying?"

The child's freckled face was twisted up. "I still don't see why country kids have to be so low-down."

Ella said, "Listen, honey. My broke garter hurts, but I'm not crying. When you get big you'll be just as good as anybody."

Chester said, "Is that your reader? No, it's your arithmetic. Listen, you study hard at home and you'll get ahead of those town kids."

"Please don't cry," Ella said. "I'll tell you something. Those pep squad girls, when they go to a real big town like Wichita Falls or Abilene, *they* are the country hicks, so the joke's on them."

Chester said, "And listen. I bet if those kids from Wichita Falls or Abilene go to a really big city like Dallas or New York, *they* are the country kids, so the joke's on them."

"And those snooty ladies in Dallas and New York," Ella said. "They don't know how to dress up, so they go to Paris, France, to dress up. *They* are the country hicks, so the joke's on them."

They got their little brother calmed and started on toward home. By the time they came in sight of the house, Willie had straightened his shoulders and stopped sniffing. He told them, "When I get big I'm going to be just as good as anybody. Nearly." He clutched the arithmetic book to his chest.

The Night Old Santa Claus Came

Imagine a white schoolhouse sitting on a hill. It had two large rooms. The one on the north was full of desks, blackboards, a bookshelf, a teacher's desk, a pedal organ, and everything needed for the seventeen pupils who attended Mama's school. It smelled like chalk dust and ink and glue.

The other room in the schoolhouse was ours. It was the only place at Anarene for us to live, but it was a good home. It had a kitchen and closet curtained off at one end with a kerosene cookstove and linoleum on the floor; the rest of our room had a lumber floor and two beds, one for me and Bill, one for Mama and Roy, and in between our wood-burning heater stove.

Roy was five years old. I was going on eight. Bill was nine. Mama was ancient, at least thirty, maybe even thirty-one. The pupils who came were different ages, two in high school, two in the first grade, the rest scattered in between. They walked in across the prairie and through the mesquite brush from every direction each school morning. From schoolhouse hill you could only see where four other families lived; the other kids had long walks, and one rode horseback.

At one end of the white-painted schoolhouse rose a flagpole, where we flew the U.S. flag on good days; at the other end stood the cistern with its squeaky pully and fuzzy rope to draw drinking water. Out on the flat ground we had three swings and a seesaw, a baseball field to play scrub, a garage for Mama's Model-T, and the woodpile and toilets. From schoolhouse hill you could see a long way, and it looked lonely out there—not much happening, except a few white-face cattle grazing.

That winter Mama said she hoped it would snow at the right time so we would have a white Christmas, but we would take whatever God sent. He did not often send the best snow to West Texas, but usually north wind and blowing sleet.

Mama was rich. Since she was the principal as well as the teacher and also mopped the schoolhouse floor, she got paid a hundred dollars a month. They had said when we first came there that you could not be a teacher at Anarene unless you could whip the biggest boy in school. They did not know her, she had fierce eyes. She was beautiful, but she could look at a big boy and say, "I thought you were older and more responsible than that," and he would start blushing and stammering.

But usually she gave rewards. If a big girl made ninety on spelling, Mama would let her sit in one of the long desks and teach a smaller kid his reading lesson. Or if a big boy did good in Geography, Mama would let him bring in wood or stoke the fire or draw water for the water keg.

We had been thinking about Christmas and one Saturday Mama gave me and Bill and Roy each fifty cents for gift money. We could spend it any way we wanted to, but Mama said, "Remember, it's better to give than to receive." Even more exciting, we were going shopping that day to the great city of Wichita Falls. She needed to buy some bright crepe paper and things for decorations. She did not ask the school trustees about such things, but used her own money because she made such a big salary.

Mama knew how to get to Wichita Falls and all the streets and stores, for she went up there sometimes to junior college. She had got her certificate that showed she was smart enough to teach school a long time ago by taking a test at the capital of Archer County. But she said that in her spare time she might as well further her education. So she got assignments from Wichita Falls and did them at night after us kids went to bed and sent them in through the mail. Anyway, me and Bill and Roy found ourselves in the biggest nickel and dime store in the world with fifty cents in our pockets.

Everything looked bright and colorful and shiny, hundreds of things in trays and hanging up wherever you looked. And the store smelled good. I could have walked around in there for weeks just looking.

Roy was dumb. He could not see past his own nose. We were not supposed to spy on what each other bought, but I could not take care of him and not let him get lost without seeing what he did. And here's exactly what he did. He bought himself a thirty-five-cent windup caterpillar tractor made out of tin with rubber tracks. Then he lost a dime and never could find it. The last nickel he spent for a sack of yellow candy corn, which he stuffed down before he even got back to the car. Me and Bill told him how dumb he was and said, "Boy, you're going to be sorry when it comes time to put gifts on the Christmas tree." It didn't seem to bother him, but we said, "You wait and see!"

I got Mama a new spatula to turn pancakes and Bill got her a handkerchief with flowers embroidered in the corner. I got the other two kids a pewter whistle with a bird on top; you could put a little water in it and it would make a tweeting sound. But I didn't know whether I wanted to give Roy a present or not; a kid of five ought to be more responsible than that.

The schooldays got long during the week before Christmas, but we all had to work decorating the room for the tree and program the night all the parents would come. Mama said that our studies must not stop, so each pupil must show each day that he learned some lessons before he could help decorate. By the time for the last recess each day we had all earned the right to work on green and red pasted chains or twisted crepe-paper chains or Christmas posters for the walls or little cut-out figures for the tree. A big girl named Myrtle Farmer made a star and put silver tinfoil on it. A boy named Tots, who could draw real good, made beautiful scenes on the blackboards with colored chalk. Some girls got to string popcorn which Mama popped, and we all teased them and accused them of eating some.

During those days Mama changed our breakfast Bible reading too. Each morning in our room when we washed our hands and sat down to eat, she would read a few verses, then say a short prayer. Usually she read straight through the Bible, including somebody begat somebody and they begat somebody else. Then we would eat our oatmeal with canned milk and maybe have hot chocolate. Now she skipped over to Isaiah and explained that it meant that Jesus was coming. Three days before Christmas she started reading about the Christ in the New Testament.

The last schoolday before the holiday was the day to get the tree. Two big boys, Auzy Brown and Garland Andrews, went to hunt it on a creek a long way off. They had got their algebra and other lessons caught up, so they left early. The only trees with leaves were chaparral bushes, but Mama said leaves didn't matter, except we had to have a tree that could come in the door and would not be too high for the ceiling. The smaller boys could not go, because the big boys were taking an ax. We watched from the schoolhouse hill and when we saw them dragging the tree over the prairie, we ran to help bring it. We struggled and pushed from every side to get it in the door and stood up. Later in the day some boys went to get mistletoe.

Mama had a habit of going with a coal-oil lamp into the schoolroom to work on her college after us kids went to bed. Bill said part of the time she prayed in there and asked God to make her know how to be a good father as well as a mother and to be a good teacher of young minds. Bill could have been wrong; a boy of nine is not so smart, but it could be true. Anyway, before the holidays Mama practiced on the organ at night in her spare time. She could play good enough for us to sing in school, but she was afraid Mrs. Meaders, the lady who usually played for community programs, would not get over her flu before Christmas, so Mama had to be ready. We would lay in bed nearly asleep and listen to her away over there in the other half of the schoolhouse, softly playing, "O, Little Town of Bethlehem" and "Silent Night."

On Christmas Eve morning before breakfast Mama said we would read a little more than usual. She read: "And there were in the same country shepherds abiding in the field, keeping watch over their flock by night. And, lo, the angel of the Lord came upon them, and the glory of the Lord shone round about them; and they were sore afraid. And the angel said unto them, Fear not; for, behold, I bring you good tidings of great joy, which shall be to all people." And she read all of it about the shepherds coming to visit the new baby Jesus.

After breakfast we started wrapping presents, each one working in a different place, me on one bed, Mama on one, and Bill behind the kitchen curtain, to keep the presents a surprise. Roy tried to play with his caterpillar tractor, which now had the spring broken and one track lost. Then he played with the stove wood some. Finally he stood out in the middle of the room and started bawling.

After a minute Mama went over to him and asked, "What's the matter, honey? Don't cry."

He didn't want to say. She knelt down and petted him and kept saying, "Don't cry. What's the matter?"

Finally he said, "I love you, Mama."

"I know you do, honey. Don't cry."

"I would give you my tractor, but you already seen it and it wouldn't be a surprise."

She got the whole story out of him and said, "I ought to spank you good." But she smiled a little and went to her purse hanging on the nail. She got out a nickel for him to buy her a present and asked me if I would go down to the store with him.

We put on our coats. Roy no sooner got out the door than he started running. It was about a minute run to the store. Before we got there he was laughing and talking just like he'd never done anything wrong in his life. He bought Mama a Peanut Pattie candy bar about the size of a pancake, only thicker, with peanuts sticking out of the top and wrapped in clear paper.

On the way back up the hill he began to open the sack and I said, "What are you doing?"

"Nothing, I'm just going to look at it."

I said, "Leave it in the sack. What are you doing?" I had thought at first that it was useless for me to go with him, since there are no rattlesnakes in winter and you won't get on a cactus if you stay in the road; but it was a good thing I went—to protect Mama's present.

He said, "I just want to smell of it."

"Roy," I told him, "don't you unwrap that! What do you think you're doing?"

"I'm just going to take a little bite. Mama won't care."

"Don't you dare! Haven't you got a lick of sense?" I got tough with him. "You put that back in that sack and don't you touch it! I'll knock you right on the seat of your pants!"

He knew I meant it. I watched him all the way home and until he got it wrapped in red paper and tied with a string and had put Mama's name on it.

God did not send us a white Christmas that day, but the air was still and cold and clear, like you could see a hundred miles. Later, when dark came, the sky was like purple velvet and the stars were like diamonds, and you could imagine looking up there that you could hear the tune of "Silent Night."

Mama had pumped up and lighted the two gasoline lanterns in the schoolroom, and the schoolhouse hill seemed the most wonderful place a person could possibly be when the people started coming in across the prairie from every direction, driving and walking, most of them laughing. There must have been a hundred, or at least forty. They brought presents to put on the tree for each other. Everyone said how great the schoolroom looked with all our decorations.

It looked as good as a five and ten cent store, not so shiny, but happier. Our chains and ribbons, mostly red and green, looped around on the walls, and the popcorn looked like snow. It was a whole roomful of people, all smiling, and everyone talking at once, until the program started. The lady with the flu was well, so she played the pedal organ and Mama announced. We all sang "Jingle Bells" and other songs. Then the kids who had practiced up gave readings. Two girls and a boy, who could sing good together, sang "Hark, the Herald Angels Sing." Bill, who was good at memory, said, " 'Twas the Night Before Christmas."

When Santa Claus came in, dressed in red and white, saying, "Ho! Ho! Ho! Have all you boys and girls been good this year?" it was thrilling, but us big kids knew it was Mr. Charlie Graham dressed up that way. The dumb little kids like Roy thought he had just got in on his sled from the North Pole. I had learned about Santa Claus a long time ago, before our daddy died. I even knew where Mama kept the red suit and beard, in a box on top of the green metal bookcase.

The program lasted real late, at least till ten o'clock. All the grown people told Mama thank you before they left. You could hear their voices and laughter going away into the clear, cold night. When we got in our room, after we had looked at our gifts a minute, Roy began talking about hanging up stockings; he'd been talking to the other kids about it.

Mama said, "Boys, we've had a big Christmas. I don't think we need to hang up our stockings this year. We will have some goodies to eat in the next few days."

Roy said, "Well, I want to hang mine up."

"We've had a big Christmas," she said. "Don't you think we should just go to bed and have a good, lazy night's sleep?"

He didn't know what she meant about getting a night's sleep; she meant she didn't have to practice the organ or do any college lessons tonight and she didn't want any other duties in her spare time. See, she had several things to do all the time, being principal, like getting the trustees to haul firewood and getting all the right textbooks and getting chalk and stuff, then keeping up with all the lessons with two in high school, and making state reports, and getting the broken window fixed, and entertaining the community, and practicing the organ, and furthering her education, and doing all the things mamas like to do such as wash clothes and cook oatmeal and make stew and put patches on your overalls. So she said to us, like it was the last word, "Well, I'm going to bed. Tomorrow I'm going to bake chicken and make dressing." Me and Bill sniggered.

Roy, that dumb kid, took his socks up to the curtain which marked off the kitchen, got two clothespins, stood on a chair, and hung his socks to the top of the curtain. I could read his dumb mind; this was between him and Santa Claus. After Mama blew out the lamp, me and Bill lay there laughing. Boy, was that kid going to learn something! If your mama says old Santa Claus ain't coming, then he sure ain't coming anymore tonight! I would have laughed forever if I hadn't been so sleepy.

We nearly always waked up when Mama was building the fire in the morning, because the stove clanked. When she saw us sitting up in bed, she said, "Christmas gift!" It was a joke meaning you had to give them a gift if they said it first, but nobody really did it. Suddenly Roy hopped out of bed and ran toward his socks. I and Bill got to sniggering again.

About that time Roy squealed. His socks were so full he had to take them down one at a time. He ran and started spilling goodies out onto the bed.

Me and Bill looked at Mama. Why in the world had she done that? How could she be such a traitor? It wasn't fair. We liked candy and things as much as him, and he was the one who hadn't acted grown up, but he got a reward for being dumb.

"Jump up, lazybones," Mama said to me and Bill. How could she be so cheerful when she had acted like a traitor to us? "It's a nice day," she said. "Get your clothes on."

I didn't even want to speak to her as I walked over the cold floor to the chair where I left my clothes. A crazy thought was going through my mind: Could it be possible that there really is a Santa Claus who fills up the stockings of dumb little kids? I got my shoes and socks out from under the chair. I couldn't get my socks on. Something was the matter with them. Lumpy. I nearly cried as old as I was because my mind was still going over the idea if there is really a Santa Claus for dumb little kids.

In my socks was one orange, one apple, fourteen pecans, nine little pieces of hard candy, one big piece of wavy ribbon candy, eleven English walnuts, four Brazil nuts, twelve almonds, and a third of a Peanut Pattie.

We all offered Mama a piece of our candy, and she said she would take a small piece of peppermint, because she didn't care for anything that was too sweet. When she got a chance, she winked at me and Bill. I believe it was a year before Roy ever figured out how come old Santa Claus put a third of a Peanut Pattie in his sock that night.

The Love Story of Sally and Melvin

I take my pen in hand with honest intentions, if not great skill, to tell the straight facts and events that happened at Wellingdale. My hope is to straighten out the lies and rumors and ridicule and these stories you can hear that some people think are so funny.

Some will say the whole matter is ridiculous and outrageous and only a good thing to laugh about. Well, the truth is better to laugh about than lies or even to cry about. Certainly there is no cause for shame.

Wellingdale never did get to be an important town, but it was not on account of Sally. It was because some citizens knew that their taxes would be raised if we paved the rest of Main Street. Then when the freeway passed us by, some businessmen said it was better to have lower taxes and less civic improvement. It was purely political, and not because of Sally.

I am not a Chamber of Commerce type of booster and have no business interest in the town of Wellingdale or its good name as a town. However, many people, friends and ones I know, have been born here and raised here; many have died here. The town is about the same as all people, no worse and no better, and should not be the subject of ridicule. As to my qualifications, I had one whole year and one summer at Andrew Jackson Junior College, and earned a valid teaching certificate for teaching English and social studies to the children of this state. Also, I actually saw some of the things which happened.

It is hard to know where to start. I cannot start with the big Wellingdale mad-dog scare, for no one would know the background. Therefore, I shall try to start at the beginning and bring in the Main Street mad-dog fight later, after I have told everything up to there.

Melvin Suggins lived with his old mother till she died on their place at the edge of town. Melvin had two older sisters, both of whom left and went to the city, one marrying a district manager of some kind and one working as a real estate saleslady. But Melvin was not an admirable person. He never did anything wrong or underhanded, but he had no confidence. One time he stubbed his toe down in front of the lumberyard and danced around in the street on one leg, yelling, "Ouch! That smarts!" Right where everybody could see him. He was kind of clumsy, not so much bad-looking, but his nose and ears were sunburned red, and he always wore overalls. Even the uglier girls around Wellingdale would not date him.

I am not sure if his mother had made a verbal contract with this fellow about the pigs on the Suggins place, or if Melvin made it after she died. Anyway, there was a contract for one big sow at ten dollars and her six baby pigs at three dollars each. The trouble was this: one more pig, the seventh, a runt. The fellow would not take it and said he had not contracted for it.

The pig had a lot of energy to be a runt. When it got hungry, it would squeal so that you could hear it clear up to Beal's filling station. Melvin cut up an inner tube and took a piece and sewed it with twine to make a nipple that would stretch over an old-fashioned milk bottle. That's the way he fed it. It would climb up in his lap to suck that bottle.

One day the pig took it into her mind to follow Melvin uptown. She squealed till he came back and opened the yard gate and let her out. She followed close, sometimes bumping into his ankles. People pointed and said, "Would you look at that? Isn't that pig cute?"

Nobody knows how she got her name, maybe from a song like the fiddle tune "Sally Goodin," or maybe it just popped into somebody's head. The first time I heard it, Melvin was going down the middle of the street with the pig and a man on the sidewalk yelled, "Hey, Melvin! Is Sally taking you for a walk?" Anyway, later they would be in the street and if Melvin saw a car coming, he would yell, "Sally, come here!" So everybody took it for her name.

It was cute when she was a pig, but after some months she did not look like a runt or a pig; she was an old red hog. Melvin would take her down the alleys where they put out garbage in a barrel to burn. We had three grocery stores and two cafés in Wellingdale at that time. Sally loved to eat old cabbages or half-spoiled cantaloupes or shriveled apples or two-week-old bread. Those barrels always had a sour smell about them, though some of it, I guess, was good food. Melvin would take a tow sack over his shoulder and load up some of the goodies to take home for her to eat on the Suggins place. She got fat.

In the high school we had a slick-haired biology teacher who thought he could explain everything out of his books. He put it in the town gossip that Sally had got "bonded" on Melvin when she was very young and now thought that Melvin was her mother. But the coach said, if that was so, why did Sally shy away from Hogan's big boar all the time. Hogan had this pure-blood Duroc boar he would rent out for two dollars a day when anyone wanted their sow bred, and when Sally and Melvin passed the place, the boar would come up to the fence grunting. Sally would get excited and try to get Melvin to hurry on past or get him to go to the other side of the street. The coach said she did not think Melvin was her mother, but her boyfriend. I don't know who can read a hog's mind, but I think she just regarded Melvin as her best and only friend.

It seemed like the bigger Sally got, the more confident she got, though she never left home without Melvin. In warm weather, if there was water and mud in the chug holes, she would run ahead of him down the street and root and wallow in the mud holes. Then she would come back to him and look at him, as if to say proudly, "Look what I found. Don't I look nice?" She kept his trouser legs dirty clear up to his knees from rubbing against him.

At the lumberyard, in the shade of the false front, men would sit on the benches in the cool of the evening. There were four benches, two on one side of the big door and two on the other. Melvin would sit at one end, and the other men would sit at the other side of the door at the end bench, talking and spitting tobacco and whittling thin shavings off pieces of cedar or white pine or redwood. Sally would sprawl by Melvin's feet, resting her snout on his shoes. Even if he got there first, Melvin would take the end bench, as if he did not want to cause anyone inconvenience in case they did not want to sit by him.

People began to talk—to gossip and argue. Somebody, undoubtedly a merchant on Main Street, brought Constable Elmore Bunson into the picture and told him something must be done. Is Wellingdale a hog pen and a laughingstock, or is it a decent, God-fearing town? What kind of town has a big, sloppy red sow going up and down Main Street?

The constable at Wellingdale was a political job. We had no crime rate. Since the freeway passed us by, there were hardly even any speeders. Elmore just took orders, or rather suggestions, from the best families, the old families, and the merchants. His biggest job was to catch stray dogs. Then, when he could get his pickup started, he would put on his jacket with the badge, strap on his gun, and take the dog out in the country by the creek and shoot it.

Elmore stopped Melvin on Main Street right in front of the hardware store. He said, "Don't bring that dang hog to town, Mr. Suggins. I have complaints. It's a public nuisance!"

Melvin said, "Why, other people keep swine." Sally got real close to Melvin's legs and watched with her little pig eyes.

Before I relate about the encounter with our constable, I feel obliged to mention a strange and violent scene which went on at a meeting of the Ladies Sewing and Quilting Circle. I say "violent" because some of the ladies could do violence with their voices and eyes. It is a delicate matter to tell, for I was not there, and only speak second hand. And gossip can be a very bad thing. The Sewing and Quilting Circle is more than a hundred years old. It is democratic. All the women who take pride, or want to take pride, in their needlework belong, regardless of their station in life. They give each other patterns and show how they do a certain crochet stitch and help piece quilt tops and tell where you can buy knitting yarn or yard goods at a certain price.

They got on the subject of Sally and Melvin, laughing at first. Then a woman who is active in church and civic functions made a sharp remark against Sally. (All these women shall remain nameless.) Then a woman who is a colored lady said Melvin Suggins had no friends and they should not begrudge him a pet. Then another woman raised her voice against Sally and Melvin both. Then a woman who is one of the best-educated people in town, and a would-be poet, said, "Do we love another because that one is clean and intelligent and deserves it? No! All love is blessed!"

There was shouting in the Ladies Sewing and Quilting Circle. (They were meeting on the bottom floor of the old Masonic Lodge building, now abandoned.) There were also tears and embarrassment. It was not at all the usual kind of meeting for the Sewing and Quilting Circle. The remarkable thing was the way the members split over the question, paying no attention to class or wealth or education.

It is to their credit that they patched it up. Several women apologized for raising their voices. One woman gave another a nice pair of pot holders she had made. But probably the reason they hushed it up was embarrassment and the understanding that those who favored Sally and Melvin could never defend themselves without looking like a bunch of fools.

Therefore, it seems to me that the ladies had no political pressure, except maybe for a wife talking to her husband. And the businessmen along Main Street talked to each other. They were the ones who gave the job of warning Melvin to Constable Elmore Bunson.

Elmore said, "They don't bring ugly hogs right to the middle of town."

"Ugly?" Melvin said. "Mr. Bunson, I don't care whether you are a constable or a duke or a count or a duchess. Other people keep loose animals—dogs and cats and chickens—in this township. There is no law."

"You will find out! This danged old sow is against the peace and dignity of the state! Suggins, this is your warning!"

"There is no law," Melvin said.

Sally stood there against Melvin's legs, looking at the strange intruder Elmore when he spoke, then up at her idol when he spoke. She knew an argument was going on.

"Suggins, be reasonable. That danged sow will go over two hundred right now. You can get twenty-five dollars, and let them do the butchering!"

Melvin turned redder than usual. He tried to say two or three things, but only said, "Damn you!"

"Well, you have had your warning. The next time I warn you, I'll strap on my gun." He slapped his hip significantly and stalked over to his parked bicycle, which he mounted and vigorously pumped away. Often Elmore had to ride his bicycle when his pickup would not start.

Elmore's warning was questionable. The only time anyone knew about his using his gun was against stray dogs that were a nuisance. That was his main official function—dog catcher. Over toward the freeway at the old highway crossing people seemed to come from far and wide to dump their unwanted dogs and cats. The cats would go wild and live on field mice and lizards and such; the dogs seemed to gravitate to Wellingdale, looking for a human friend.

The thing Sally did which most offended the sensitive and thoughtful people was rooting up the gladiolas in the yard of the Winters sisters. They lived alone in a nice two-story house with a white picket fence. The house was practically the showplace of Wellingdale on account of the beautiful red gladiolas they had. Other people had flowers, but not gladiolas. The youngest sister, Dorothy, did the shopping and took care of most of their business. The other sister, Violet, mostly stayed inside, though often a passerby could see her at a front window, just looking out.

A person cannot understand without knowing what had happened away back in 1940. Violet Winters had been our Homecoming Queen and on the honor roll and everything. Curtis McDonald had been great at sports, as well as on the honor roll, and had been voted the graduate most likely to succeed. Violet went away to what they used to call a finishing school for a year, and Curtis went to the university. Then the next summer they got engaged. People said it would be the ideal match. I guess it was the only engagement story ever to make the front page of the *Wellingdale Bi-Weekly Banner*.

To make a long story short, he had to go into the Army, so they planned to wait till he got out. Only he didn't return. He had won a medal out in the Pacific, a battle star or something, and had been promoted under fire in combat. Then he went in with the first wave in a landing on a distant tropical island. According to the *Banner,* he never got to the beach, and they did not recover his body.

Men of that generation around Wellingdale would show an old school picture or a newspaper picture of the baseball team and say, "That's me there. And that's Curt McDonald." But some of the women would say, "Who knows? Maybe it would not have been a great romance. Maybe Violet and Curtis were both too proud for their own good."

Anyway, a person can understand that the gladiola thing really offended some of the better people of the town. I did not see it and can only report what I heard from several sources. Melvin was squatting down in the middle of the street, tying one of his shoes, and did not see that Sally had bumped into the yard gate and opened it. She ran in as if she knew that there were bulbs which could be rooted up and eaten. It took Melvin a minute to find her; then, uncertain or embarrassed, he stood at the open gate shouting, "Sally, come here! Miss Winters! Miss Winters! Sally, stop that! Come here!" In another minute or two Dorothy Winters came out of the front door with a broom and proceeded to drive the hog out.

Some people exaggerated the damage, for to them it was almost sacriligious. I walked by three days later, and the gladiolas still looked beautiful through the picket fence. I did not look closely for damage; the white face and dark eyes of Violet Winters were in the front window, and I did not want to stare at the yard.

Constable Elmore Bunson tried to make good his warning without the use of his gun. One day he got his pickup started and came down to confront Melvin and Sally on Main Street. When he stopped and got out, he took from the pickup bed a long device he had made to catch stray dogs. It was a rake handle strung with a cotton rope, which made a loop at the end. He could put the loop over a dog's neck, then pull and choke the dog into submission. I saw the entire incident from less than a block away.

"Halt in the name of the law," Elmore demanded.

Melvin asked, "What in the world do you think you are doing?"

"I've got to take that danged hog off the public streets. You'd better not resist, Suggins."

Sally seemed to realize that this was the same intruder they had argued with before. She planted herself in front of her owner, her feet spread, ready to fight. Clearly she believed that the constable was after Melvin with that peculiar weapon.

"Don't touch my animal with that thing," Melvin said. He was trying to get between the constable and Sally, but she would not let him.

"You'd better not resist, Suggins! I've got to do my duty!" He moved right and left, trying to get his catcher into position.

When he lunged, Sally dodged, then ducked under the rake handle. She was rushing at his legs, and the constable barely managed to jump in time to avoid her. He nearly fell down.

Sally circled and stationed herself in front of Melvin again. It was surprising how fast she could move.

I could hear laughter up and down Main Street as the battle went on. Elmore kept yelling, "Suggins, I'm warning you!" But Melvin was not trying to do anything except get his pet hog out of the fight and take her home.

Elmore finally got the loop over Sally's head. She heaved up, jerked the thing out of his hands, and slung it halfway across the street. When the constable bent over to pick up his contraption, she charged. She hit him about knee-high with all her weight. Elmore went sprawling on the sidewalk.

It was obvious that there would not be any hog catching that day. Elmore yelled, "I'll get a warrant! You can't do this, Suggins! You'll see! I'll get a warrant!" He got his device, got his pickup started, and left with as much dignity as he could muster.

It seemed on the following day that Elmore might get important support in his campaign, for Sally went to the toilet on the sidewalk right in front of the ice cream parlor. They said she was just as natural and casual as could be. The merchants had not been happy before; now they were saying, "That's the limit. Miss Sally has got to go." There was a lot of laughing about it, but the store owners were serious.

We were never to learn whether our constable would get some type of court order, whether he would bring his gun to the next encounter, or what action he might devise against Sally and Melvin; for only one week after the latest warning there occurred what has since been called the "Wellingdale mad-dog scare."

It was twelve o'clock high noon. I was coming out of the hardware store. Elmore Bunson came pumping up Main Street, screaming at the top of his lungs, "Mad dog! Get the kids in the house! Mad dog!" A person could hear him blocks away. People came out of the stores to look. Elmore tried to guide his bicycle with one hand while he waved them back with the other, yelling, "Inside! Mad dog!"

He stopped long enough to shout at Mr. Riley at the hardware store, "I got to go get my gun and pickup! Mad dog! Get the kids in the house! Mad dog!"

Mr. Riley said to me, "If we have to wait for him to get his old pickup started, we won't have much protection."

A commotion was starting at the south end of Main Street, mostly shouting. Later we found that the hydrophobic dog had torn a lady's washing off the line and slung it around. We could see down there a man quickly climbing up a telephone pole.

The dog came raging, a heavy, black, short-haired mongrel. He was groaning half the time as if in pain, and half the time growling and barking furiously, running from one side of the street to the other. White foam on his mouth blew back on his neck and shoulders. He seemed driven to find something to slash and tear. At the feed store, a sack of chicken feed stood against one awning post; he scattered it in the street, moaning frantically.

At the hardware store door we were startled to hear shouts up in the other direction. "Melvin! Get inside!"

Down the middle of the street came Melvin Suggins and Sally. He had a tow sack over his shoulder, a quarter full of discarded vegetables and stale bread. Sally had just been in a mud hole and was rubbing against Melvin's legs as he walked.

"Melvin, mad dog! Get inside!" Several people yelled at him. "Mr. Suggins! Mad dog! Get off the street! Mad dog!" Mr. Riley shouted, "Come in here, Suggins! Bring the hog if you want to."

Maybe it was clear to everyone. At least it was to me. Melvin thought they were teasing him. He would not look at anyone. I do believe he closed his eyes, as if he did not want to embarrass a person by looking at them and identifying who was laughing at him.

The big black dog saw them and came charging. They were right where the pavement ends, just one block this side of the lumberyard. That's where the fight started. The dog seemed to take them as the whole reason for his anger and the cause of his pain. He was howling as he ran, and Sally jumped in front of Melvin and met the dog with her heavy shoulder. They both fell down.

Sally was heavier, but the mad dog was taller and furiously determined. Melvin swung his tow sack at the scrambling dog and began yelling. "No, Sally! He's mad! Come back! Come back! Run, Sally! Come on, Sally!"

The dog was attacking both of them, but Sally thought he was after Melvin, and she kept warding him off. Meanwhile, Melvin knew that any creature could get hydrophobia from one bite, and he kept trying to protect Sally, swinging his tow sack and yelling, "He's mad! Run for it, Sally!" But the truth is that she was quicker than Melvin and always stayed between him and the danger. You couldn't keep from being surprised at her quickness. Sometimes she would run bouncing up and down, front and rear, front and rear. Then she would glide, her little feet going like an engine or a sewing machine.

The dog was pitiful, barking and growling and almost crying; but intent on destroying both of them. White froth built up on his mouth, and I could see it on Sally's side and flank.

They raged up and down the street. I saw a wound on her shoulder and one front leg dark with blood. She began to fight with open mouth; then the dog was flung back and had to fight with one crippled leg. Melvin's sack broke open, scattering stale vegetables and bread. He was crying, "Please, Sally, it's all right! Come on, run!"

When they came nearer the hardware store we went inside and closed the door. I did not get a place at one of the windows till Mr. Riley decided to go to the back of the store and load up a shotgun. When I got a clear view, the two animals were down, tangled together. Melvin kicked the limp dog away. Both of the animals' throats were torn, and their life's blood was draining out on Main Street. Melvin squatted beside his pet and he was saying something to her while she died that we could not hear.

When we went out there, he said simply and softly, "Please do not bother her. I will be back after a while."

When he returned in about an hour, the body of the dog was already removed by our constable, sand was scattered on the blood, and people were speaking in hushed tones up and down the street. Melvin brought a wheelbarrow and a pick and shovel. He loaded Sally's body with great effort and pushed her toward the cemetery the other side of town.

The Wellingdale Cemetery land was donated by the Wellings family back before the turn of the century. It was twenty acres, which was too much, and only about an acre was fenced, that near the main road. Melvin took Sally back behind the fence on cemetery land. Evidently he took half the night digging a grave and burying her and setting up a cedar post at the head of the mound.

I happened to be driving on the back road the next day. I pulled over in the ditch and stopped and went down there to the mound, just because of a sentimental whim. Leaning against the post was a bunch of wildflowers, Indian Paint Brushes. Those particular flowers grew thickly out on the Suggins place.

But I have some more to reveal about the townspeople of Wellingdale, or some of them.

Very early the next morning, about five to be exact, when all decent people should be still asleep, I happened to be driving on the same back road. I stopped, just to look again at Melvin's wildflowers and at the crude marker. I could not see well, but it seemed as if something had been added to the mound. The closer I walked, the more curious I became. Something red. I could not believe it. A big spray of red gladiolas, loosely bound with a black ribbon, lay over the clods. They did not grow but one place in town.

Of course, I was gone from Wellingdale for over a year and did not return till two days after Memorial Day or Decoration Day. On that day the three churches of the town always got together and had a service and a picnic; then those who wanted to went out to the cemetery and put flowers on the graves of their dead. It was a kind of joyous occasion. One often saw kinfolk who had moved away to the city.

It happened that I was driving along the back road beyond the cemetery land the night after I got back to Wellingdale. It was about 3 A.M. Sitting there beside the road, I was wondering whether Melvin had remembered Sally. The moon was full in the sky to the west.

I could distinctly see the cedar post sticking up. But as I walked toward it, the mound of earth seemed to have grown to twice its size. If I had been surprised on my last visit, now I was astonished. Melvin's bunch of Indian Paint Brushes had its special place, leaning against the headpost. The big spray of gladiolas was in front on top. Farther down on top was an expensive bunch of hothouse lilies. Banked around on the sides were roses and chrysanthemums and every kind of garden flower and wildflower that grows around the town. I saw lilacs and Sweet Williams and Johnny-jump-ups and Shame Marys and Hollyhocks and Sweet Peas and Monk's Caps and Blue Bells and Honeysuckle and Woodbine.

Looking at the perfect black ribbon bow on the gladiolas, I could see the white deft hands of Violet Winters. And I could see her dark eyes looking forever out the window, her pale face becoming bony and wrinkled in the years as she waited for him, who would always remain young in pictures.

But who brought the expensive spray of lilies? Only two places in Wellingdale had hothouses on their grounds, the Wilsons and the Pevelers. I remembered that the Wilsons had lost their only child to diphtheria, a little boy only four years old. And the Pevelers—their youngest daughter, a spoiled girl of seventeen, had eloped with a hippie and was never heard from again.

As for the honeysuckle, one could not help thinking of the Carters, whose front porch was always enclosed with the fragrant flowers. They were black folks and the salt of the earth. He worked at Beal's filling station; in fact he actually ran the business. But their eldest son had gone into the city and got in with a bad crowd. He was in prison.

The roses and such could be from any of dozens of flowerbeds in town. One bunch of Black-eyed Susans was held together with a rubber band. Some of the Daisies and Dandelions were carefully placed; others were flung as if the bringer were afraid of being caught.

The moon was going down. I found myself looking over my shoulder to make sure I would not be caught here. Every flower someone had brought represented a risk, that someone would be caught. It struck me that there was a defiance in it all, a determination to say some secret in spite of the risk and prying words of gossip.

I confess that I had not come merely to look, but had brought a modest bouquet, thinking to place it beside Melvin's, just as a token. I put it at the foot of the mound, not wishing to cover up any of the others or disturb them.

Then, because of what I saw, I turned and hurried back toward the road. Over at the corner of the cemetery fence the dark form of a man or a woman had emerged, then had peered toward me, then had drawn back to hide behind the heavy corner post. When I got to my car, the form was kneeling at the mound. I drove off without my headlights on. Who it was, I don't care. Whoever would put flowers on the grave of a dumb old nasty hog is kind of strange, it seems to me, and not very sensible.

If anybody wants to ask why I seemed to turn up at the cemetery late at night, it's none of your business. I'm a respectable woman and a schoolteacher to the young people of this state for thirty-seven years.

Solid Gold

Will came in the front door of the house and went through to the kitchen before he found his mother. She was putting a skillet of corn bread in the oven and propping the iron door with a cane-bottom chair. The spring in the oven door wouldn't keep it closed.

"Abe Jones is going to college, Ma."

The old woman straightened up and wiped her hands on a washed-out flour sack that hung from a nail. "I'm glad he ken go. Ain't many people working on shares can afford to send their kids to college."

"I don't see any difference in them and us. Pa ought to be able to do without me better than the Joneses can without Abe, having his own bunch of cattle."

"The Joneses have got three more boys at home. You're the only one your pa and me has got left to depend on."

"I don't help Pa much. He could get a hand to help when he brands or anything, and it wouldn't cost him as much as it does to feed me."

The old woman went back and forth from the kitchen to the dining room, setting the table. She didn't look at the boy. "It'ud be mighty lonesome around here with just your pa and me, Will."

"I guess it isn't lonesome around here now. With Abe gone I won't have a friend for ten miles."

"I know it ain't easy for you, Will. It ain't easy for me, either."

"If I don't go this fall, I won't ever get away. I'll be right here when I'm sixty, working just like Pa is now."

The old woman washed her hands and wiped them again on the faded flour sack. The knuckles were large. Blue veins stood out on the backs. The palms were cracked and stained. "I got eighteen dollars left from them pullets, Will. You could have it if your pa was to say you could go."

"You help me talk to him, Ma. He never does pay any attention when I bring it up. You help me and maybe he'll say it's all right."

The old woman shook her head. "No, Will, I ain't taking your side against Pa. He may not understand you, but I ain't so sure you understand him either. I ain't taking no sides in it."

"What if he says I can't go?"

"He's your pa, Will."

Dinner was steaming on the table when the old man came up from the barn. Will and his mother waited in the dining room while he washed the heavy grease from his hands on the back porch. The old man was tall and skinny of build. His Adam's apple stuck out almost as far as his chin. His tousled light gray hair was a contrast to the dark bronze of his face and neck. When he rolled back his shirt sleeves to wash his arms, the skin showed as white as that of a baby. He called to the woman inside.

"I'm going to have to go into Olney this afternoon, Ma. Got to have a blacksmith fix a couple of iron straps to hold that binder tongue together."

The old woman came to the door. "You going to get groceries while you're in town?"

"Ain't nothing you need before Saturday, is they?"

"Nothing we have to have, I reckon."

They went in and sat down at the table. The old man spoke to his wife. "You want me to take that watch of yours and leave it to be fixed?"

She shook her head. "It'ud cost a lot of money. I reckon we'd better let it go awhile."

"It ain't much good if it won't run."

"I ain't got no use for a watch anyway. It's just as good a keepsake of Grandma whether it runs or not."

The old man chuckled. "You think so high of it, I'd of thought you'd want to get it fixed."

"It's solid gold," she said. There was a flash of light in her eyes which had not been there before.

The old man hitched his chair closer to the table and bowed his head. "God, we thank Thee for this food and all the other blessings of life. Amen."

The three filled their plates with boiled beans and potatoes and thick slabs of corn bread.

"Going into Olney with me, Will?"

"No."

"What's the matter? Don't you like Olney anymore?"

"I don't get anything out of going into that town."

The old man set his glass of buttermilk back down beside his plate. "There's something bothering you, Will. Speak up. What is it?"

"Abe Jones is going out to Lubbock to college, Pa. He's catching the bus tonight."

"And you want to go along. We've had that all out before, son. With them heifers I lost last winter, and the grass lease money coming due in January, you ain't got a chance of going this year."

"If I don't go this year, I won't ever go."

"We ain't got the money, Will. Can't you understand that?"

"Lots of boys work their way through college. I can do it with my forty-seven dollars I have to start on."

"What about that saddle you were going to get?"

"I won't ever need a saddle if I go to college."

The old man was still eating, but slowly, and he didn't pay any attention to the food. "I know it don't seem right now, son, but you may find out when you're older that hard work is worth more to you than going to school. I only went to fourth grade and now I have my own bunch of cattle. You stay here and work with me. Your brothers have all gone off and left me and you and your ma with the place. You stay here and work with us, and when we're gone it'll be all yours."

Will had filled his plate with food but hadn't touched any of it. "I don't want the place when you all are gone. I wouldn't take it right now if you were to offer it to me."

The old man laid the worn knife and fork down slowly. Deep wrinkles cut across his forehead and between his eyes. "Listen, boy, you're seventeen years old. By law I can make you do anything I think is right, but I ain't. I'm just saying one thing, and that's the last. If you ever leave here, don't come back."

The meal was finished in silence. The old man got up, swiped his sleeve across his mouth, and started out the door. "Sure you don't want me to take the watch, Ma?"

"No, there ain't no need."

A minute later the woman and the boy heard the popping backfire of a Model-A Ford. The noise faded out down the road. Will arose without a word and went up the stairs to his room. He jerked a battered tin suitcase from under the bed and swung it open on a chair. Into it he dumped the contents of a bureau drawer. He took a black, half-cotton, half-wool suit down from its hanger on the wall, placed it on top of the wad of clothing, and snapped the suitcase shut. Then he placed it at the head of the stairway and went down.

His mother was washing the dishes. "Pa never give the pig its water," she said. "Must of forgot it. You take it down, will you, Will? I'm going to lie down awhile; my head's splitting."

Will took a five-gallon bucket from the porch and filled it at the pump in the backyard. He carried it down to the pig pen below the barn and poured it into the wallow that the pig had rooted out in the shade. He stood and watched the pig drink and then lie down and roll over in the muddy water with low grunts.

Will climbed the gentle hill to the house, threw the bucket toward the water pump, and went inside. His mother was not in the kitchen or dining room. He climbed the stairs again and looked briefly at the room; then he reached down for the suitcase. It was not in the exact place where he had left it.

He knelt down and opened the rusty metal catches. Everything looked just as it had. He raised up the black suit which was on top. A wad of dollar bills was tucked in among the clothing. Will picked them up and straightened them. A tiny, round gold watch fell out. It had a black silk string for a band. He counted the eighteen dollars, then wrapped the watch back in the money, and put them inside the suitcase.

He picked it up and went slowly down the stairs. His mother was lying on the bed in the front room. Her eyes were closed. Her breathing was regular. He stood by the bed for a long time and looked down at her. He looked at her graying hair, her wrinkled face, and her worn hands. He started to bend over her, then straightened up quickly and tiptoed to the front door.

He went outside and down the dusty road that the Model-A Ford had taken thirty minutes before. The suitcase made a rattling, tinny noise, beating against the side of his leg as he walked.

Cimarron, the Killer

"Talk about your horse sense," the old man said. "You ain't seen it. Ain't nobody seen it, without they seen Cimarron the way I did. He was a horse that had feelings, just like a human. You wouldn't believe it!" He glared suddenly at the disbelief that he suspected and began working at his jumper pocket, from which he soon extracted a roll of bills slightly smaller than a pound coffee can. The one on the outside was a twenty, but I got enough of a glimpse to tell that the bill under it was a one.

"That's a cool three hundred bucks," he said. "Money talks. This old lady, Ma Patrima, sent it to me right out of the clear blue sky. She wrote and said I ain't never forgot that horse ner who give it to me, and this will pay you for part of what he was worth. Money talks," he repeated as he wedged it back in a pocket, as if he had proven what he was going to tell.

"First time I seen Cimarron was in Stamford, Texas. I was riding and bull-dogging then, and making a fair living at it. A bunch of us old boys went out to the stockpens, like we did to look over the rodeo stock. In them days they shipped rodeo stock by train a lot. They had unloaded these broncs and a lot of fellers was perched on the fence looking. One of the handlers says, 'That's Cimarron; he's a killer.'

"He pointed at this big dun horse, a young one, maybe three, not over four years old. I say 'dun'; in the north they generally call them 'buckskin,' but on the ranges in the Southwest they call them 'dun' or 'coyote dun.' He wasn't a smooth dun, if you know what I mean. He looked flea-bit or moth-eaten, like some of them do. All it is, a dun has got black skin, you see; if he sheds a little or gets scarred up a little, that black shows through his dun hair and he looks flea-bit. That's all it was. Outside of that he was strong, wide awake, held his head high. His mane and tail was jet black.

"Well, of course, I didn't know at that time but what I might have to crawl on him the next day, so I says, 'How come he's a killer? Who'd he kill?'

"This handler says, 'I hear he's killed many a man.'

"Then some town dude spoke up and says, 'He sure looks like a killer.'

" 'You ain't seen nothing yet,' the handler says. 'Wait till you see him in that arena tomorrow.'

"I says, 'Does he belong in the bareback broncs? He's big enough to go in the saddle-bronc string.'

" 'Shoot,' the handler says, 'I hear they ain't never nobody been able to get a saddle on him.'

"Well, I could of told him better, but I shut up. You can put a saddle on any horse. I worked a many a year on the range where you rode pitching horses—they bucked on the northern ranges, but they pitched where I worked—and you rode them because that's what they give you to punch cattle on. I been around a few horses in my day, some that never seen a man till they was grown and trapped, and I been around a few horse trainers too. You can put a saddle on any horse. You can hear a lot of bull around a rodeo. I figured I'd just wait and see what kind of a killer this horse was.

"Next day I noticed something funny. Before they put the bareback broncs in the chute, they kept them in this corral behind the stands and one place you could see between the stands and see the arena. Cimarron was standing there with his head high and his ears straight up, looking over that fence, watching what went on in that ring.

"I never drawed him. Idaho Joe did; he was an old hand at the game and a good rider. Finally the time come and the announcer announced him. They used one of these pasteboard funnels, you know, for a megaphone in them days. The announcer yelled, 'Idaho Joe coming out of chute one on Cimarron!' That was before the days when they announced him as 'Cimarron, the Killer.'

"Well, the horse began to snort in there. I could see him between the planks, and he wasn't giving Idaho any trouble, just standing there giving him a chance to get his circingle like he wanted it. The crowd heard the snorting and got real quiet.

"When they throwed open the gate that dun come out screaming. You don't hardly ever hear a sound like that anymore. It was part rebel yell and part Comanche war whoop. It was a neigh with kind of snarls in it, you know. Well, the crowd come to their feet. And I mean they seen an exhibition.

"He went high and he twisted right; he come down and he twisted left and landed stiff-legged. He switched ends, all the time swinging that heavy black tail and mane like a flag. He kicked high and mighty, that dun did. He zigzagged and sunfished and jackknifed. All the time screaming like a banshee! He would rare up and paw and come down humped like a horseshoe. It was savage!

"Well, old Idaho got behind, as the saying goes. He got to riding over here when Cimarron was already over yonder. He hit the ground rolling and scrambled for the fence. When the hazers got the dun out, Idaho walked back out to get his hat. The crowd was still on their feet and they clapped; I guess they knew a good ride when they seen it. Idaho had stuck about seven seconds, and if I ain't mistaken that was the longest time Cimarron was rode that season.

"I was on the circuit with him most of that year; in fact, I drawed him myself at Phoenix. Now, I'd seen him in three performances and I'd been studying him. But you couldn't keep up with that horse; he was a gut-twister. I mean it. I'm not just making excuses. Well, I stayed maybe four or five seconds and when I hit the ground, he come down right on top of me. I hit on the side and I seen his broad belly straight over me when I landed. Now that is one of them times when all your life is supposed to flash in front of your eyes. Seemed like he was bound to stomp me or kick the fool out of me. He straddled me with all four feet, like you threw a four-legged table down over me; then he rared up and twisted back, screaming, and bucked out across the arena, trying to get his circingle off.

"They come running. 'Are you all right? Are you all right?' I says, 'I'm fine; how are you?' The crowd clapped, but it wasn't clear if they clapped for me or for Cimarron.

"I tell you, that horse could make you cuss and hope at the same time. He was a picture bucker, you know. Now some picture buckers are actually easy. They're too simple. The crowd guesses it, and the judges know it for sure; you won't make no score on them. Cimarron wasn't like that. He was rough as a cob and anybody could see it. It would make people yell in the stands, you know; in fact, it would make old hands at the game climb on the fence to watch and even they would yell. That dun would bring the crowd to their feet and put his rider in the dust. Like I say, it would make you cuss and hope at the same time; if you could stay on him, you could win any contest they was, hands down.

"Some of the riders called him a killer that first season, but it wasn't till next year he got the title officially, you might say. I ain't sure where it was at; Boise I think; I've got my places mixed up that long ago. But I remember that Ed Burleson was running the show. Ed always liked to run a fast performance.

"Anyway, they had these two clowns out there during the bull riding and they had this straw man they would throw at a bull and let him toss it a few times. It was just a pair of old overalls stuffed real fat with straw. Well, the bareback riding followed the bull riding, and Cimarron was the second horse. That straw dummy was still laying in the arena.

"I don't remember who had drawed him, but the dun put up his usual fight. That scream would go through people like lightning. The rider, whoever it was—seems like it was an Oklahoma boy—went into the dirt, and Cimarron went bucking off across the arena. The hazers come in between him and the rider, of course. Then Cimarron spotted that straw dummy and he lit into it like a case of dynamite.

"That was the most savage stomping you could ever see, and it sounded like all the hate an animal could have for a man was screaming out of that horse. It would almost make you sick to your stomach. Straw flew around like a whirlwind hit it. The coveralls was a limp rag tromped into the dust.

"After that was when they started announcing him as 'the killer.' They put it on the posters and billboards too: 'Cimarron, the Killer,

Never Been Rode.' You could hear talk from the fellers that hang around a rodeo and also from the paying customers: 'They say he's killed many a man.'

"One year I was dragging this empty trailer for a feller. He had been in the money up at Calgary, and I hadn't even made expenses, and he had sold his roping horse. So he give me fifteen dollars to drag his empty horse trailer behind my old pickup all the way from Canada to Texas.

"I was coming through eastern Colorado, the other side of Las Animas, when I seen this bunch of horses out in the pasture, maybe a hundred yards off the road. I pulled over in the bar ditch to look at them; no special reason. They probably belonged to old man Padgett, who had some rodeo stock out there. I seen two things that got me interested about the same time. There was this big dun among them that looked familiar. The other thing: this kid, just a small kid in a straw hat, was walking out toward the horses. He had a bunch of oats in his hand, not threshed oats, but oats out of a bundle. I'd say the kid was seven years old, dark complexion, barefooted.

"This dun horse come to him. The kid give him the oats, heads first, you know, and the horse commenced to chew them with the straw sticking out of his mouth. Then the kid come around to the near side and jumped up and got hold of his mane over the withers and begin to dig his bare toes into that horse's front leg; he clambered around a good bit and finally got on his back.

"I says to myself, 'Couldn't be the horse I thought he was.' Then I seen the double-X on his left hip. I got out of my truck and walked out that way and says to the youngster, 'Hi there, cowboy.'

"He just grinned at me. His straw hat was too big for him and hanging on both ears.

"I says, 'What's the name of your horse?'

"He grinned some more and then it come to me that he was a Meskin boy; some of them don't speak nothing but Meskin. I says, *'Cómo 'sta, vaquero?'*

" *'Way-no,'* he says through that grin.

"I says, *'Cómo se llama el caballo?'*

"He told me; it's the same in Meskin as it is in English, only he says it, *'See-ma-roan,'* and there was about a dozen R's in it.

"I looked at the dun's right knee on the inside and he had this little scar I'd noticed on Cimarron before. Just a scratch, sort of like a black question mark. Another brand, you might say.

"I walked back to my pickup mumbling to myself, then set there and looked. That savage dun outlaw was trotting around giving that Meskin kid a little ride. I chewed that problem over for days and never did make heads ner tails out of it. That crazy horse liked Meskin kids, or else maybe he just hated gringo rodeo riders.

"It was about two years later that I got to be a hero up at Cheyenne. I was running low on cash and was helping some with the stock the day before the big show started, so as to get my entrance fees. Some of the broncs had been in the mud or else had cockleburs in their mane and tail. They needed to be cleaned up a little. I had the misfortune to put my loop on Cimarron, or I thought it was misfortune. But I didn't even tighten the rope when he turned and ambled up to me, looking at the currycomb and brush. It's a fact; he held his head down where I could brush every place good, and he would turn this way and that like a man in a barber chair. Well, I figured, this crazy bronc don't only like little Meskin boys, but he likes to have his hide scratched good.

"When we drawed for bareback broncs next day, I got him. The fellers ask me what next-of-kin they should notify and where should they ship the remains. I'd been hoping to ride in the money, and now I went to hoping he wouldn't cripple me up too bad to where I couldn't enter the bulldogging.

"He didn't jump around in the chute, just snorted. The crowd got quiet. They knew about Cimarron, the Killer, never been rode. He come out with that chilling scream, and the crowd come to their feet to see the meanest, wildest animal that ever performed. I've told you how he could pitch and twist and swing that tail and mane. He jarred my eyeteeth, and I could hear the stands whistling and yelling.

"But it was funny. Whenever I was losing my seat one direction or the other, he would jump that way. The horn blowed and he bumped into the pickup horse and dumped me off behind the pickup man's saddle. Then Cimarron charged the fence and splintered two or three planks. The hazers managed to get him out before he could destroy the arena. I thought the crowd wouldn't ever stop cheering.

"It was in the newspapers: BRONC BUSTER CONQUERS CIMARRON, THE KILLER. And my picture with the manager handing me first money for bareback riding.

"I had found a big secret, how to have a cinch on top money. I followed that horse and give him a good combing and brushing every chance I got, but, dammit, I couldn't draw him. And didn't want to let another cowboy in on the secret. He went right on throwing all the riders into the dirt and putting on a great show, only the posters and handbills said: NEVER BEEN RODE BUT ONCE!

"In a few years I went to having bad luck. An old rangy steer broke three of my ribs in Fort Worth; he thought he was supposed to bulldog me, instead of the other way around. Then I busted a knee against a fence in San Antonio. I worked some in the oilfields, then got a job as a night watchman in Denver.

"I was living with my sister and her old man, and one day I went out to fix a flat on my pickup setting beside the gravel street. This ice wagon was coming up the street and wherever the ice card was in the front window it would say twenty-five or fifty or some weight and the feller would carry it in. I seen that he wasn't driving the team, but he would yell at them and they would pull up to the next ice card. They pulled right up behind me, but I didn't pay much attention. I was bending over trying to see how to get the jack set under the axle, and one of them horses bit me. Right on the bottom!

"I jumped about three feet high. Fact is, it wasn't a hard bite, about like a young dog you're playing with. Some old flea-bit dun. It was Cimarron.

"The ice man come out. Actually, I couldn't explain it, but I hated to see that horse hooked to that ice wagon. The feller started complaining about me bothering his team. I says, 'I like that old worn-out dun horse and will give you thirty dollars for him right where he stands.'

"He laughed and says, 'He ain't for sale. That's the smartest delivery horse in town. I would not part with him for a cent less than fifty dollars.'

"I says, 'He's ready for dog food, but I like him and will give thirty-five. That's my final offer.'

"He says, 'That horse ain't but eight years old, and I would not take a cent less than forty-five.'

"We could have checked his teeth and got his age within two years, but I says, 'I was on the rodeo circuit with him fourteen years, and he was four the first I saw him.' That shocked him out of all his trading powers. I give him forty dollars for the horse right there on the street and rode with him over to the ice house. Then I rode Cimarron, the Killer, back to my sister's place with just a little cotton rope around his neck and a half-hitch around his nose. I put him in the backyard.

"Well, I'd done a damned fool stunt, as my sister told me several times. Spent every last cent I had on an old horse I had no use for and no pasture to put him out on. All from being soft-headed. All because I figured he had four or five more years and didn't want him to spend it pulling no ice wagon.

"About that time we had to go to a funeral down in Abilene, and we left the horse at a dairy farm for a week. Down there we got to see Ma Patrima, that I hadn't seen for thirty years. She was my second cousin and had been some kind of big star.

"She had started out in Oklahoma with Miller's 101 Ranch and Wild West Show. Then she traveled for years with Ringling Brothers and Barnum and Bailey. Patrima wasn't even her name. She had made up the name of Hermosa Patrima for the posters and handbills. When she got to be the oldest person on the lot, they started calling her Ma. Now she had got sort of wrinkled and dumpy-looking and she was working as assistant manager and general swamper for a one-elephant circus that made these small Texas towns.

"I offered to give her Cimarron. Told her he was an old rodeo horse that had gone gentle as a baby, but could pull in harness and help raise a tent or anything. I guaranteed he would earn his keep. She didn't know for sure that they needed him, but anyway she sent a feller to get him a few days later.

"About a year or so later I seen Ma Patrima in Clarendon. Of course I asked about Cimarron, how he was working out. Well, she frowned and shook her head. 'He earns his keep,' she says. 'He's smart, always looking around. But he bothers the clowns. He don't hurt them. He just noses into the dressing tent and bites them. They want me to sell him for dog food, but I hate to do it.' I made her promise not to sell him without telling me. I had a good job as night watchman at a oil-field supply warehouse in Wichita Falls at that time.

"Well, I never heard from Ma Patrima ner the horse for a couple of years. Then I seen where this little circus was coming to Archer City, a kind of one-horse town about twenty or thirty miles south of there, so I drove down there. Some of the streets was blocked off. I walked up and found Ma Patrima on the courthouse lawn, following the parade while it circled the square. Right away I asked about Cimarron, but she pointed at the front of the parade.

Leading the show was this smooth cream-colored Arabian-looking horse with a lot of black mane and tail. He didn't even have a bridle on. Standing up on his back was this twelve-year-old girl, all gussied out in tights and spangles.

" 'Pegasus,' Ma Patrima says, 'and that's my granddaughter Rosalee on him.'

" 'Nice horse,' I says. 'Whereabouts is Cimarron? Is he down at the grounds?'

" 'Look at that gait on Pegasus,' she says. 'How he lifts his knees, but easy so she won't fall off.'

"It was a classy horse all right, this Pegasus. His neck was sort of arched and his chin tucked in a little. I didn't see a soul showing him which way to lead the parade. But if Ma Patrima thought she could get away with selling my old rodeo horse for dog food and then talk me out of it, she was crazy as a loon. By the time we followed them down to the block where the carny tents and the big tent was set up, I meant to have it out with her.

"It's a fact; that Pegasus got down on his knees to let that little girl Rosalee hop off. She went skipping away in her pink tights. Pegasus come up to me and Ma Patrima.

" 'Looky here,' I says, 'I want some kind of answers! Don't lie to me! Whereabouts is Cimarron at?'

"Her face was sort of twisted up and she says to me, 'You damned old fool! Look at me! I'm dumpy! I've lost my figger! Look at you! You damned old stove-up rodeo hand! Look at your potbelly and your spindly legs!'

"About the time I got good and insulted, I seen that she was crying.

"She says, 'Dammit, can't you see when he was bothering the clowns, he just wanted somebody to help him? You can bet your sweet life if I hadn't lost my figger, I'd get me some greasepaint and I'd go back to work. In front of the crowd, where I belong!'

"I was mixed up as a batch of cement. Pegasus reached out and bit me easy on the shoulder. His neck wasn't arched and his chin tucked in like before. I went and rubbed on his left hip where it looked too smooth. Grease come off in my hand and there was a double-X. Then I looked inside his right knee and rubbed. A perfect little black question mark scar.

"I says, 'I'll be damned!'

"Ma Patrima says, 'Please do not use that language around us ladies.'

"I seen that the granddaughter Rosalee had come back, licking a ice cream cone. So I says, 'I mean I'll be danged!'

"Well, it wasn't but a few months after that when Ma Patrima wrote me. The old horse had took his last bow. She hadn't never forgot who give her the horse. She said the money wasn't half what he was worth, but it was all she could spare.

"Cimarron, the Killer. He killed many a man. And ladies and children too. He slayed them and laid them in the aisles from Canada to Texas. When he got through killing them, they stood up and cheered.

"Sometimes, even now, when I'm all alone by myself, I can hear the crowd cheering. After all, I was a hero once. If I hadn't lost my figger, I'd get me some of that greasepaint and go back to work."

Yore Grandpa Was a Sporting Man

Buck Holmes stomped back and forth on his back porch, shaking the loose flooring with his cowboy boots and causing the tin patches on the roof to rattle. Every time he looked at the big black and tan hound that lay on the edge of the porch, he cursed. He said with fervor, "I ought to kill that fool Perkins! I'll horsewhip him, that's what I'll do! I'll cowhide him!"

Buck was not a handsome man. He had one top front tooth missing where a yearling steer, which he had been trying to bulldog, had stepped in his face at a rodeo fifteen years ago. When he had calmed down, he stood with hands on skinny hips, looking at the hound. The dog looked back with big serious eyes, his jaws drooping, his forelegs before him on the porch; one paw was twisted outward unnaturally and was matted with dried blood. Buck rubbed his red beard stubble, slowly shook his head, then yelled in through the screen door, "Myrtle! You got anything for Old Rip to eat?"

His wife came to the door. She was a big woman with a broad kind face and straw-colored hair. "Why, it's Old Rip, isn't it, Buck! Old Rip's come home."

"Yeah, but I'd just as lief he hadn't. Look at his leg."

"I'll swan!" Myrtle said. She opened the screen to peer at the old dog. "What could have done it, Buck? Is he been in a fight some place?"

"He's been in one of that Perkins's wolf traps. Confound that old man! I'll get even with him if it's the last thing I do!"

"Well, he never meant to catch him," Myrtle said in a soothing voice. "He's just trying to trap and make a living."

"Make a living! Look at my dog, Myrtle! The best dog I got! Ruint! And you tell me old Perkins is got to make a living. Trapping all the wolves and putting them up in a cage! How's a sporting man going to get in a decent wolf hunt?"

Old man Perkins lived in a tent over on Webb Creek and trapped shunk, opossum, coon, and badger in the winter, and coyotes the year around. In the summer the skins were no good, but Baxter County paid a bounty of two dollars for a pair of coyote ears. The coyotes Perkins caught in the autumn he sometimes caged up and saved until cold weather when their fur would become thick and salable.

"Fightin'est dog I ever had," Buck went on. "I knew he was getting old, but I didn't expect him to end like this." Suddenly a pleading note came into his voice. "Look at him, Myrtle!" He turned and smashed his bare fist against the gray weatherboarding. "Look at my best dog!"

"Good lands!" Myrtle said. "Don't do that, Buck. You'll hurt your hand. I'll get something for him to eat."

She went into the kitchen and brought back a slab of yellow cornbread. Buck broke it into chunks on the porch. The big dog hobbled over eagerly. "Look at him walk! And him the fightin'est dog I ever had!" He shook his head slowly as he watched the dog gulp down the cornbread. "I aim to get even with that Perkins. I'll cut him down like a broom weed. I'll take me a bear trap over there and set it in the door of his tent and see how he likes to get caught."

Buck stood over the hound, without the swagger he usually had in his bearing. His bony hips weren't pushed out in front as usual. "I haven't got the wolfhounds I once had, Myrtle. There was Old Rosy. I've never had another dog like her. She was the trailin'est dog I ever had, and the smartest. And there was Old Tip; he was the runnin'est dog I ever had, and a good all-around dog, too. Now here's Old Rip, the fightin'est dog I ever had, and he's as good as done for. It's like a sign, that's what it is. The sporting in this country is about over."

Myrtle wished to pacify him. She said hopefully, "Well, there's the pups, Buck. Maybe one of the pups will turn out good."

"The pups! Myrtle, you oughtn't to even mention the pups when

I'm talking about dogs like Old Rip. The pups! Slim Wilkinson, for instance. He will do good to get his full growth without bothering to turn out good. He'll fall in the cistern and drown or else break his back from jumping around like a fool."

"He might turn out to have a good nose," Myrtle suggested. "He's always smelling of something, seems like."

"Yeah, he's always smelling of tobacco spit, or where you throw out dishwater. You look at my dogs a minute, Myrtle. Right now I got Ike and Bob and Wing and Fan and Trailer and Rome and Pete and Jip and Ringer. Ringer would be a top dog outside of running rabbits. And then I got the four pups, four if you count Slim Wilkinson. I got *enough* dogs, Myrtle. They make a good pack if Old Rip is with them. But look at him. I guess the sporting in this country is about over."

Old Rip sopped up the last cornbread crumb, as well as some dust out of the cracks, then hobbled down under the porch to lie down. Watching his pitiful attempt to walk, Buck moaned, "Why couldn't it have been one of the pups, instead of Old Rip."

Buck's "pups" were over a year old. The largest, Slim Wilkinson, was almost as big as Old Rip, and still growing. He was white with a scattering of large and small black patches. About the young hound, Buck would say: "That Slim Wilkinson is the clumsiest fool dog I ever had. All I got for him is hopes he might change. If he was to tighten up in the joints some and stop that crawling up to you on his belly with his legs flopping out at the sides and grinning and slapping his tail on the ground, then he might be a passable dog."

But Buck Holmes's four boys, none of them the connoisseur of hounds that Buck was, loved the pups, which they had helped to raise. Elmer, an unlikely youngster of nine years, even went so far as to think of the loose-jointed Slim Wilkinson as his favorite.

The boys mourned Old Rip's crippling almost as much as Buck did, for they knew the old dog was a great one. They knew it because Buck said it. They did not think of their father as an irresponsible tenant farmer or an unsuccessful rancher, both of which he was, but as a man who could not be judged by any ordinary standards at all. Indeed, their pa had done everything worth doing, such as riding the meanest horses in the world when he used to follow the rodeos, and he knew everything worth knowing, such as how to break a dog from chasing rabbits. Their pa could still do anything worth doing; he had built a dog trailer as good as a factory-made job and had covered it with the chicken wire from the garden fence; it didn't matter if the chickens got into the garden because the grassburrs and ragweeds always choked out the vegetables anyway.

For several days Buck did nothing but feed Old Rip and mope around the house, occasionally muttering some vile threat against the trapper Perkins. Then one day just after noon, he walked out, followed by the four boys, to the windmill a hundred yards from the house. They turned and faced the house. Then Buck began to yell, "Old Rip! Hyah, hyah! Hey, Rip! Hyah, Rip!"

The boys took up the call. Dogs poked their heads around the corner of the cane stack and from under the barn and smokehouse. Old Rip scrambled out from under the back porch and ran toward them eagerly, but he was favoring his right front leg. When the old dog had covered a third of the distance to the windmill, the pups bellied out from under the smokehouse, led by Slim Wilkinson, and came pounding down the same trail. They got to Buck and the boys as soon as the old dog.

Buck squatted on his boot heels, patting the old dog and wallowing the loose skin on the dog's neck; but he was shaking his head. "He can still run, kids, but not like he used to. And he'll get to where he knows it, and it'll kill his sporting blood. He'll be just another old pot-likker hound."

Slim Wilkinson was bounding around gaily, like some kind of jubilee was in progress. He finally settled down on Elmer, the only one of the boys who would let the young dog lick him in the face. "Pa," Elmer said, "did you see the way Old Slim Wilkinson came scooting down here?"

"Good night! Elmer!" said Wayne, who was next older than Elmer. "This sure isn't the time to say anything like that."

Buck's hand was still over the old dog's shoulder. "Kids, I sure would like to have one last good wolf chase while Old Rip's still got some sporting in him."

"Boy!" Elmer said, "Old Slim Wilkinson is the runnin'est dog of all the pups, isn't he, Pa?"

"Goodnight, Elmer!" Bert said. "You haven't got a lick of sense. You oughtn't to say 'runnin'est.' The runnin'est dog Pa ever had was Old Tip and a long time before you were born. You ought to know better than to say some fool pup is the best at something, without Pa says it first. Goodnight! Pa, I ought to kick Elmer a little and try to learn him something about dogs."

"Naw, don't be kicking." A crafty look had come into Buck's face, along with the dejection. "Kids, isn't this Saturday? And doesn't Perkins always walk in to Baxter City on Saturdays?"

"Yeah," Red said.

"And doesn't it take him all day to buy grub and pack it back out to his camp?"

"Yeah, he never gets in till dark."

"Kids, I'm going over to Perkins's camp to see if he'll pay me for catching Old Rip. Red, you go up in the barn loft and get me a tow sack and throw it in the car. I been promising you all I'd take you wolf hunting some day. Well, we might go tonight."

He refused to answer any of the boys' questions. Five minutes later he fired up the old car and headed out the wagon road toward the highway.

"Pa's going to take that tow sack," Elmer said, "and throw it over old Perkins's head, and beat him up."

"Goodnight, Elmer! Perkins isn't even at his camp now," Red reminded him.

"He said he'd like to set a bear trap for that Perkins," Myrtle said. "I hope Buck don't go over to his camp while he's gone and make some kind of trouble."

An hour later Buck came back. He swung open the car door and stepped out with some of the swagger he used to have. The back of his hand was marked with a long red scratch. He stood at one of the back car windows, the glass of which was missing, while the boys gathered around. In the back of the car on the floor lay the tow sack, full, a heap of something that didn't move, but seemed to tremble slightly.

"Pa's got old Perkins in there," Elmer said, awestruck.

"I got me a growling, spitting cyclone in there," Buck said. He sucked at the scratch on his hand. Then he said, with a drama in his voice which sent goose bumps up the spines of the four boys, "Namely, a wolf! Catch up the dogs, kids. Get your chores done. We're going wolf hunting tonight."

They hurriedly cut the cookstove wood, slopped the hogs, gathered the eggs, and milked old Bessie, and began to put the hounds into the trailer, so they would have them all in before dark. The old hounds saw what was going on and came running up to get into the trailer. Sensing that something important was afoot, Slim Wilkinson scrambled into the front seat of the car.

"Slim Wilkinson, doggone your hide," Buck said. "I reckon you can go, but you dern sure can't drive."

Elmer, who had never been on a hunt before and who was as excited as the pup, had preceded Slim Wilkinson into the car. "Pa, could old Slim Wilkinson ride in here with us if I'll hold him in my lap?"

"Hold him in your lap, nothing! He's twice as big as you are. Stop hugging that clumsy pup, Elmer, and come out of that car. We're not leaving till sundown."

At supper Buck was thoughtful. He had eaten half of his first helping of red beans, when he lay down his fork and cleared his throat. "Kids, I better talk to you a little bit. I better tell you some things about tonight, so you'll know."

"Stop smacking, Bert," Myrtle said. "All you kids stop eating, so's you can hear your pa better."

"Kids, it's something about sporting I want to say. I want to start with your grandpa. He wasn't a good-looking man. He had big red ears, like Elmer here; or come to think of it, all you kids has got sort of red ears. But that isn't the point. Your grandpa had something real unusual about him; he was a sporting man. It was a kind of magic he had. But, kids, you know he had a dog—Old Tiger." Buck screwed up his face and fingered one of his big red ears, finding it hard to say what he was trying to. "Well, kids, I've had lots of dogs myself, and I've had three kind of like Old Tiger. But that thing is passing away. It's going. And the last of it is out yonder in the dog trailer with a busted foot—Old Rip. He's the last."

Down Myrtle's broad, simple face two fat tears ran and dropped from her chin down to her heavy bosom.

Buck went on. "It's hard to talk about that sporting thing, but you could tell it plain when you saw it. If it was in a dog, that dog would do things you wouldn't think any dog could do. You take Old Rosy. Red, you remember Old Rosy; she was still alive when you was little. Well, say we had Old Rosy here, and there was only one wolf in Baxter County, and we take Old Rosy out hunting; I tell you she would pick up that wolf's trail. That's how good she was.

"Well, kids, so that's why we're going on this hunt. We've got a wolf, and we'll have a good hot trail. Old Rip will get him, with the others helping. You see, Old Rip won't hunt much more; after a while he'll get sad about his foot. And the other dogs will get to understand about his foot, and they won't respect him anymore. The sporting in this country is about over. So that's why I want you kids to go with me and know what we're doing; we're just going to take Old Rip out and turn him loose, and see that magic work one last time."

They all ate in silence for several minutes. Then the four boys began to talk again. The solemnity of the occasion, as explained by Buck, could not alter their thrill at the thought of the night ahead of them.

After supper, Buck and the four boys went out to the car, Buck with his dog-calling horn slung over his shoulder on a leather thong. The mesquite brush in the west made a ragged silhouette against the setting sun as they started out.

"Whereabouts we heading for, Pa?" Red asked.

"I believe we'll go over to Chaparral Ridge. There's a wagon road goes right up there, if it hasn't grown up too bad. This wolf will stick to the high ground mostly, and maybe we can follow them quite a ways in the car."

The car was noisy. When they hit a rough place it sounded like a chain-drive grain binder. One of the headlights blinked off and on. A half moon began to brighten up overhead.

They came out on the north end of Chaparral Ridge. It was a wide, uneven stretch of land, partly clear of brush, which came up out of the rolling hills to the west and sloped more sharply away on the east to flat bottom thickets and Webb Creek a mile away. The ridge extended south three or four miles.

Buck turned off the ignition. "Here she is, kids. Now, Red, you get by the trailer door. When I give the word; swing her open." He took the tow sack from the car and walked out across the clearing, holding the sack away from himself and unwiring the top as he went. The coyote was a good load. Old Rip began to whine like a baby.

A hundred and fifty feet away, Buck threw the sack down and jumped back. The sack writhed. The coyote came out like a steel spring uncoiling. He became a part of the dim moon shadows on the ridge, and Buck waited an eternity of ten seconds.

"Let 'em go, Red! Hyah, Rip! Hyah, Rip!"

Boys and dogs ran forward together. Old Rip went past Buck in a fast, but limping, run, wound back and forth across the coyote's trail with his nose to the ground, and with a long bay of discovery, took off trailing. The other dogs followed. Slim Wilkinson bounded around between the boys, barking, kissed Elmer on the nose, then pounced on the tow sack and shook it savagely. The other dogs were out of sight when he started after them in a long, leaping gait.

The sounds from the dogs became fainter and fainter. Buck and the boys got into the car and headed on south down Chaparral Ridge.

They stopped once and heard the chase still ahead of them, then drove a half mile farther.

"They're down there in the flat, Pa," Bert said.

"Yep. I believe that wolf is taking it into his head to make some circles."

"I can tell which one is Slim Wilkinson, can't you, Pa," Elmer said. "He sounds glad."

"Don't talk so much, Elmer," Red said. "Goodnight! We can't hear the dogs with you talking."

"Kids," Buck said, "I want you to listen to Old Rip. He's that one with the deep mournful sound. Hear him! He don't bark much."

They could hear the bark like a deep-throated sob, with a musical note in it. It came across the night air at intervals of fifteen seconds, and each time it tapered off and died away slowly.

"Kids, the first time I heard that note, it was up north of Baxter City. Your grandpa was standing by me. I wasn't any bigger than Elmer here. And it wasn't Old Rip barking; it was Old Tiger. Listen! Hear it? Old Rosy had that note, kids, only it was shriller in her. And Old Tip had it too."

He was silent a minute, then said, "They're coming this way."

The trailing bark of the dogs came directly up toward them and then seemed to be turning again. Old Rip missed one of his regular barks.

"Hey, kids!" Buck said.

Old Rip broke into a sharper bark. He was running fast.

"Hey! That wolf picked the wrong place to cross his trail. Old Rip's right on him, kids."

Then not two hundred yards ahead of them, the coyote broke against the skyline at the edge of the ridge. Old Rip was ten feet behind. The coyote turned and slashed at him, then ran on. He was more than a match for Old Rip in speed. But the other dogs were coming up now.

"Kids!" Buck yelled above the sudden roar of the car engine. They barely had time to get a handhold before Buck had it in second gear. "He'll turn around again, and if Old Rip gets hold of him, he's a goner."

Buck came plowing around a clump of trees and skidded the wheels. He hit the ground running, like a boy instead of like a man with twinges of rheumatism. As they ran up the rise toward the tumbling mass of dogs, one dark form broke away and struck out south.

"There's one of them pups taking out, Pa," Red said.

"If it is I'll stomp his rump into the ground," Buck said, puffing. He came up to the melee of fighting dogs. "Here! What's going on here? What is this?" He shoved dogs aside roughly with his legs and hands. "Fan, Pete, Ringer! This isn't any wolf you've got; it's Slim Wilkinson!"

As soon as Old Rip was untangled from the snarling mass, he struck out south, trailing in the direction the coyote had gone a minute before. The other dogs took in the situation and followed him. Slim Wilkinson, who had been at the bottom of the heap, scrambled about as if hunting for the fight he had been in. He rared up clumsily on Elmer's chest and licked him in the face, bounced about a moment, barked, and ran after the other dogs.

They got into the car and followed the chase south along the ridge for a mile and a half. The coyote went out into the hills to the west. "If we had some horses we'd go out that way," Buck speculated. "We'll wait and see if he's coming back to the ridge before we try it in the car."

Elmer and Wayne wanted to build up a fire while they waited. Buck agreed, though the night was not cold. They sat around the fire of dry mesquite wood and heard the voices of the dogs echo back from over a mile away.

Buck talked of the ways of coyotes. "When a wolf is fresh, he's bad about circling back and cutting his trail. Or sometimes, he'll backtrack and then cut off his trail in another direction. That's a good trick, because a good trailing dog hates to go backwards on a trail worse than anything, and if backwards and forwards is the same way, thay don't know what to do."

Buck was squatting with his hands spread out to the fire. His back was in darkness and the light flickered over the front part of him as he talked into the flames. To the four boys he seemed a magician talking.

"But about the most fouled up you can get a wolfhound pack, if they're not really good, is to get two smart wolves ahold of them. Them wolves will tie their trail up in knots like they was knitting a sweater. Your dogs will be back-trailing and going ever which way. Sometimes, if you got two extra-good dogs—I mean *real* wolfhounds— they'll split up the pack, and they'll take both of them wolves. I've seen Old Rip and Old Tip do it when they was both in their prime. And once Old Tip and Old Rosy did it when Old Rosy was over ten years old."

They sat by the fire half an hour, and the chase wound around again toward Chaparral Ridge. When the dogs came in near enough that their barks could be heard clearly, they sounded tired. Buck and the boys wet on the fire and kicked dirt over the steaming coals, then stood listening while Old Rip and the pack came slowly over the ridge a quarter mile south of them. "Come on, kids," Buck said. "Let's drive up a ways and see if we can get closer."

They drove up and stopped to listen. The coyote had taken to the thick brush in the flat again, between there and Webb Creek. He was running straightaway. "He won't circle anymore," Buck said. "He's too tired. We got to get over there some way."

The ancient wagon road over the ridge ran into the highway two miles farther south. They bounced down it, part of the time in the road, part of the time out. The dog trailer swung crazily behind them. They turned out on the highway, came back north two miles, and stopped to listen again. The chase had turned up Webb Creek. "Where in the Sam Hill is that crazy wolf going?" Buck said.

They turned in at the Welty place, drove past the house, and on down to where the Welty's north fence cut across Webb Creek. There they climbed through the fence, then ran up the creek toward the barking of the dogs.

"They got him bayed, haven't they, Pa?" Red asked.

"I think so," Buck said, puffing. His boots were making a lot of noise on the uneven ground. "But I don't like it."

"Say, Pa," Bert said, "that's right close to where Perkins has got his camp, isn't it?"

Buck grunted in answer. Up ahead they could see the dim flash of a lantern. They scrambled down into the dry creek bed and ran along its gravel-covered bottom. Elmer, panting along behind the others, said, "Pa can whup any man in the country."

They came out of the creek bed and stopped. No more than thirty feet away was an eerie scene, the center of which was Perkins and a kerosene lantern which sat on a rickety cage. The skinny old man was nailing a slat back onto the cage with his right hand and cradling in his left arm a double-barreled twelve-gauge shotgun. Around the edge of the dim circle of light the dogs moved, barking and whining in frustration.

Perkins raised the lantern high, showing his ragged white beard. His voice was a cackle. "My coyote got out. But he come back. Yore dogs ain't much good at catching coyotes, air they?"

On the floor of the rickety cage crouched a dark heaving form. The coyote's small eyes gleamed like points of fire.

Buck stood silent a minute, then blurted out, "You caught my best dog in one of your blasted wolf traps!"

Perkins laughed shrilly. "I ain't got no wolf traps. Just coyote traps. Besides, I turned yore ole dog loose. He! He! He! Yore best dog! He! He! I can outrun any dog you got, and me eighty-two year ole." He shifted the shotgun over into the crook of his right arm.

"Pa, I don't see the pups," Elmer said. "Where's Old Slim Wilkinson?"

"And Ringer," Red said. "Ringer's not here, Pa."

Buck did not answer them. He was watching the old man and the coyote in the cage. Then he said, loud enough for Perkins to hear, "Kids, I sure hope that old man don't ever try to shoot that old rusty gun he's got, because it will probably blow up in his face." With that he turned and started back toward the car. "Bring the dogs, kids." They could hear Perkins's shrill laughter behind them.

They called the dogs and herded them back to the trailer. Bert said, "Boy, I sure wish we had caught that wolf, Pa, don't you?"

Wayne said, "Aw, we don't care anything about catching him, but just chasing him. We don't care, do we, Pa?"

Red said, "Let's don't talk about it."

"Pa," Elmer said, "we got to find Old Slim Wilkinson. Do you reckon he could be after a wolf?"

Buck shook his head. He was limping badly from the rheumatism. "I reckon him and the other pups and Ringer got after a rabbit and got lost. Ringer is bad about rabbits, and I guess they followed him."

"Well, I thought Old Slim Wilkinson was out in the hills, because I can tell when I hear him," Elmer said. "And I didn't hear him come back across the ridge with the rest. Let's go find him, can't we, Pa?"

Buck agreed, halfheartedly. They drove down the highway and turned back up the wagon road toward Chaparral Ridge. Buck drove slowly. The blinking headlight had gone out. They pulled up on the south end of the ridge and stopped.

They could barely hear a faint moaning bark away out in the hills and farther north. "It's Slim Wilkinson!" Elmer said. "He don't sound glad now, but I can tell him!"

As they climbed back into the car, he said suddenly. "Pa! Maybe Old Rip and Old Slim Wilkinson split up the pack!"

"Goodnight, Elmer!" Wayne said. "I'm going to bust you right in the mouth!"

They drove up a couple of miles, and Buck pulled into a clearing at the west edge of the ridge. He shut off the motor. "That's Slim Wilkinson doing most of the barking," he said. "Like Elmer says, you can tell him; and I sure don't like to hear it." He looked up at the clear half moon. "It's not right. That note! It's like a half dollar made out of lead. I'd as lief see a man spit in his own grandma's face, as to hear Slim Wilkinson bark like that. Liefer. It's not right."

Old Rip was whining back in the trailer.

Buck climbed out of the car and took the steer horn from his neck. He raised it to his lips, hesitated, then lowered the horn and stood listening. "Kids, I don't understand it at all. He sure puts me in mind of Old Tiger."

Old Rip was whining like a baby.

"Kids, I don't see how a sorry dog can bark like that, especially chasing a rabbit." He stood listening while a tenseness came into his body, and he spoke with a quick wonder in his voice, "Kids, no dog would run a rabbit for two hours like this. And listen to that note!"

Elmer was jumping up and down. He uttered a sound that was half scream and half laugh.

Buck whooped like a rider when he comes out of the chute on a mean bucking bronco. "Kids! Turn them dogs loose! Slim Wilkinson can't catch a wolf by his self."

Red threw open the door of the dog cage, and the hounds came pouring out, tumbling over one another with short, excited yelps. The hounds lined out immediately, running silently, in the direction where Slim Wilkinson had been heard. They were a stream of jumping white spots in the moonlight, until they disappeared in the brush.

"Reckon he's in sight of it, Pa?" Bert asked. "Or is he still trailing?"

"I can't tell," Buck said. "He's too tired. But listen to that note, kids. Listen to that fool pup!"

They stood listening to the bark of the persistent young hound, punctuated occasionally by a weak bark from Ringer or another pup. Suddenly, the other dogs broke in with sharp, fast running barks. It was like a band of fiddles and banjos and guitars, all trying to tune up at once.

Buck and the boys piled into the car and headed west for the roughest ride of the night. There was no overgrown, washed-out wagon road this time, for no one had ever been fool enough to take a wagon along the route Buck took. They straddled mesquite bushes five feet high. They went in and out among the trees as a snake goes through a weed patch. A long section of prickly pear leaves was dragging from the trailer. They could hear the dogs just ahead, even above the threshing machine noise of the car. The boys poked their heads out the windows and dodged back in to avoid the limbs.

They came right up to the howling, jumping, happy pack of dogs. There seemed fifty of them, rather than fifteen. Buck and the boys walked into the center of the confusion. There on the ground lay a big, well-chewed coyote. His fur was ruffled and wet. Blood flowed freely out of his throat.

On one side of the coyote sat Old Rip; on the other side, Slim Wilkinson. The big pup's tail twitched back and forth in the dry grass. One long ear dripped blood, slashed by a mesquite thorn or the fangs of the coyote. His red tongue hung out of his mouth six inches. Slim Wilkinson was grinning.

Buck took out his knife and cut the ears off the coyote. "Kids, I believe we'll take these ears by, and wake up old Perkins, and show them to him—just for the heck of it."

When they were putting the dogs back into the trailer, Elmer said, "Pa, do you think Old Rip could ride in the car with us, and maybe Old Slim Wilkinson too? He could set on my lap."

Buck nodded. "You might turn out to be a sporting man, Elmer. I believe you might." When they were in the car, Buck took Slim Wilkinson by the loose skin on top of his neck and shook him slowly back and forth. "Kids, this clumsy fool pup is the grinnin'est and eagerest dog I ever had."

Crime and Punishment

I had to ride in the back seat with the groceries on account of my size. Roy, no matter how much you warned him, would stand up on the seat so he could look out the window, so he got to sit by Mama, where she could catch him in case he stood up and she had to slam on the brakes. Then, Billy, he had to sit by the front door so he could get out easy to open the gates when we came to our turnoff. We had gates at each pasture fence, five in all, and they were stretched tight, and Billy could open them better than I could.

We had a big sack of flour and a bunch of pasteboard boxes and brown paper sacks on the floor and on the seat with me. Vinegar to make pickles, lye to make soap, baking powder, soda, fruit-jar lids, everything. Sticking out of one sack was bunches of delicious grapes. They were kind of green and white and clear. You could tell they were good. I could almost taste one, just looking.

"Don't bother the groceries, Ben," Mama said while she backed out. "Do you hear me?"

"Yes, ma'am."

One grape on top looked like it was about to come loose, because it was just hanging by a little skin on one side. Then it might fall down in the bottom and get smashed. To save it I slowly pulled it off and slipped it in my mouth. It was the juiciest, best thing, like soda pop, only better, and you had something to chew on besides.

Mama was a fast driver; even in town she drove about as fast as you could run. She had driving rules for herself. She kept her eyes straight ahead through the windshield.

I saw that there were five bunches of grapes down in the sack, and it seemed all right to take one from the top of each bunch. They could have dropped off anyway. They were delicious. When you bit down on one, the juice would squirt all around in your mouth. You could not imagine anything so good.

Roy said, "Did we get any candy?"

"No, dear. Candy is bad for your teeth. We got something more healthy than candy, but it tastes better also. You wait and see! It's a real treat. Seedless grapes!"

"I want a seedless grapes," Roy said.

"No, dear. We will have them for dessert. I got enough for all of us. We will have them at the end of dinner and at the end of supper."

"How many do we get?"

"About a dozen each. At each meal."

"How many is a dozen?"

Billy said, "A dozen is twelve, you nut."

"Don't talk naughty, Billy." She almost took her eyes from straight out the windshield. "A dozen is more than all your fingers, dear. Isn't that a lot? And they're delicious."

She was sure right about that. I saw that the bunches looked funny with one missing on the side of every one, so I took one from the other side of every one to even them up. They were the best things you ever put in your mouth.

"Don't bother those grapes now, Ben," Mama said. "Do you hear me?"

"Yes, ma'am."

I decided to take just one all around the top of each bunch. It might not be wrong, because they might not be the best ones anyway. They were so sweet that you couldn't hardly stop.

Mama made signals with her arm whenever she turned the corners to get out of town to the highway. She could make Stop, Turn Right, Turn Left, Slow Down. She made the signals even out on the wagon roads, but especially on streets and cement roads.

I saw that the tops of all the grape bunches looked suspicious, like somebody had been eating some, so quiet as a mouse I turned each bunch upside down. The ones that had been on the bottom looked even whiter and clearer and jucier. You could almost taste them, just looking. I pulled off a few that stuck out from the rest to make it look even.

Billy said, "Mama, he has his hand in a grocery sack."

"Don't bother the groceries, Ben. Do you hear me?"

"Yes, ma'am."

Mama went buzzing down the highway, looking straight out the windshield. Sometimes, when she did not have to make a hand signal, she held her hand over the horn button, ready to blow. She never did honk at people, because it is impolite, but she had to be ready to honk at a dog or a cow.

When we got to our turnoff, I saw that the bottoms of the grape bunches looked suspicious, and the idea hit me: Mama might find out! I thought about a whipping. Us kids had a way figured out to take a whipping if you had to. Mama would hold you by the left arm and beat you with the switch in her right hand. You had to run around and around her as fast as you could and yell like she was killing you; then she might let up before long.

Quick as we got through the turnoff gate and went buzzing down the wagon road I began to turn the bunches of grapes on the side, quiet as a mouse. I had to pick off a few of the side grapes. They sure tasted good. I kept turning the bunches around so they would look better and picking off a few so it would look even.

Roy said, "Mama, don't you like candy?"

"Just a minute, dear." She was coming to that left turn where you go up over the cattle guard and don't have to open a gate. When she made her signal and got going straight again, she said, "Yes, I like candy, but it is bad for the teeth. Seedless grapes are just as good. You'll see. They are even better than ripe peaches. Or dewberries. Or wild plums."

She was sure right about that. At the third gate I began to look at the grape bunches, trying to see them like Mama would if she stopped looking out the windshield and started looking at the grape sack. They looked like somebody had been gobbling around on the ends and sides, more than half gone. It was too late. I might as well go on. If I only got one lick for each bunch, that wouldn't be too bad. It was worth it. By the time we pulled up in the backyard, I was swallowing the last grape.

Mama began to unload the groceries, giving Billy the jug of vinegar to carry in and Roy a can of black pepper. She began to pick up the grape stems out of the sack. She said, "Benjamin Franklin Capps!" If she said your whole name, you were in trouble.

"I cannot believe this! How could you do it? I do not believe it! Go right now this minute and get the hatchet out of the smokehouse and cut a good switch from that peach tree on the end where all the sprouts are. You hear me? I do not believe it!"

I found a switch about the right size, about as big as a pencil on the big end and long as my arm, about the size to switch Roy or a puppy dog. When I brought it, Mama said, "That will be five extra licks, young man." When she called you "young man," you were *really* in trouble.

She snapped the switch in two. "Go right now this instant and cut a switch as big as my thumb and this long!"

I was getting scared and feeling low-down, so I cut a big sprout that any mama would be pleased with. I felt it was my duty. But on the way back, I got to wondering if I had gone too far. That's when I saw the old pie plate under the smokehouse. It was a metal pie plate that kept on getting holes in it and had been patched two times with harness brads. We put things that were no good, but too good to throw away, under the smokehouse. Right beside it was a gunnysack wadded up.

Seeing that I had gone too far in cutting a big switch, I took the pie plate and wrapped it around and around with the gunnysack; then I unbuckled one strap of my overalls and tucked the pie plate with padding on my bottom. When I handed the huge peach tree sprout to Mama, she took it; she probably did not notice my large behind. Her eyes looked like she was looking straight through a windshield.

We started going around and around, and I tried to guess right when she would hit so I could yell louder then. But no matter how loud I screamed, it sounded like somebody was beating a pie plate.

Mama stopped. Her turn-signal hand darted into the back seat of my overalls without even unbuckling the strap. "Benjamin Franklin Capps, I cannot believe it!" She nearly turned me over jerking the metal pan and gunnysack out. "Young man, that is ten more extra licks! I do not believe it!"

Nobody could tell about the whipping I got, there in the clean-swept backyard. It did not help me to run around and around her. That peach tree limb swished and whistled and caught me however much I ran and jumped and cried. I was thinking, Will she ever stop? Before one lick had started to ease up, I got another whack!

You can think when you are truly crying. I thought, even when my bottom was burning so much I couldn't tell the difference from this side and that side, *I'll never eat another seedless grape as long as I live.* About five whacks later I thought, *I'll never do another bad thing in my whole life.* Nobody could tell the plain, whole truth about that whipping. We stirred up the dust and made a whirlwind there in the backyard.

Mama was breathing hard when she laid the huge peach tree sprout on the back porch. She began to carry the rest of the groceries into the kitchen and said, "Let that be a lesson to you!"

I was standing there by the cellar door, trying to stop crying. Roy and Billy stood there watching me with their hands on their hips, trying to look like Mama or a schoolteacher or something.

Roy said, "Let's jump on him and beat him up. He ate our grapes too."

"No," Billy said. "We just have to suffer because we have a brother with a criminal mind."

"And a pig mind too," Roy said.

On top of all my other troubles that day, I got a stomachache for some reason.

The Meanest Horses in the Country

When a bunch of men who have been working cattle a long time are sitting around shooting the bull they will finally get to talking about rough horses. They will remind each other of things they forgot years ago. Then some old boy will say, So and So outfit had the meanest horses in the country! They had this one horse. . . . Some of those stories are true. Among cowhands you get about the same percentage of liars as in the population as a whole, no more and no less. But as for knowing what outfit really had the meanest horses, that's another question. If in that bunch of men is one that has worked on the J's he will sit there and look down his nose in pity at the rest. If two of them have worked on that particular ranch, they will look at each other and shake their heads and shudder; then they may grin and go to remembering names like Whirlwind and Hong Kong and Dodger and Cotton-Eye Joe and Rusty.

I wintered on the J's and along in March it began to rain. The manager, Amos Lockhart, sent me over to Stubby's, which was the east line camp, to ride bog. Stubby had tried to farm over there at one time and had built a two-room house out of logs and mud, but his farming had broke him and he'd been working for the J's for years. They said the ranch paid him a hundred dollars for his house. It was all right for a line camp.

Stubby was a short fellow, built like a badger, and he had a name for being a great talker and kidder. When he had lost all his money and used up all his credit trying to farm, his wife had run off, so he said good riddance, and after that he always laughed a lot and made sarcastic remarks. They would let him get away with murder, but he was actually a good hand.

He gave me the welcome of a long-lost brother, and I wasn't long in seeing why. He had to cover six miles each way up and down the Beaver Fork, then clear over the divide to the Wichita River, and all the washes and draws that led into both streams. It took plenty of hunting, because if a cow is going to get bogged down, she'll do it in a low place where you can't see her. Also, she may be starved and helpless, stuck in a buffalo wallow with four inches of water, but when you snake her out, she has a way of blaming all her troubles on the first thing that moves. And here she comes on the prod, right at the man who saved her bony carcass from the buzzards. It's not exactly a job for one hand alone.

It suited me to leave headquarters at that time, since I got away with two decent horses, one named Blackie, which I figured was a gentle all-around cow horse and which I meant to hang onto as long as I worked for the outfit, one a dun named Sleeper, which was hard to saddle and hard to mount, but one which pitched a little and then settled down. I couldn't pull a cow out of a mudhole on Sleeper, but when I rode him I worked on the ground and let Stubby do the pulling. I had learned that on the J's if you got hold of a horse with only a little devil in him you'd better be thankful and shut up.

We rode bog for two weeks, half the time in a drizzling rain, and pulled four or five critters out of the mud each day. As many cows as Old Man Jackson had, he never would have missed that many, but we made him money. I remember Stubby shot one that couldn't stay on her feet, then got out his knife and began to whet it. When I saw he meant to skin that mud-caked beauty, I told him to count me out; the Old Man would just have to get by without the money one dirty hide would bring, for all of me. Stubby laughed. "Blankenship," he said, "that's what I like about you, always thinking about your employer. I'm going to make me some rawhide chair bottoms. Get hold of that leg and hep me."

We had two sunny days and it began to dry off. On a Friday afternoon we rode into camp, and Billy Tuttle was sitting there in a buckboard with a load of grub.

Stubby rode over and looked critically into the bed. "Where in the hell's the meat?"

"One side of bacon," Billy said. "Red beans. White beans. What did you want?"

"One side of bacon? Look at that! One sack of prunes! You all trying to starve us? That ain't enough grub to feed two working men!"

Billy Tuttle was a little fellow with a nose like a weasel. He grinned like a man will when he knows something you don't know. "One working man," he said. "Amos Lockhart says for Blankenship to come on back to headquarters this Sunday."

That held Stubby for a minute.

I asked, "What does he want with me?"

"Wants you to help with the horses."

"What horses?"

Billy grinned, then began to laugh silently. He had a way about him, if he thought you were teasing, of laughing, just shaking as he grinned, making only a slight hiss now and then.

"You tell Amos Lockhart," Stubby said, "we still got work out here."

Billy said, "I don't know about that, but I think the order came from the Old Man. He's started to worry about spring roundup."

I said, "I'm not going to tame that herd of wildcats for other cowhands to ride."

"I don't know about that," he said.

Stubby said, "You tell Amos Lockhart that Blankenship is leaving his black horse here, because I need me another horse out here."

"That'll be a cold day in July," I told him. "Listen, Billy, you tell Amos Lockhart I couldn't make it and Stubby will be in on Sunday in my place."

Billy sat there grinning and shaking.

"I don't believe he's got the nerve to tell Amos Lockhart a thing," Stubby said. "Billy, you may aim to sleep here tonight, but we can't feed you. We just ain't got the food."

We helped him carry in the grub and unsaddled and unharnessed the horses; then about dark we rustled up something to eat and pulled up our chairs around the plank table by the light of two coal-oil lanterns. Billy Tuttle ate a half a gallon of cold red beans we had. It's amazing how much some little fellows can eat. Makes you wonder where they put it.

I took the edge off my appetite and mulled it over. Finally I asked him, "Is that all he said about me coming in?"

"Yep. Come back to headquarters on Sunday." It seemed like he considered saying more, but he was spooning it in, and talking got in the way of the serious business.

Stubby said, "I guess you know why Amos Lockhart said Sunday. He's a bigger tightwad than the Old Man. What he don't know is that we don't work around here on Saturday anyway. It takes one day to get ready to rest up on Sunday."

"Well, at least I won't have to wash any more dishes at this camp," I said.

"I believe it's your time tonight."

"I was thinking we have enough clean ones to last till I leave."

Stubby rolled himself a cigarette, lighted it, and flicked the match at the front of the cookstove. He said, "I don't see how you can set back in your riggings so easy, Blankenship. It looks plain to me that you're going to catch it."

"Why? I haven't done anything."

"They're fixing to make a bronc stomper out of you."

"Not me. I didn't hire on for anything like that."

"Can't you ride the mean ones?"

"I ride them like they come." The fact was I figured I could stay on a bad one as long as anybody. On the other hand, I had known a few older men that got their liver and gizzard scrambled together from being too confident about bronc riding when they were young.

"What wagon did you go with last fall?" Stubby asked.

"Snuffy Detweiler's."

Stubby shook his head sadly. "That's what I was afraid of. Who rode the rough string for that bunch?"

"Hell, every hand on this place rides a rough string. You're lucky to get one gentle horse."

"But think about it," he said. "Didn't they have one hand, and he had to take the outlaws?"

"That Comanche Indian boy, I guess."

"Whereabouts is he at now?" Stubby asked.

"I don't know. Gone back to the reservation, I guess."

"Yeah. How about that? I wonder did they ever hire anybody to take his place?"

"Stubby, they don't make a man do that unless he asks for it. They can't do that. I didn't hire on for anything like that."

"Don't tell me your troubles. I just want to know where we should ship the remains."

Billy Tuttle was turning his weasel nose from one of us to the other, keeping busy eating and grinning and shaking silently.

Stubby said, "I didn't even know you were scared of bad broncs."

"Listen, I had Dodger in my string last fall, and I worked him every time in his turn. I guess you might have heard of Dodger."

"Did he throw you?"

"A few times. But I worked him."

"That's what I thought. There's an eye up above watching you, Blankenship. They've figured out what you're good for. Why do you think Amos Lockhart sent for you?"

"Help wangle the horses a little, I guess. Help shoeing. Maybe help the blacksmith make some new branding irons. How would I know?"

He went to laughing and slapping his leg. "How would you know? Ha! Ha! He! He! Ho! Ho! Ho! How would you know? Ho! Ho! Ho! Ho! Making branding irons! He! He! He! He!"

I said, "Stubby, being out in this line camp so much by yourself, you have blown your cork."

He would look at me and laugh the next day, and he was still going after it when I rode away Sunday morning, riding Blackie and leading Sleeper. He thought because I was young they would be able to work me into doing something I didn't aim to do. I liked Stubby, but I remember thinking he was running his joy and merriment into the ground.

Headquarters was sprawled out over twenty acres with a building called the Old House in the middle. It looked like a dozen line shacks grown together. One long wall was adobe two feet thick; most of the rest was lumber, but jammed into it about the middle was a two-story log house. If you went in the back, which was the only way I ever entered, you passed through the woodshed into the dining room where the hands ate, with a kitchen off to the side; straight through the dining room was Amos Lockhart's office, and evidently the remainder of the Old House was storage space where they kept everything from chicken feed to barn paint to cow dip. The Old Man himself lived in a good-looking stone house a couple of hundred yards away with a collection of poor relations that came and went; mostly they were a crowd of dudes and not necessarily poor; only if you were kin to Old Man Jackson at all you were a poor relation.

I sneaked into the dining room for supper that Sunday afternoon, figuring I'd just as soon not get any instructions from Amos Lockhart till the next morning, but he caught me as I was leaving. He yelled, "Hey, Bud!" and came stalking out of his office door. He had got the idea my nickname was Bud.

"I see you got in all right," he said. Then he edged on out through the woodshed with me, asking stupid questions about how old Stubby was getting along. When we got outside he stopped and shifted his cigar around in his mouth, and I figured he was about to get down to business.

Amos Lockhart was a large man. It seemed that he had to dress clean and neat to keep from looking like a bum. He had something sloppy about the way he walked, like he was double-jointed. Usually he had a cigar stuck in his mouth, and always he had a narrow-brim felt hat jammed down on his head. I guess he wore that kind of hat to show he wasn't a hand but a manager. Whether he slept in it or not I don't know, but he ate in it and once I saw him thrown so hard from a horse it would jar your eyeteeth and that hat stayed on his head like it was glued on.

"Bud," he said, "guess what we got down in the picket corral?"

I said, "I thought I saw a few horses down there."

"About a dozen or so. We caught Dodger. And that roan Pepper. I've got a crew out right now bringing in all the horses."

"I reckon it's time for spring roundup before long," I said.

"Yeah. I want you to go down in the morning, Bud, and ride Dodger. That fool has got to be broke fresh every spring, but I never saw anybody that could handle him the way you can. Give Pepper a whirl too. Make sure all that bunch is rope broke. Billy Tuttle will help you. Joe Christian will be back by noon, and I'll send him to help you too."

"Something I wanted to mention, Mr. Lockhart," I said. "Of course, I didn't hire on to be a bronc rider. I don't claim to be one. I just want to make a hand. I don't mind to help with the horses a couple of days or wherever I'm needed, but I don't claim to be a bronc rider."

"That's what I told the Old Man," he said. "I says, 'That Bud Blankenship—we kept him over the winter, and he'll pitch in and help where he's needed.' But, listen, don't downgrade yourself when it comes to riding. That's what I like about a rough young feller like you, Bud; you pitch right in and do your duty."

I started to say something about being kept over the winter. Thinking about all the hay I'd handled and all the cows I'd tailed up and all the fence I'd fixed and all the miles I'd ridden in the cold wind, it didn't seem like the right way to put it. But he didn't mean it the way it sounded. He meant they "employed" me over the winter instead of "kept." It's supposed to mean they rate you high if they keep you the year around.

I guess I should have taken the bull by the horns and told him I didn't mean to cripple myself up being a bronc stomper, and not only that, but I could ride any outlaw on the place if I took a notion to, and if they didn't like my attitude I would ask for my time that minute. The only trouble is that ranch managers and such people don't give you a clear-cut case; they string you along so you can't tell when it's time to get sore and put your foot down. Amos Lockhart was a master at it.

He went on in a confidential way, "I want to talk to you about a rumor that's going around. Did you ever hear anybody say this outfit has got the meanest horses of any outfit in the country?"

I laughed a little. "Well, yes, sir, I've heard it said for a joke."

"That's what I told the Old Man." He shifted his cigar around in his mouth as if he was trying to find a place for it to set easy. "Detweiler said one of his men told that story about the meanest horses last fall, and two weeks ago I was over in Kimble City hiring some hands and a clerk in a store mentioned the same rumor. A tale like that don't do the reputation of this place any good, Bud. We got to tame these horses down a little."

"It's mostly a joke," I said.

"Sure it is. Not a word of truth in it. Every ranch has naturally got its share of pitching horses. I hope the boys that work here don't spread those tales around. You're a good judge of horses, Bud. What do you personally think? Has this outfit got good horses or not?"

"Well, of course, the ones that run loose all winter . . . Then some talk has it . . . Maybe some horses that are supposed to be broke when they are bought are actually outlaws other outfits couldn't handle. I'm not complaining myself. I expect to take them like they come."

"Right," he said. "You get good, strong saddle stock and they won't be all gentle little lambs. Any good horse wants to shake a few kinks out on a cool morning. You got to expect that. Well, we want to tame them down the best we can. I know the hands on this place don't mind a horse to pitch a little. The Old Man wants us to be well mounted. He's just bought thirty or forty head of first-class horses. I want you to go up to Sealey Station with me to get them on Wednesday. So you throw a saddle on that bunch down in the picket corral in the meantime and give them a little workout."

We left it that way, whatever way it was. The news that the Old Man had bought thirty or forty head of first-class horses did not ease my mind. I was thinking, You can buy thirty head or forty head or thirty-seven head, but if you say you buy thirty or forty head that's not very clear news. And what do they mean by "first-class horses"? I took it with a grain of salt.

At sunup the next morning Billy Tuttle and I rode down to the picket corral a quarter of a mile below the Old House. It was a round pen made out of mesquite poles the way the Mexicans used to make them: the butts charred so they wouldn't rot, then stood side by side in a trench, and the tops bound together with rawhide. It looked crude with the bleached, crooked posts, but it was handy, with a stout snubbing post in the middle and a short wing running out from the gate.

A dozen horses came up to the fence and studied us, looking for some feed. They'd been up three days, only getting out long enough to be driven to water, and somebody had been hauling hay to them. It was a typical bunch of J's horses. Besides Dodger and Pepper, I saw two blazeface bays named Brat and Caesar, a big paint named Goodfellow, and a red horse named Youngun, as well as several others I'd seen before but didn't know their names.

Dodger is an overgrown flea-bit dun with black scratches in his hide. When he sees me come in the gate he immediately strolls around behind the others and acts like he's looking the other way. He knows me all right. I mean one thing to him: work, after he's spent a gay, free time kicking up his heels all winter.

I feel good. That time of year it's cool and fresh-smelling early in the morning. You feel ready to tangle with anything. I make a loop, get it straightened out to suit me, and get it all cocked and ready. Then Dodger gets interested in smelling of the ground.

I move over and wait. He moves over and looks out to the far prairies. When I'm ready he ducks his head again.

I say to Billy, "Run them around the fence. I'll see if that crowbait can smell of the ground while he's running."

When he's in the clear I get lucky and put my first loop on him. He drags me a ways while I plow up two nice garden rows with my boot heels; then I swing around the snubbing post. He pitches a few jumps, practicing, and I take up slack on him till he has to simmer down or choke himself.

We leave him there a few minutes to think about it, while we get my saddle and bridle. Evidently he decides to bide his time, because he takes the bit and doesn't paw or kick when I throw on the saddle. All he does is hump up and lay his ears back. I whomp him on the shoulder with the flat of my hand a few times, talking to him. "Dodger, you remember me. Relax, old friend. We're going to treat each other nice, me and you. Lovey-dovey!" Billy Tuttle stands and grins like an idiot, laughing silently.

We get him out through the gate, and Billy mounts his horse and holds Dodger's bridle, while I climb on top of him.

Dodger has seen about twelve years and he's had experience getting cowboys off his back. He has a mean reputation and looks rough as a cob. Actually, he doesn't buck to jar a rider. He comes down soft-legged as a cat, but when he hits he's ready to go some place else. He's quick for a horse his size. You can't afford to get behind. You'll never catch up.

Soon as Billy lets him loose, he goes at it. I rake him with my spurs. He jumps like he's never had a man on his back before. Billy lets him clear the wing fence, then hazes him away from the rocky ground and down toward a flat that has a good stand of dry grass.

Dodger means business. I get that feeling of jouncing power and action that I haven't felt in months. Kind of surprising—you know it but don't really remember it. Jump left. Jump left. Jump right. I relax, try to be loose and quick. Jump left. Jump left. Jump right. I'm saying to myself, I've got to watch out and outguess this wild brute. Jump left. Jump right. Jump right. I lose my balance and my left stirrup. I'm clawing leather. The next time he comes up, the cantle of my saddle hits the inside of my left knee and he flips me out into empty air. I light on my shoulder with a good jar. It hurts a minute, but I don't find anything busted.

Instead of running, Dodger is trying to get rid of his saddle, so Billy catches him only a hundred yards away. It comes to me, as I'd already learned once and forgotten, that you don't want to get ahead on this horse either.

When Billy brings him to me his ears are still thinned down and closed up and flattened back. I whack him on the shoulder a few times and talk to him. "Dodger, calm down. You're not treating me right. You know I can ride you. Old friend, you're going to get me mad."

I climb back on board, and he's waiting for me, warmed up and in tune. Like they say, same song, second verse, only I aim to do more of the calling this time. He's jumping high and twisting, but every time his front feet hit bottom I rake him good. It seems like he tries on purpose to get in the rocky ground, but he can't run through Billy's nag, so he plunges down toward the grassy flat, pitching for every cent he's worth. Dodger's got a hard mouth and a neck ten times as strong as my left arm. I don't try to hold his head up. I pull and let off, pull and let off, to get him off stride. Let him try to outguess me. I yell a little. "Pitch, you devil!" He circles the flat twice and luck is with me. I stick. He stops to blow, but I kick him into a run.

I run him hard out west above the creek, about a mile and a half, then make a turn and head back. This big dun can go. Billy can't stay close to us. By the time we make it back to the picket corral, Dodger is showing sweat and obeying the rein. We unsaddle and unbridle him and put him back in the pen.

After that I rode four more horses and two of them, Pepper and Brat, threw me, Pepper twice. The second time Pepper put me down he kicked me in the hip. I couldn't walk for a minute, but when I finally got back on him he was worn down enough that I could handle him. I worked him into a foaming sweat before taking my gear off of him.

A picket corral has got advantages and disadvantages. One thing, you can't sit on the fence worth a hoot, which is just as well if you plan to get the work done; cowhands waste a lot of time sitting on fences. The trouble with this corral was the plank gate. It had caught all the heavy sitting by itself and had not merely sagged down to the ground but actually into the ground. You had to lift it and drag it to get it opened or closed. Along toward noon we saddle up the big paint Goodfellow. When I started to lead him out the gate he was jerking so it was all I could do to hold him. The other horses commenced to follow him. Billy yelled, "Wait! Whoa, there! Hold it! Wait!" trying to lift the gate and push it shut. Every time he'd get it clear of the ground another horse would bump it, trying to crowd through, and he would lose his hold. Every mother's son of those broncs got out.

I tied Goodfellow and told Billy, "Let's take them to water while they're out." We dragged the gate back against the wing and Billy mounted and took off after the eleven horses, which were kicking up their heels and heading for the wide-open spaces.

I'd been told Goodfellow wouldn't pitch, but that's as far as the guarantee went. He shied sideways till I finally got set in the saddle; then he ran away. Before I found my right stirrup he was halfway up toward the Old House. Even after I got situated well enough so I had a decent chance to ride him, I couldn't slow his mad run nor do much to guide him. He circled the bunkhouse and dashed back past the picket corral and toward the creek bottoms, a mile away, like he had forty miles to go and already late. I got his neck pulled around so he was running half blind, and he ran smack dab through a bush six feet high. I never used a spade bit, but only a curb bit with a short port. It always seemed to me that if you couldn't ride, why take it out on the horse? But I began to wish now I had a bit where I could tear his head off.

After going through the bush I started throwing my weight to the side and managed to guide him toward the tank where Billy Tuttle had caught up with the horse band. Goodfellow saw the other horses drinking and headed for them like a bat out of hell. I thought he would drown us both, but he splashed into the water knee-deep, stopped, and began to try to nose out enough loose rein where he could drink, just like a gentle old saddle horse. Billy had enough sense not to mention the detour I'd taken.

About that time we could barely hear the cook pounding on the cast-iron wash pot he used for a dinner bell. I was ready, but it took us an hour to get all that fine horseflesh back up into the pen again.

After dinner I rode two that I knew wouldn't pitch; then Long Joe Christian came down with a load of hay, and the Old Man himself came down with him.

The Old Man's eyes fastened immediately on the sagging gate and he called Long Joe over. "Quick as you get that hay off the wagon, start to work on this gate. Hang it a foot higher. Have Newt make you some bigger hinges."

He had a kind of dry voice and could size a thing up quickly. He stood a little shorter than the average man, a little lighter, had white hair, and usually wore a big hat. The thing about his clothes was that he wore hundred-dollar suits and always had a red flannel rag wrapped around his neck. Rumor said he had rheumatism in his neck. He wasn't as young as he once was. But that old man had followed the free grass west for thirty years, sacking up the money as he went; then he had bought a few hundred square miles of land. He had forgot more about raising cattle than many a man ever learns. An owner that way has something distant about him even when he's standing right in front of you. It's because you can't add him up.

He said to me, "You can go ahead and work these horses while Joe fixes the gate, can't you? Tie them all up to a post if you need to. Billy can go get you some stake ropes."

"Yes, sir, I think we can."

He smiled. He had false teeth. You could never tell when he was about to smile, nor what he might smile about, like he had his own private sense of humor. In that, he was different from Amos Lockhart, who never smiled, but Old Man Jackson didn't waste much time on jokes. He said, "I saw you giving Dodger a little go-round this morning."

"Yes, sir, I worked him a little."

"That's a good strong horse," he said. "Needs a little training."

The question was going through my head whether he considered that I was in charge of bronc training, but he went on talking.

"We start roundup the second week in April. We've got to get these mounts in shape. That's one thing about this outfit; we start roundup on time. I want to be sure everything is well shod. These barefooted horses that run in the bottoms all winter, Blankenship, their toenails get too long. Cocks their pasterns. I want the hoofs trimmed right. I want shoes that fit. I want them set down solid and tight. One thing I believe: You take care of your horse and he will take care of you."

It was a cinch he didn't consider me to be in charge of horse shoeing. Newt Tanner handled that.

"I just bought thirty-six good horses," he said, "to improve our saddle strings. Lockhart tells me they'll be in on the railroad Wednesday. All first-class stock. Some of them may need a little training." With that he went over and began to study the poles in the picket fence; he walked around it once, then walked back up toward the Old House.

One by one I saddled the remaining horses that hadn't been ridden and tried them out. Long Joe Christian, usually a solemn fellow, would get excited when one of them would pitch. He'd stop whatever he was doing and yell, "Ride him, Blankenship! Spur him! Look at him go! Hang on there, boy! Give him what for! Yip-eeee!"

I thought I'd give Dodger another turn that afternoon before he backslid on me, but I'd already waited too long. He pitched wild as ever and dumped me twice, in spite of Long Joe cheering me on. One time he threw me in the rocky ground but I came out with only the back of my hand skinned up. When I managed to stick and got him to running I gave him another half hour's hard run. By the time the sun hit the horizon I felt like I'd put in a day.

Next morning I couldn't hardly get out of my bunk. It felt like a stampede of goats had run over me. I had a dozen blue spots, and I couldn't hardly bend enough to get my clothes on. I thought, Well, that was a long one-day bronc-riding career I had. But by the time I got up to the woodshed and got washed up and had some breakfast everything loosened up enough to where it seemed like I might be able to make another day.

The first horse I tried was Goodfellow, and he ran away with me again. The run served to get me warmed up and feeling good. Then I started in on the buckers and got thrown three times. Pepper kicked me again, a glancing blow on the right knee. It made me sick to my stomach for a minute.

Sometimes that morning I would think, I didn't hire on for anything like this and they are taking advantage of me. They can't do this to me. Why should I let these broncs bang me all up? Let Amos Lockhart ride these outlaws and see how he likes it. If the Old Man figures these horses have got to be tamed before the second week in April, let him do it himself. They can't treat me this way. They think they can but they can't. They think they can beat around the bush and I won't ever have a chance to tell them to go jump in the lake. I guess they'll think twice if I quit when they're trying to get hands together for roundup.

But then I would climb on one and he would pitch high, wide, and handsome, and it would dawn on me: I can ride him! He's doing his best, but I've got his number! Pitch, you devil! And I would hear Long Joe get all excited, yelling, "Go after him! Look at that buckeroo ride! Whoo! Eeee! Spur him, Blankenship! Spur him!" That's the way it was on Dodger when I would get by his tricks; then he would start pitching high and I would know I had him. When he would go up I would sit there on top of the world and I could see twenty miles every direction.

That afternoon a crew brought in the main horse band, something over a hundred head. I don't reckon anybody knew the exact number unless they checked the ranch books. It made quite a sight, that running conglomeration of horseflesh, every color, some still patchy and shaggy with winter hair. Range horses lose their hair early in a wet spring when the grass is good, but some of them seem to need a little work and sweat to shed it all. I recognized some of these: a wild yellow horse named Hong Kong, Blue Baby, that I had ridden a few times, Cotton-Eye Joe, Pewee, and a wicked red roan named Whirlwind. We put some of them in the plank corral at the barns, some in the bull yard, some more down in the picket corral, and the rest down on the creek with two bell mares and a wrangler. The horse business around headquarters was picking up.

On Wednesday morning Amos Lockhart, Billy Tuttle, and I started early for Sealey Station to get the new horses that were coming in on the train. It was only seventeen miles and we figured with any luck to be back by dark. Amos Lockhart rode a long-legged gelding that set a good pace. Blackie could stay with him trotting, but Billy Tuttle's horse had to break into a lope now and then to keep up.

Sealey Station was a sprawling, dusty town on the Fort Worth and Denver line. We went to the loading pens and watered our horses. No cars were on the siding, so we went down to the station. The agent stood on the loading platform, scratching himself and yawning. Amos asked, "When's the train coming in?"

The man looked at his watch, looked up the track, and said, "Before long, Mr. Lockhart."

"You got three cars of horses due in?"

"Might be," he said. "I could look it up." He wandered into his office.

Amos Lockhart climbed onto the loading platform and clomped back and forth, chewing on his cigar.

When the agent came out he said, "I got three stock cars."

"When is the train due?"

Amos and the agent were both looking at their watches as if they were checking up on each other; both watches were as big as turkey eggs. The agent said, "Pretty soon now."

Amos stomped around awhile and suddenly said, "Let's go to the restaurant, boys, and grab a bit of dinner. I think the goddamned train's late."

We went to Kate's Diner and ordered the specialty of the house, which on Wednesdays was Kate's hot hash. Also we took advantage of this being a railroad town where they had ice and ordered iced tea to offset the hash. Amos went outside a couple of times to listen for the train. Billy Tuttle took seconds on the hash, though his eyes had already turned red from eating all that pepper.

Back down at the station Amos Lockhart climbed on the platform and asked the agent, "What time is that train supposed to be due, anyway?"

The agent said, "It's due now."

"Looks to me like if it was due when we got here, it's an hour late now."

The agent didn't say anything. He was sitting in a cane-bottom chair in the doorway, eating a sandwich and looking at a copy of *Harper's Illustrated Weekly*. Amos lighted a cigar. I figure he thought it was frivolous for the man to sit there looking at a magazine when the train was late instead of standing up and worrying.

We waited and Amos fretted and I began to figure we wouldn't get the horses home before night and we'd have to camp out without even a coffeepot. About the middle of the afternoon the agent came out of his den and said, "Mr. Lockhart, there's been a wreck up the line."

"A train wreck?"

"Yes, sir."

"What about the horses? Is it that train? When are we going to get the horses?"

"Well, we won't have anything that's scheduled today, Mr. Lockhart. That's all the information at this time."

For the next hour Amos went in and out of the office and stalked around on the platform. Finally I told him, "Me and Billy might walk around town, Mr. Lockhart. I might buy me a few pair of socks I need."

"Stake out the horses first," he said. "And listen for the train. If it comes in, I don't want to have to hunt you up."

We staked the horses out close to the loading pens and we hadn't got to the nearest saloon before I learned that maybe I hadn't been as bright as I'd thought. Billy didn't have a cent on him. I'd figured to tank up on fifty cents' worth of beer and go on a little toot, but I was going to have to finance him too. We went to a small place and stood at the bar drinking. They had a gallon of pickled boiled eggs sitting there, and Billy had eaten seven of them before I realized they were costing me a nickel apiece.

I got him out of there and we went to a large saloon called Pete Kimble's Emporium. After we had a few I lost my tight attitude about money so that I didn't even know whether Billy got enough to eat or not. Some gent who was kibitzing the same poker game we were found out we worked for the J's and asked if they still had those bad horses. We admitted they had a few. He said when he worked down there four-five years ago, they had about a hundred. He claimed he had got both legs broke trying to ride J's horses, but he'd been soaking up so much booze you couldn't believe half he said. When he tried to take his pants off to show his broken legs, the bartender put him out on the street.

Later on Billy and I were walking along singing and we noticed every light in the town was out. We found the hotel, but the front door was locked. We banged. We called for service. Nobody answered. After a short council of war we decided the hotel front porch was dry and cheap and up out of the snakes and would make a good bed.

It was daylight when Amos Lockhart woke us up, talking sarcastically. He asked if I bought any socks. He thought I felt stiff and sore because I'd slept on that wood flooring; actually that cause was nothing up beside of the lumps and bruises I carried from my two-day bronc-stomping career. I didn't press the point; he was in a bad mood worrying about the train. He knew the Old Man was counting on the new horses to improve the saddle strings.

After breakfast we walked back to the station, and Amos went inside. Billy and I lounged around. Evidently a message came in on the wire, and Amos got to arguing about it with the agent. Amos's voice carried when he got mad. I heard him say, ". . . sue this goddamned railroad! Can't even haul a few horses!"

You couldn't understand the agent as well, but you could tell he wasn't backing down. It sounded like he said the railroad would sue the Jackson Ranch.

Not long after that a locomotive gave a long whistle up the line and we could see her coming. We went to the loading pens and the train bucked two cars onto the siding. Everything looked all right, except the caboose was missing.

We unloaded twenty-four horses out of the two cars, big healthy horses, some of them skinned up a little on the legs. They looked like they belonged on the J's, every color, strong, with an independent air about them. A couple of them had short pieces of frayed rope on their necks and one had a short piece on his foreleg.

Amos stuck his head inside one car and began cussing. It sounded like he was about to throw a running fit. The floor was strewed with a jumble of splintered wood and pieces of rope. "What kind of ignorant fools would make a car full of horses ride on a mess like that?" he demanded. Both cars were the same. I figured no kind of fools would have loaded the horses without cleaning the junk out of the cars. In fact, I had begun to smell a rat.

We got the two dozen horses strung out south. We would find out the details on what happened three days later when two hands from the Dipper Ranch sixty miles up the line drove in the last twelve of our new horses. Here's what happened: When they loaded the stock in Colorado they built stout plank gates for partitions in the cars, putting two horses in each temporary stall and tying each horse. The horses evidently did not enjoy the ride nor any of the arrangements, for they proceeded to smash up everything they could reach. They broke a bottom slat in the wall of one car and kicked one of those plank partitions part way out. The train passed a single stock car sitting by a two-bit loading chute. The plank partition hooked the empty car and carried it to the switch, where it derailed itself and one car of horses, turned over two more cars and the caboose, and knocked down a railroad water tank beside the tracks.

Amos, Billy, and I made a hard day driving the improvements to the J's strings to the ranch. Those horses knew they could outrun a horse that was carrying a man, and each one of them had a mind of his own. It was nearly sundown when we turned them over to the wrangler in charge of the remuda on the creek below headquarters.

Like they say, birds of a feather flock together, and this bank of outlaws from up north that had wrecked a damned train fell right in with the J's horses as if they were all kissing cousins. It looked like a family reunion.

Billy Tuttle and I were lucky to have our claim in on bunks, because the bunkhouse was getting crowded. The men from the line camps were coming in and new-hired hands were reporting. The next day what you might call the big horse circus started. By the middle of the morning dust rose up in clouds around that place. Out at the bull yard and down at the picket corral they were riding horses. Behind the barn a bunch of horses were tied to logs to try to teach them not to jerk against a rope. In the plank corral we were shoeing and branding.

Somehow, missing only two days around headquarters, I had got out of the bronc-riding business. Sid Wilcox and a Mexican named Vasquez were riding the bad ones in the bull yard, and a fellow from Utah, nicknamed Utah, was doing the same down in the picket corral. Evidently it had just happened in the natural run of events and I was satisfied to keep my mouth shut, though it was a cinch I could outride Sid Wilcox any day in the week.

We threw every new horse to shoe him or reset his old shoes. They would have to be tied down for branding anyway—the Old Man was determined to burn a small "J" on the left shoulder of every horse he owned—but these, the way they fought, had to be thrown for shoeing even. While they were down Amos Lockhart would check their teeth. He had a book in which he wrote a description, old brands, and age of every new horse. Newt Tanner did most of the shoeing and checked the fit of every shoe. He had seven crates of horseshoes sitting against the fence, two kegs of nails, a sack of coal, a forge and anvil, and a tub of water.

Stubby was one of the ropers. He liked to foreleg a horse and drop him quick, but Amos didn't want to bust them hard, so we would catch them by the neck and choke them down, then try to get them to walk into loops on the ground. One big rusty-colored horse we maneuvered around for fifteen minutes. Finally we got all the ropes on him and started to pull him over. He began to rare and pitch, got one front leg free, jerked two men down, and swung the rest of us around like kids playing pop the whip. One man ran into the forge and knocked it over, or he was slung into it. Amos and Newt got on the ropes to help us throw the horse. By the time we could get a breather and look around, there was Amos's horse book over by the spilled forge, burning like a pine knot and about to set the fence to blazing.

Amos grabbed it up, beat on it, then soused it in the tub of water. The rest of us did our laughing as silently as we could. When Amos would get worked up and sweaty, he looked like somebody you'd picked up off the ground behind a saloon. He said to Stubby, "If you ever have to rope that rusty son-of-a-bitch again, I want you to foreleg him and bust him where he'll crack the ground! It'll take me all night to copy that out into a new book!"

Another horse we got the ropes on was fighting and jerking and kicking up the dirt, and I noticed a little fellow hanging onto the rope in front of me, bobbing like a cork. Suddenly I realized he had on a hundred-dollar suit and a red flannel rag pinned around his neck. The Old Man. When we got the horse down, he looked around at me, smiled, and said, "Good healthy horses." I kept waiting for him to say that they needed a little training. He checked every detail as Newt fitted a new set of shoes.

We shoed and branded about fourteen horses that day. Well along in the afternoon we knew a kind of commotion was going on down at the picket corral. Long Joe Christian tore off down there in a wagon, flailing at the team. Shortly afterward they hauled Utah, unconscious, back up the hill and laid him on the ground in the shade of the bunkhouse. Some of us went over to see what was wrong. He'd been thrown hard and looked dead but evidently had only got the wind knocked out of him. He finally sat up and said he was all right. His eyes looked blank and crossed.

Amos Lockhart said, "He'll come around. Let him rest awhile." Then he said to me, "Bud, you better go on down there and top off some of these horses. We got to tame these horses down a little and not many days to do it."

It looked like suppertime to me, but I went down to the picket corral and rode one horse that I knew wouldn't pitch.

It's a long lane that knows no turning, they say. That evening a new light was cast on the horse situation. It made some of the old hands happy, some mad, some relieved, some jealous. The news came from a new-hired man, Willie Caudle. He had long legs and an eager way of talking. Actually, he was halfway a greenhorn and worked sometimes as a bookkeeper for the county clerk, but he worked on ranches now and then when they were hard up for hands. Willie had no sooner come on the place than the word began going around that a great man named Red Paden would arrive in a day or two in a blaze of glory and our horse problems would be taken care of.

I walked into the bunkhouse with three or four other fellows. Willie Caudle was sitting on his bedroll on the floor, and I asked him, "Who is this Red Paden jasper?"

"Boys," Willie announced, "Old Man Jackson is bringing in a pro."

Someone asked, "A pro what?"

"Yeah, what's that? A whore?"

"Maybe it's a lawyer."

"Boys," Willie said, "the Old Man has hired a real first class rider. A pro bronc buster. And, man! I want to tell you that Red Paden can ride!"

We questioned him, but he wouldn't back down an inch on the news.

Stubby said, "If he's so famous how come we never heard of him?"

"I never said he was so famous," Willie said, "only that he can ride. He'll ride any animal that's got hair on it!"

Somebody said, "I guess you think he's quite a lot better than these boys around here?"

"All I know is he can really ride! You can't hardly get old Red Paden off a horse's back till he gets ready to leave!"

Stubby said, "He better stay away from these Jackson horses if he don't want to ruin his record. They'll kill him."

Willie Caudle must have had about forty dollars on him, and he laid every cent of it on the line before bedtime. They bet him different ways: that Red Paden wouldn't stick on Hong Kong the first time, that he wouldn't last a week with the outfit, that he would never ride Whirlwind, that he wouldn't ride Dodger twice in a row. They prevailed on Snuffy Detweiler to hold the stakes.

Next morning I went down to the picket corral. The ground was getting pretty well tromped up around there, which was good. In my education as a bronc rider I was learning, unfortunately, not only about staying in the saddle, but also about looking around for landing spots. If a man's coming straight down, water would be the best, or tall grass. If he's coming in on a slant to hit sliding, it's better to find loose dirt than to loosen the dirt with your own tender hide.

I tried to get Red Paden out of my thoughts. He might be only a dream of Willie Caudle's overactive mind, I kept telling myself.

Utah came down that morning also, but it seemed clear that I was expected to ride the bad ones. His eyes still looked a little glassy. Billy Tuttle and Long Joe Christian had orders to help us, to move the ones we considered tamed to the remuda and bring back horses that hadn't been saddled since last fall. Keep us plenty of pitching horses handy. That wasn't hard to do; they'd been adding fresh horses and taking out only the tamest, and that corral was getting more and more concentrated with ornery horseflesh.

I had bad luck with the first one, that ugly red roan named Whirlwind. Billy is trying to hold his head and is getting jerked around and lifted off his feet. When I get my boot in the sitrrup I jump for the saddle, which is a schoolboy type of trick.

Like they say, I am shipwrecked before I get aboard. He's exploding like a string of firecrackers, going around and around, with me trying to hang on the side. I get a chance and lurch upward, but he twists to meet me and socks the side of the saddle horn into my chest. Crack! A rib goes. I can feel it pop like breaking a dry stick in your hands. I'm all over that crazy horse for a dozen hectic jumps but never get my seat in the saddle. Then he dumps me on my head on the off side.

While they're catching Whirlwind I tenderly probe my chest. My rib is numb and prickly. I can hear those cowhands in the bunkhouse saying, "Yeah, Blankship gave it a try, but he didn't last till he got on the first bronc." I'm not positive I can ride this particular bearcat, but I figure I can sure give him a better run for his money than that.

Utah, Billy, and Long Joe all three get hold of him. Billy, feeling guilty about the sorry job he did before, takes off his shirt and wraps it around the nag's head, while the other two ear him down. This time I get set solid before they let him loose. He bucks hard and wicked for six or eight circles, and I can feel the action in my rib. Then he shucks me off.

The third time I ride him. The third time's the charm, they say. He runs out of steam, but instead of working him I slide down and lead him back to the corral, because I'm getting sick to my stomach. I take it easy awhile, helping the other three while they do some riding.

That was the most miserable day I ever spent. An idea kept nagging at me, as if the Old Man was saying, "These boys just couldn't do the job, so I had to send for a professional, Red Paden." It aggravated the devil out of me that I kept thinking that nonsense. And the rib gave me holy hell every time I rode. A jolt that started in a bronc's stiff knees would rise straight up to my rib and stop there. But I had got my thick-headed stubbornness worked up to where I thought, I'll see this whole bunch in hell before I say anything about my rib.

Although Long Joe did little riding, he did most of the cheering. He would get carried away, and it did me good to hear him pulling for me. But for some reason, when I was up on Brat and he was pitching like a turpentined cat, it suddenly came through clear to me what Long Joe was yelling. "Go get him, Brat boy! Higher! Buck, you devil! Atta boy! Yip-eeee!" The halfwit was cheering for the horses! If that bronc had thrown me then, I'd have fed Long Joe a fist full of knuckles.

An hour or so before sundown Amos Lockhart turned over his teeth checking and record keeping to Snuffy Detweiler and came down to see how things were going at the picket corral. I saw him coming and roped out Cotton-Eye Joe, a nag homely as a mud fence which I had found to be an easy pitcher, though very shy to handle. Amos didn't say much but just stood and watched.

Cotton-Eye Joe kept frisking around and wouldn't let me get near him with the saddle. We got a rope on a hind foot and tied it up on his neck so that he only had three feet on the ground. Utah eared him down. Billy and Long Joe got on the other side and held the saddle blanket on and tried to push him toward me. It didn't do my rib any good even to pick up the saddle. I got ready to swing it when he would hold still a second. He stumbled and jumped and tried to rare up. Then he planted one front foot square dab on my boot.

I'd been stepped on before. A horse will usually let up, thinking he's on a rock or something. But Cotton-Eye Joe was trying to catch his balance. He came down on the top of my foot, put all his weight on it, and gave her a little twist. I thought that wall-eyed elephant would never get off.

I dropped the saddle and limped back and sat down to take my boot off.

Amos Lockhart said, "I wouldn't take that boot off if you don't have to."

"Why not?"

"If it swells up on you you'll never get it back on."

Yes, I thought, you big, ugly, double-jointed bastard, if it swells up to where I can't get my boot on or off, I guess you figure I can go ahead and work. My rib felt like a hot iron and my foot felt busted and I was not in a respectful mood. I got my boot and sock off. It didn't look bad, but pressing on it I could guess I had another cracked bone somewhere down inside.

Amos helped them get the saddle on. Utah mounted up, and Cotton-Eye Joe ran away with him. Billy chased after him. I don't know how far they went, but they were both late to supper.

I couldn't stand any pressure on my foot, so I took my pocket knife and cut small slits in my boot. The next day was Sunday. I spent the morning soaking my foot in a bucket of hot Epsom salts, trying on my boot, and enlarging the slits.

That was the day Red Paden came. Evidently he spent a while hanging around the Old Man and Amos Lockhart, but Willie Caudle gave us the news that he had arrived, along with further information about his great riding skills. Late that afternoon I got a chance to talk to him. Some of the boys were walking around looking at the horses in the different pens, giving him the grand tour.

Red Paden was redheaded, of course, and short. His legs didn't look long enough to grip a bronc good, but he looked strong. The fellow actually had muscles in his jaws. He stood straight and had a look about him like the statue of an explorer or a politician. He wore a black silk shirt with small pearl buttons and a pair of California pants. His boots had shiny brass caps on the toes. His hat was creased to a low crown, flat on top, with a chin strap made of plaited calfskin that could be tightened with a silver concho. He looked good for a night on the town, but these were his working clothes.

I don't act too forward with a stranger. Maybe it was because of my game foot; I was an honorable veteran of the J's horse wars. Anyway I limped right up to him, stuck out my hand, and told him my name.

I asked, "You're Red Paden, aren't you?"

"Yep."

Shaking hands with him was like shaking hands with a pair of blacksmith tongs.

"They say you're a pro."

He grinned. "What kind of a pro?"

That had me stumped for a minute. "That's what we been wondering. What do you do?"

"I work with horses."

"Riding and training? Like that?"

"Yep."

"I guess you've been riding a lot in rodeos or a circus or something."

"I've been in rodeos some. Small ones."

"They say you're a real professional bronc stomper."

"About average, I guess. I do my best."

He was grinning and not arguing, but I didn't seem to be able to get down to the nubbin of it with him. I knew I wasn't exactly polite to ask so many questions, but I know too that a new man coming into an outfit doesn't know who he can tell to go to hell and who he can't.

"What I mean is," I said, "we've got a lot of experienced hands around here, used to riding them as they come. They're about average or better."

"They say this is a good outfit," he said.

"It's a good outfit but we got some real rough horses. I don't mean to be a nuisance asking so many questions, but some of the boys were just curious and wondering why you were brought in."

"I reckon every ranch has some rough ones," he said. "A lot of good horses want to warm up a little and get the kinks out on a cool morning."

Words right out of the Old Man's mouth! I thought, Lord have mercy! What kind of a sucker is this? No more idea than the man in the moon what he's got into!

I asked him one more question. "If it's not being too nosy, did you hire on for a regular cowhand?" I didn't have the gall to ask him how much wages he was drawing.

He said, "Well, I'm just supposed to work with the horses, I guess."

That's all I could get out of him. I didn't know whether to feel sorry for him or ask what gave him the idea he was so great. A little later a bunch of us were washing up for supper in the woodshed and they were asking me about Paden. I told them, "I don't know what he can do or what he's supposed to do. He doesn't claim a thing."

I hadn't seen Willie Caudle. He had his face down in a pan of water, bubbling and spewing. He raised up and said, "Red Paden won't tell you, but listen to me; that old boy can ride! When I say ride, I mean ride! Man, you ain't seen it!"

The straw that broke the camel's back with me was when I found out that night where our hero was sleeping. The bunkhouse being full, Amos Lockhart had told him to bring his bedroll into his office. He was bunking somewhere in the Old House.

I thought about all those hundred-some-odd Jackson horses. I knew some personally that should have had a price on their head, dead or alive, but most of them I wasn't even acquainted with. I hadn't even touched with a saddle blanket any of that bunch that wrecked the Fort Worth and Denver train. I felt of my sore rib and my busted foot and thought about Utah's glassy eyes; then I thought about Red Paden's short legs. A sweet kind of dead certainty came over me, like you're looking down somebody's throat in a game of stud.

I figured I could use the money, so I went around in the bunkhouse announcing, "That dude won't last ten days on this place." Some of the boys had been impressed with the new pro rider. Sid Wilcox, who was not known as being overly bright, took me up, and we each put up an IOU for thirty dollars with Snuffy Detweiler on the question: Would the man last ten days?

Actually, the worst thing about Red Paden was that he was not cocky and smart aleck. One like that you can pin down and everybody can gang up on him. You know what you're dealing with. You can hate him with pleasure and wait, knowing that Providence is bound to provide his comeuppance. But this fellow didn't brag a lick; he had Willie Caudle to do all his bragging for him. And could he help it if the bunkhouse was overflowing and he got a bed somewhere in the bowels of the Old House? What a disgusting turn of events!

My only consolation was that I would make sixty dollars for this hard month of horse taming and roundup, my pay and Sid Wilcox's.

The next morning Amos Lackhart sent Utah over to the sheds where they were repairing and tightening up the three chuck wagons, and took Red Paden, me, Long Joe, and Billy Tuttle down to the picket corral in a buckboard, carrying our saddles and a bag of gear Paden had. Amos said, "Mr. Paden, you can give each one of these horses a saddle or two, and when you think one is in fair shape, the boys will put him out in the remuda. Bud Blankenship here has been working these horses; he can tell you as much as anybody can about him. If you need any more help or anything send Billy or Joe here after me." He left.

Someone had put my horse Sleeper in with the broncs by mistake. I'd figured on going up to the stables and leading Blackie down if I needed him, but I didn't intend to give Paden the satisfaction of breaking Sleeper when I'd ridden him all winter. I said to Paden, "I'll catch out one to use for a hazing horse if you don't mind." I happened to catch Sleeper.

When I had him saddled, Paden asked, "You want me to ride him first?"

"No, I'll try him," I said. I gave a nice riding demonstration; then Sleeper calmed down. It didn't help my rib and foot but did wonders for my feelings.

By the time I dismounted, Billy Tuttle had roped Dodger. Whether he did it on purpose or not, who knows? If you haven't ridden a tricky bronc in the past few days, you forget how sharp you have to be and how quick he can turn. You need to get ready for Dodger.

While Paden was saddling him, he asked me, "How's this one?"

"He pitches," I said. "Name's Dodger. He won't jar you, but he's quick."

"Might make a good cutting horse if he was trained," Paden said. His saddle was full stamped and fancy with silver-plated conchos. He had on spurs and also had a quirt hanging on his wrist.

I get on Sleeper and they help Paden mount Dodger. When they let him go he starts fast, and I haze him in the direction of the creek. He pitches corkscrews, switches ends, and ties knots in the air, and Paden stays on him like he's pasted on, cutting that bronc's bony rump with the quirt at every jump. He's ready for all of Dodger's tricks. I figure he must have suspected that his first horse would be a dilly. The next thing I know Paden has taken charge of Dodger. He's jerking him this way and that and whipping him, finally gets him to running. But before he can get lined out too fast, Paden turns him on a dime. Back and forth across the flat they charge like they're playing polo. Dodger is mad as a wet hen but he's doing exactly what he's told.

Paden pulls him up at the gate of the corral in a cloud of dust and climbs down. He says, in a friendly voice but businesslike, "I believe Dodger is about ready to go into the remuda. Let's time him to the fence and I'll give him one more ride after a while."

He rides that swirling fool, Whirlwind, that broke my rib, and then he rides Pepper. On each of them he looks like he's a part of the horse, if you can imagine a part of a horse with a black silk shirt on.

Then he says, "Let's give Dodger one more little workout."

When Dodger is bridled and saddled and the rope taken off his neck, Paden says, "Step back a little, boys, and let's check to see if a cowhand could mount him without any help." Dodger has his ears keened back and he's walling his eyes. This horse has got a mind and a memory. Paden pulls the left rein up so short Dodger is looking at his own tail, and before the horse can make half a turn, he is stepping into the saddle.

I run limping around the wing to where Sleeper is tied and scramble into the saddle, but he starts shying and acting up. Meanwhile Dodger is bucking straight for the rocky ground; I figure it's not a matter of conniving as much as it is wanting to stay away from that grassy flat where he was whipped back and forth.

Paden is flailing his quirt. Dodger is not tired, but plenty scared and sore. He's bowing his back like a barrel hoop and hitting the ground stiff, teaching himself new stuff. One iron-shod hoof comes down on a flat sandstone outcrop and slips. Dodger goes halfway down. Paden grabs for the horn. Dodger jumps and turns and hits hard. Paden is off balance. Then Dodger snorts and cracks his back muscles and sails Paden ten feet high.

The horse is halfway to the Old House trying to pitch off his saddle before I catch him.

When I come back Paden is standing up, sopping with a bandanna at the side of his neck where he peeled off a few inches of hide on a rock. His hat is mashed. His shirt is dirty. I try not to take too much satisfaction in the sight, but Red Paden looks a lot more human.

I took Dodger down past the wing and Paden mounted him again. He rode him that time, and wore him down, but put him back in the corral without saying any more about his being tame enough to put in the remuda. After that we caught out Whirlwind the second time. No telling whether Paden was losing part of his confidence or getting tired or what, but he got a strap out of his war bag and put it on his right stirrup; then when he got the saddle cinched down, he brought the strap under and tied the stirrups together. He couldn't do much spurring in that getup, but he made up for it swinging his quirt. It looked to me like you got jolted worse too, with your feet tied down that way, and I wondered if maybe Paden got the muscles in his jaws from clamping his teeth tight to keep from biting his tongue. But, anyway, he didn't get thrown again that day.

The only thing that happened to him was that Pepper kicked him. It wasn't his fault. Pepper just hauled off and kicked him. He was walking past with his rope in his hand and his eye on another horse. Suddenly, swish, wham! It hit him in the hand he was holding the loop with and in the side, knocking him off his feet into the litter and horse apples. I don't believe he even saw which horse did it.

He got up and brushed off and acted like it didn't surprise him or bother him much, but he looked at his right thumb. Several times I noticed him feeling of his thumb, about like a person gently mashing a peach to see if it's ripe.

The next day Billy Tuttle and another hand took off in a freight wagon with a six-mule team to haul enough grub and supplies to stock the chuck wagons. To take Billy's place at the picket corral, Amos Lockhart sent down Willie Caudle.

Red Paden showed up with a bandage on his thumb and a stick about the size of a pencil bound into it to keep it straight and still. Like they say, it stuck out like a sore thumb. The skinned place on his neck had scabbed over and looked ready to heal if nothing bothered it. Since I was still nursing my rib and foot, I felt kindly toward him, but before the morning was an hour old I began to lose the feeling because of the way Long Joe would cheer him and the way Willie Caudle would say Mr. Paden this . . . Mr. Paden that . . . Once halfway to the creek Paden dropped his quirt and Willie ran after it like a trained pup. I was thinking, No wonder he can stick on these horses; with his stirrups fastened together he's practically tied on.

When he saddled up the big paint Goodfellow, you could guess the horse was too scared to pitch much. Paden didn't ask anything about him and I didn't say. I actually didn't keep quiet out of meanness, but because it sounds silly to talk about a horse running away with a grown man.

Goodfellow sprinted sideways about fifty yards, then lined out like a catamount was after him. I tried to follow on Sleeper and felt like I was standing still. Paden couldn't seem to understand; when he would try to turn Goodfellow, he would nearly lose his seat. You get that horse in a runaway mood and he's got no connection between his head and his feet. I came up on a rise and saw them pounding across the draw ahead. Paden was swinging his quirt. Goodfellow was looking south and running west.

They plowed into a brushy mesquite tree and came out the other side. Paden's hat was knocked back on his shoulders, hanging by its chin strap. They circled two miles out ahead of me and came back still running. Paden was cutting him on the rump now, making him go. I saw that his black silk shirt had a big rip in the back.

When I got up to the picket corral Paden had Goodfellow trotting around almost like a cow horse. Then I saw another small item of damage. Paden had a red welt across his forehead. Well, I thought, I may be forced to admit he can ride, but he may admit he's got into a regular fandango of horses before he's through. A while before dinner he got a needle and thread out of his war bag, took his shirt off, and commenced to sew up the rip while the rest of us took seven horses to the remuda and brought back seven. One we brought was Hong Kong, an ugly devil, with a head as big as a side of bacon.

In the middle of the afternoon, the four of us stood inside the picket corral gate, resting a minute, looking at the horses. Red Paden said, "That yellow horse looks a little wild."

"That's Hong Kong," I said. "He's got a reputation."

I'd never seen him saddled but he had been pointed out to me a couple times. The word had gone around that the last hand who drew him in his string had never stayed on him and had got in the habit of skipping him.

"What does he do?" Paden asked.

I said, "I don't know, but he's got a bad name."

"Let's give him a whirl," he says.

Some horses are spoiled and conniving and wise. We find out that Hong Kong is crazy. If he has a brain, all he's got in it is the idea that he damned sure won't go along with our plans. He snaps Long Joe's lariat. He grunts and kicks and coughs and slews around. He falls down and we pile on his neck and put on a hackamore.

Out by the wing, with two men on his head, with a hind foot tied up, a leather blind hung over his eyes, he is saddled by Paden. The rambunctious fool is jerking and staggering and snorting like he's trying to say, "No! No! No!"

Paden is cool and businesslike, taking his time. He steps smartly up, gets set, and says, "Let him loose, boys."

When his hind foot goes free and the blind comes off, Hong Kong takes two wild jumps. Then it seems like it comes home to him that he really does have that weight tied on his back that he can't stand. He bawls like a wounded jackass and rares up. I'm sitting there on Sleeper, who is pussyfooting around, worked up by the noise. Hong Kong comes straight at us, his mouth wide open and his lips drawn back, his yellow teeth shining. He snaps twice like he's going to eat us alive. His teeth hit my knee and Sleeper's shoulder, but by now Sleeper has enough sense to get out of there.

Hong Kong whirls, and it must be that he closes his eyes, because he pitches straight into the picket corral fence. He hits it with both front feet, squawling like a ruptured foghorn. He's fighting the fence and bucking at the same time. You'd think a mad Jersey bull couldn't get through that fence, but two posts break, the rawhide ties come loose, posts bend over and spread out. Through they go.

It seems like Hong Kong opens his eyes and sees he's back inside and doesn't like it any better in there than outside. He rares up and circles and sees the hole in the fence. He heads for it.

Paden has done all right up to now, but the jagged end of a post is pointing into the corral like a spear, ready to hang his leg. He gets out of one tied stirrup and swings his leg up just in time. Hong Kong comes out through the hole in one jump. Paden has his free leg along the bronc's back and is floundering over the brute's shoulders to keep his balance. He's grabbing all the saddle he can get.

Hong Kong is going away fast and furious. It seems like he remembers that bawling and fighting won't get a man off your back. He starts pitching seriously, long twisting leaps, scrambled up with short hops that jar grunts out of his chest. Paden can't get his place in the saddle.

There's a time to get off a horse. If he won't let you get set, the time is right now. Paden is making a mistake trying to ride it out instead of starting over. I see both of his feet in the air and his shoulder on that yellow devil's withers. He's sliding downward and I think that's it. But bad luck hits him. One side pocket on his California pants slips down neatly over the saddle horn. Hong Kong is exploding the dust out of the ground with his hoofs. Paden is hanging by his pants, upside down.

Of course he's lost his reins. I unlimber my rope, but Sleeper doesn't want me to build a loop. In fact, he's nervous as hell about even going in the direction of that dirty yellow horse.

Hong Kong's left knee is pounding Paden in the side of the head. It must be that the chin strap on his hat loosens, because the next thing I know that fool bronc's got a big hoof inside the hat. Fortunately, the chin strap breaks. Two jumps later Paden's California pants rip out and he drops. Hong Kong goes on pitching with the hat on one front foot.

Paden goes to the ground like a load of wet laundry. I head for him instead of the horse, because it looks like he needs help, but he begins to pull himself together and gets to where he looks more like a human being than a loose pile. By the time I hit the ground, he's halfway sitting up, with that bandaged thumb sticking out. He makes small movements, testing to see if everything still works, and looks around him as if he doesn't remember seeing this part of the world before.

I don't want to help him any more than he needs, because he might be easy to insult right now. I ask, "You all right?"

He says, "Yep," and grins, but has a puzzled look around his eyes. The scab has been knocked off and the place on his neck has got dirt in it.

Long Joe and Willie are coming on the run, so I go after the bronc. Hong Kong is down on the ground a quarter mile away, trying to roll, but he can't get over the hump of the saddle. Every time he flings his feet in the air, the saddle skids on the ground, and it doesn't do Red

Paden's full-stamped saddle any good. When I ride up, Hong Kong flounders to his feet and runs.

About that time I heard Long Joe yelling to beat the band. The broncs had found Hong Kong's new gate in the picket corral. That concentration of ornery horseflesh was spilling out one by one. I kicked Sleeper into a run and went back but lost the race. Long Joe had a saddled mount tied at the end of the wing, but he was too late too. They all took off. We got two ropes and laced them in to patch the fence, opened the gate, and rode after our hookey players. Red Paden was wandering back up toward the picket corral, and Willie Caudle was down there looking for Paden's hat.

With the help of the two horse wranglers, Long Joe and I penned our horses again before sundown. Hong Kong was with them, naked as the day he was born. Me and Long Joe went to supper. Willie and Paden got in after dark with his saddle, the girt busted.

As the old saying goes, If at first you don't succeed, try, try again. The following day Paden had his britches sewed up and his hat creased back and his saddle fixed, and he rode Hong Kong. We took that booger away down in the open and got two hazing horses around him. He snorted and bawled while he pitched, but Paden worked him down.

That day we brought in some of the new horses. Most of them didn't have a name and wouldn't have till some cowhand got a bright idea, but the dirty brown one that had caused Amos Lockhart's record book to catch on fire had already got the name of Rusty. He and all the other members of the train-wrecking squad were now scattered and mixed with the other bands of horses so that you couldn't tell them except by their fresh brands. Rusty turned out to be rough to handle, saddle, and mount, but no great shakes as a bucker. He would go up and down, front and rear, like a kid's rocking horse. I don't guess Paden could see it, sitting on top of him, but Rusty's neck action looked strange, like he had a hinge in his neck. Paden had unlimbered his quirt, then jerked back quick on the reins. Whack! Rusty's head swung back and socked him in the nose.

I rode up closer to him in case he needed help. His nose looked flat as a pancake and blood ran down on his mouth and chin. It looked bad, but he stayed in the saddle and rode him down. I figured the nose wasn't as bad as it looked, or else Paden had more pride than he had sense. When he finally got down, his nose was red as a beet, his shirt front was bloody, and he was blowing through his mouth. Willie Caudle swabbed him off some, but Paden wouldn't let anybody touch his nose. He went on riding.

On Thursday Cotton-Eye Joe tried to rare up and fall back on Paden. He got free and pushed clear just in time, but he was down where the ground breaks away near the creek. He stumbled and fell and rolled into a mess of cat claw cactus. Little leaves of cactus stuck all over his back. Willie dismounted and began to pull them out while Paden stood real stiff and still. I caught Cotton-Eye Joe. Paden had got to where he didn't look nor act the same as he did at first. Seemed like he didn't stand like a statue, but more like a man getting ready to duck. He would still grin and act businesslike and say, "Well, let's give him a whirl," but while he grinned his eyes would be darting around at those J's horses.

On Friday afternoon a strange thing happens. I've ridden a couple of broncs, just enough to get my rib and foot throbbing again. Long Joe and Willie Caudle are both horseback. We catch Whirlwind and Paden gets on him. I lean against the wing fence and watch.

There's our pro rider's splinted thumb cocked out and his hat pulled down to his ears, dried blood on his neck. His nose looks like a rotten apple. Clothes all torn and sewed up and dirty. The parts of him you can see banged up, and God alone knows what kind of bruises and wounds he's got that's covered. This horse is going wild and high, and Red Paden is staying with him. He's not exactly relaxed; in fact, he looks desperate with his hat pulled down that way. But Whirlwind is giving all he's got and Red Paden is staying up there and swinging that quirt. I hear somebody yelling, "Ride him, Red! Give him hell! Ride him! You've got him, Red! Stick on there, boy!" It's me yelling. Considering that I've got a hard-earned month's wages put up against him, it's clear that I'm a bigger fool than Long Joe Christian.

The following Monday we started spring roundup. The Old Man had been able to foretell a month earlier that we would be ready the second week in April and that we would start on time. Like a wise man said, "Wherever McGregor sits, there's the head of the table." When the Old Man said we were ready, we saw that we were ready. Amos Lockhart agreed with him, and you didn't hear any of the hands dispute the fact, though Stubby did laugh. But even though all our horse strings were ready for spring roundup, they sent Red Paden along with wagon number one, which was Lockhart's wagon. I found myself on the same crew, ten men in all, not counting three reps from other outfits.

We pushed away out on the headwaters of Paradise Creek to get ready for our first gather on Tuesday. We camped on flat prairie ground. That morning it was damp and foggy. Soon as it got light enough where you could tell one horse from another, we began to saddle and mount up. Horses went pitching off in every direction in that fog. Amos Lockhart loped around and tried to keep up with it and see what was happening. He would say to some hand getting up off the ground, "Better pull your rig off that horse and catch another one. Leave him for Red Paden. We got to move out." As sure as a rider went down the second time, Amos would make him leave the horse for Paden, and he was supposed to give the bad one a good working that day.

Willie Caudle had drawn the job of horse wrangler. He was the only help Paden had. I can use my imagination about the fun they experienced trying to tame down those broncs out there on the bare prairie.

We brought in about four hundred head of grown stuff and started branding before dinner. Then we left a guard on the herd and came in to eat. Paden arrived limping at the wagon, with caked mud on his side. Caesar had got him down in a mudhole that morning, and Pepper had kicked him.

It went the same all week, with a rodeo around the wagon every morning just before the sun came up. Some of the bad ones would be ridden out, salty and mean, to hunt cows, but the worst half dozen would be left for Paden. On Friday we brought in a small bunch and we were going to move camp a good distance, so we went on and worked them and came to the camp in the middle of the afternoon for a late dinner. Everybody was squatting around eating, using every little patch of shade. Amos Lockhart charged up with his horse in a lather and yelled at Billy Tuttle, "Hitch up the hoodlum wagon, Billy, and come help get Red Paden!"

They hauled Paden in an hour later. Hong Kong had knocked him off against a tree, then had bucked on top of him. Paden's right leg was busted in two places, just above and below the knee. He looked white as a ghost. The scabs and scars and his swelled nose looked peculiar with all the blood gone out of his face. His shirt and hat were torn and one boot was missing.

They figured to take him to the doctor at Seymour, but it would be a rough trip in the hoodlum wagon, and he had to have a splint on his leg. We had a spare doubletree, which we took the iron off of and split to make two splints. Somebody tore up some canvas for bandages.

Amos Lockhart got into an argument with the cook about whiskey. He said, "Bring that bottle of whiskey you've got hid in the wagon."

The man said, "Why, Mr. Lockhart, I don't have no bottle. You know it's against J's rules."

"I know damned well you have," Amos said. "Get it out here!"

"Why, Mr. Lockhart, you know I wouldn't carry no whiskey on Jackson land."

"Dammit, man, can't you see we've got to have it? Dig it out, right now!"

Amos had a way of winning arguments with the employees. He made the cook bring the bottle and give Paden a long pull. Paden gripped the bottle in his lap and came out with a slow sigh, like he'd been waiting a year for a drink.

About six of us grabbed hold of him and stretched him out straight while the rest got the splints on his leg and bound them tight. We packed him into the little wagon with him leaning back on his war bag and soogans wadded around him. He sat there cradling the bottle, gazing at the outfit. He looked older, but his eyes weren't darting around now.

I can't say I was happy and I can't say I was sad, but I'd sure been counting the days. It hadn't been ten days since he started on the J's. It had been twelve. I thought, If Hong Kong aimed to do that to him, why in the name of all that's holy didn't he do it two days sooner?

Billy Tuttle was getting ready to go and getting orders on where to rejoin the roundup. Paden sat there and gazed. I walked up to him and shook hands and said, "Good luck, Mr. Paden." It was like shaking hands with a half sack of Bull Durham.

A pitiful grin sputtered across his face and he said, "I should wish you fellows good luck."

After that we continued to have our riding show each morning before sunup. Broncs went popping around like popcorn in every direction. The winning cowhands only had to saddle one horse. The winning horses got to lounge around in the remuda all day. Hong Kong only put in two days of work, but I worked Dodger every time in his turn except once; I would have worked him that day, but Amos Lockhart caught me lying on the ground and ordered me to catch another horse.

We finished roundup in four weeks. The first order of business back at headquarters was payday. Amos Lockhart set up shop on the long mess table in the Old House with his records and his iron-bound box full of money. I drew mine and turned around. There stood that dumb grinning Sid Wilcox with his hand out. I gave him his filthy lucre. He didn't make any smart remarks; therefore I didn't paste him in the mouth. I didn't mind so much not making any money in the last month, but I had cut up a good pair of boots in the process.

They wanted me to stay on, but the wages for a regular hand had to be cut to twenty-four dollars, because the price of beef was dropping. I told Amos I had to be drifting.

I've thought about that spring on the J's off and on since that time. The funny thing is that we never did break the horses, but we went on and made the roundup anyway. And that old goat with the hundred-dollar suits and the red flannel rag around his neck went right on sacking up the money. Sometimes I think the horses won the battles but lost the war. Then the "war" idea makes me ask: Who was on each side? How did we line up, the Old Man and Amos Lockhart, the cows, those broncs, and us cowhands? Seems like the Old Man and Amos and the cows had a business going and that business went right on; the horses and men were tools, used like wire nippers or a lariat rope.

But who can say? You don't forget an outfit like that. You mull it over, and once this idea came sneaking up to me: Maybe it was the other way around. Maybe us broncs and us cowhands had a game going and we just used the J's outfit to furnish us a place and an excuse.

You have to be camping way out on the prairie alone to think a thought like that.

Ethel Mae Is That Kind

I grant, without argument, that women are privileged to do things which cannot be entirely understood by men. This is natural. Having nothing to do all day but sit at home and think up unreasonable attitudes to confuse their husbands with, they are not to blame if they sometimes show a lack of logic in thinking. Some women, however, go too far. My wife, Ethel Mae, is that kind.

She herself first called my attention to the little man and woman. We were sitting in the breakfast nook eating, Ethel Mae, Billy, and I, and Ethel Mae said, "Oh, William! Look at that couple coming up the sidewalk."

Our house sits out nearer the street than the others beside it, and you can see the sidewalk for about two blocks from our breakfast nook. I looked out over my coffee cup and fastened my eyes on the most comical-looking two people that I have ever seen outside of a circus.

The man was short, and his legs were shorter still. His neck, however, was long enough to make up for his legs. Another inch on that neck and he would have been a freak. The woman was two inches taller than he. Her figure was dumpy, she had a big mop of red hair, and her face was plain, though not homely.

She was holding to his arm, and they were walking as close together as two people could possibly walk. They stepped in perfect unison, swinging along as if they were marching to a drum and coming up on their toes in a queer little jumpy motion at the end of every step.

I set my coffee down without taking my eyes off of them. "Well, I'll be damned," I said.

"William!" Ethel Mae said, inclining her head at Billy.

"Okay," I said, "I'm sorry." Ethel Mae is so careful about the language Billy hears that I'm surprised he's even learning to talk. I can just see him twenty years from now, when he's a big football player, breaking his arm and saying, "Gee whiz, I wish I hadn't broken my arm!"

The little couple on the sidewalk got near enough that I could see the expressions on their faces. He had a pleased look, a half grin that was set into his face. Her face was blank. If she had a thought in her mind, it didn't show.

"Looks like a farmer leading his old red cow home for the morning milking," I said.

"She has pretty hair," Ethel Mae said.

"Pretty stringy," I said.

"If you want to be so smart," Ethel Mae said, "a farmer doesn't have to lead his old red cow home for the morning milking, because she stays in the barn at night."

That's just like Ethel Mae—bringing something like that in so she can show how much she knows about something that I don't know anything about, just because her uncle owns a farm.

"And besides," she went on, "I bet you never will see a cow and a farmer walking side by side like that and right in step."

"I know one thing," I said. "If I had some film in my movie camera, I'd take some pictures that would be good for a laugh any time."

"I think they're kind of sweet, myself," Ethel Mae said.

"They don't have any sense of humor," I told her. "Look at that expression on their faces."

They were up by the house now. His pleased expression showed that he was both satisfied and proud, but he was deadly serious about it. Her dead-pan hadn't changed a bit. She still clung to his arm like he was a treasure to hold on to. They went on past our house in that little jumpy, swingy step like they had been walking together for the last ten years.

"Do you know what that walk reminds me of?" I asked.

Ethel Mae poured Billy another glass of milk.

"It reminds me," I said, "of the way they play a tune in a comedy in the movies. They have it synchronized with someone walking and it makes his walk look twice as funny."

Ethel Mae stopped eating and pushed her plate back.

"I wonder," I said, "whether he would fall down if she turned loose of him—or maybe he's holding her up. What really gets me, though, is that walk, ker-ping, ker-ping, ker-ping."

I let my voice go up and down like they do in the movies, *"Ker-ping,* ker-ping, *ker-ping,* ker-ping."

Ethel Mae was getting red in the face. All of a sudden, she slapped her hand down on the table, "Stop it, William!" she said.

Little Billy and I looked at her in amazement. She rarely ever used such sharp tones.

Then she began to sort of splutter. "Dammit! Haven't you any sense of decency at all about you? Since you're so smart I'll just tell you something: I wish I were that woman and you were that man and we were just like they are."

She must have been ashamed after she said it, because she left the room in a hurry.

"Billy," I said, "whatever you do when you grow up, don't marry a woman."

Billy swallowed enough of the scrambled eggs which were in his mouth to make his voice intelligible. "Damn no," he said.

Mother Love

It was almost midnight and Joe Cronin was sitting there in the Lucky Seven Lounge, feeling comfortable and lazy. Neither he nor Lumpy, who sat across the small table coddling his drink, had a record in this town, nor even in this state. And the lounge was a good place, not too fancy. But if you hung your hat where you could keep your eye on it, you were all right.

Joe had been wondering in a casual manner whether he ought to ditch Lumpy in a couple of days or whether they ought to get started casing a job. If he got rid of Lumpy temporarily, he would be able to pick up a high-class dame. He was tall and well built. With a haircut and a clean shirt he could do all right. On the other hand, Lumpy was the type who could never pick up a high-class dame no matter what he did to himself. Joe had made no decision on it when the phenomenon came in the front door.

It was a sweet little old lady. You would have thought it was a gag of some kind, until you saw her face. Such a face could not be faked. She looked like a minister's grandmother.

She started for the bar, stopped, started to go back out the door, looked around with puzzlement on her small white face. Her face was fragile, with tiny wrinkles, transparent as if she had been kept in a closet. A feeling of being little, gentle, and lost revealed itself in her face.

She came straight toward them as if she knew them. For some reason, Joe felt like he'd been caught playing hooky.

"Pardon me, boys." Her voice was cracked and sweet at the same time and every wrinkle of her face had bent into a smile. "This isn't the bus station, is it? I was afraid it wasn't the minute I came in." The word "boys" as she used it made Joe think vaguely of school picnics when he had been spoken to by a woman who was serving strawberry punch.

"I don't speak to strangers usually, but you remind me so much of my own boys. So much!" The woman wasn't poor. Her white hair lay on the collar of a short coat of rich mink. Her two hands gripped a large purse, and on the thin fingers several rings sparkled. One blue-white stone would have sold for enough that the old lady might have bought her own bus line.

Joe half stood up. It was the first time he had risen in a lady's presence in years.

"I do hope you'll forgive me," she was saying, "but I guess I'm lost and I don't know anyone in this vicinity. Isn't that foolish? But I feel like I know you. You look so much like my own two dear sons. Could I trouble you to direct me to the bus station?"

"Yes, ma'am," Joe said. "I'd be glad to, ma'am. It's straight on down this street, straight across the park, and it's on the corner. You can see it when you get through the park."

"Oh yes! This way, through the park, and on the corner. You are so nice."

"Would you want to sit down a minute, ma'am?"

"Take a load off your feet," Lumpy said.

"No, I better not. My dear late husband used to caution me about carrying sums of money off away from home this way. I better not. But you are very courteous."

Her eyes dropped to the glasses on the table in front of them and her smile did not diminish as she said, "I hope you boys aren't drinking anything alcoholic."

They both protested, "No, ma'am."

"Well, it isn't good for you, remember that. Thank you so much for your help." When she had turned her back and made her way out the door, Joe felt as if he were released from a spell that had been cast by her face.

He said to Lumpy, "Get your hat."

Out on the street they saw her a half block ahead of them. She was carefully stepping off the curb, looking both ways for traffic on the empty street. She walked with precision and care as if she knew her bones were brittle.

"You got your sap?" Joe asked.

Lumpy's hand went to his back pocket. "Yeah. What for? Say! I'm not hitting that little old lady! I'm not about to."

"All right. You tell me how we're going to do it."

"Well, I don't like the looks of it at all. I just don't like the looks of it."

Joe didn't like it either. It was too easy. But the fact that Lumpy objected was no reason to stop. He had found that when they argued over a job, they were more likely to take all the details into consideration. He asked, "Just what is it you don't like about it?"

"It looks suspicious. How do we know she's not a plant of some kind? Maybe she works with the fuzz some way."

"You've got the mind of a criminal, Lumpy. We've got no record here. Cops don't plant people to get mugged, either."

"There's just nobody like that," Lumpy said.

"Yes, there is. You remember back. There really is people like that."

"Well, I won't hit her. I'm not about to."

"You want out? One man can handle it. I could meet you somewhere in a couple of days."

Lumpy thought it over for several steps. "Would I still get my cut?"

"What do you think?"

She had been walking slowly, a lonely small figure on the night street. It was a block of secondhand clothing stores and small hole-in-the-wall cafés that had closed at dark. She passed under a solitary blinking red sign, and as her form was lighted clearly, the hunched shoulders under the mink, Joe could almost see her smiling face again and almost came under her spell again. "We don't have to hit her," he said. "You can hold your hand over her mouth while I take her purse and stuff."

"Why me? You hold your hand over her mouth, and I'll take her purse."

"It wouldn't work anyway. She'd scream when we turned her loose. We'll gag her. Have you got a clean handkerchief?"

Lumpy produced one.

"Is that thing clean?"

"I might have wiped my face with it once."

"It doesn't look clean to me. We'll use my necktie. It's clean. You can tie her hands behind her with the handkerchief. Take off the mink before you do it."

Ahead of them the little woman had stopped and was looking in a pawnshop window. She was leaning slightly toward it, peering like a child at some article that had caught her fancy. She toddled on. It was hard to walk slow enough to stay behind her. Might look suspicious if a patrol car came along. They were two blocks from the park. Joe said, "Let's go around this block. We can walk three sides while she walks one."

They turned up the side street. Lumpy said, "You think she might catch a chill if we take the mink?"

"It's not that cold."

"But it might be colder to her, an old lady that way."

"All right. You take the mink, then you put your coat on her, then you tie her hands behind her."

"Yeah, that's it. It might not be too bad, Joe. We don't have to tie her hard."

"Listen, Lumpy, I'll tell you about this job." He was thinking as he went along, but had found it useful in the past to pretend with his short friend that he had already thought everything through. "This little old lady is all right, see, but she's had a soft life. She doesn't know from nothing. Her husband died and left her all that loot, see. Now she's got to learn the easy way or the hard way one. I figure we're doing her a favor. I mean, you think she would ever get home with that roll in her purse and that mink and that glass on her hands? Some rough crook will take it off her if we don't. Even if she doesn't get taken this trip, she's got to learn. She's ripe. We're doing her a favor."

"I'm not against it like I was," Lumpy said. "But if her rings won't come off easy, we leave them. You could hurt an old lady's fingers that way without knowing it."

"All but the big diamond. If it won't come off easy, we prize it out of the set."

"Okay, but we don't hurt her hands."

When they turned back toward the street she was on, they saw her still making her precise, careful progress. They walked faster and came up within half a block of her as she went under the trees in the park.

"And we leave her some of the roll for a bus ticket," Lumpy said.

"We leave her exactly twenty bucks," Joe told him.

They ran forward then, coming into the irregular tree shadows, circled out from the path. It was a good, lonely area. As they came back through the shrubbery ahead of her, Joe noted with satisfaction that it was a dark spot. It was not only that he didn't want to be seen, he didn't care to look at her face again.

She was still making her slow way, serene and unmindful. Might even have been humming some little tune. When she was as near as the distance across a room, he heard the sudden explosion of Lumpy's breath in an unintelligible sound: "Guh!"

A split second later a ton of metal seemed to fall on Joe's head.

He was semi-conscious. He knew that he had just been jarred to awareness by landing on this hard place where he lay. He had pains that he couldn't locate. That taste. Someone had jammed an oil well into his mouth sideways. He considered it, the taste and the strain on his cheeks and jaw. A gag. Greasy. The cloth had been used to wipe lubricating oil or grease. Rancid. Sickening.

His face was rubbing against the floor, grinding against it. Something was moving. He had an impulse to put his hands under his head, but found they were fixed behind him. Something was cutting at his wrists and ankles. His hands were numb. He tensed his neck muscles to raise his cheek from the gritty floor, but could not hold it up. He had guessed that he was being hauled in the back of a panel delivery truck before he drifted out away from it all.

Someone was kicking at him, tumbling him. He rolled to help, to get as little of the kicking as possible. The floor went out from under him and he jerked his head up. His shoulder took the blow of the concrete floor. He clearly heard his collarbone snap. It was a piercing pain that awakened him completely. A soft weight thudded on him and rolled off. He could see Lumpy's back then, the wire on the wrists, the hands swollen blue.

He couldn't see up. Out ahead of him across the floor he could see the bottom parts of cars, a chain hoist, a hydraulic jack, dim, rough metal walls. All half lighted by an overhead light he could not see. It was a garage of some kind. He was just beginning to think that he should try to line up all the facts, what he could remember, try to make sense of it, when the voice came. It was a gentle, cracked voice.

"I think Mother did very well, boys. That one is just your size, Junior. And this one, Sonny's size. Those old naughty police won't be hunting my boys after tonight. Now, we mustn't waste much time. You can get the car ready, Junior."

"Which car, Ma?"

"The Cad, dear, of course. They know you have it. Put on the hot license plates to make sure. And put in the machine gun you took from the prison guard. You do have the plan in your mind exactly, don't you, dear?"

"Sure, I got it, Ma."

"Repeat it to Mother."

"Up on Highline Drive—we crash through the construction sign. Put the bodies in the front seat. Set it on fire. Then push it over."

"You have it, dear. Of course, we must take the wire from their wrists and ankles when we put them in the Cad. When you're through making the accident Mother will pick you up. Gracious! I almost forgot. Put your ring on the tall one's finger, dear."

Joe Cronin felt the tugging at his arms behind him, the cutting of the wire into his wrists. He heard the man's breathing behind him. He did not feel the ring that he knew had been worked onto one of his numb fingers. The facts were beginning to sort themselves into a kind of fatal, fantastic pattern in his consciousness. His screams were stopping somewhere in his throat before they even got to the oily gag. Then the gentle, old voice again:

"Now, Sonny, Mother has a job for you. We mustn't trust the fire in the car. Put the big tip on the acetylene torch and burn their fingerprints off. Then get their faces good."

In a moment there was the pop of a torch lighting, the rushing, blowing sound of flame, the glaring light of open fire.

"Ma, these guys are awake. I hate to burn them in the face with them awake."

"Well, don't do it that way, Sonny. We don't do cruel things like that, do we? Hit them on the head first. Take the lead hammer and hit them on the front of the head, as it might happen in a car."

The foot was kicking at him roughly, trying to turn him over. The last thing he heard was the little old lady's voice, slightly scolding as when she had cautioned them about drinking anything alcoholic. "Turn the front of your head up, dearie."

The Disgraceful Affair of Turpentine Jackson

To the President of the Company and other officers, Dear Mr. Blackmoor:

First, they say it is a disgraceful affair, which I don't say is true, and hope it don't reflect on the good name of the Blackmoor Land and Cattle Company. As to giving the account, this is what I have to respectfully say for the record and to put it in black and white. I think Mr. Jackson's name is Henry, as I found it put down H. Jackson, but as you know he answers to the name of Turpentine. I want to apply and say that because I paid him twice I don't think it should be deducted from my salary. This is in the amount of sixty dollars cash money. I was told and instructed many times when out of contact with superior officers of the Company, to use my own judgment, which I did to the best of my ability.

I had them put me down as Acting Foreman McWhirter, since I did not know if I have been promoted or not. Anyway, this here's a copy of the agreement or contract, so as you can understand what went on.

AGREEMENT

Whereas, it being the determination of the following various parties to settle certain serious grievances and alleged crimes and debts and damages once and for all, we the contracting parties hereto do agree and affirm:

That the party of the first part shall include the Honorable Mayor of the City of Dodge City, the Chief of Police of the City of Dodge City, the High Sheriff of Ford County, the aforesaid Sheriff also as a representative of the State of Kansas, the Commanding Officer of Fort Dodge, the President of the Chamber of Commerce of the City of Dodge City, and the Secretary of the Civic Improvement League of the City of Dodge City.

Further, that the party of the second part shall include, but not be limited to, Elmore McWhirter, Acting Foreman of the Blackmoor Land and Cattle Company, having authority over Turpentine Jackson, all owners and operators of said Cattle Company having authority over the employee Turpentine Jackson, and any keepers or guardians having influence or control over the aforesaid Turpentine Jackson.

Now whereas it is agreed that herein claims do not represent final judgments in either civil or criminal actions, the party of the first part does nevertheless present an itemized statement of account, to wit:

One bowl of chili at Welcome Tex Café. Not paid for.	.10
Defamatory and libelous statement of finding dog hair in chili at Welcome Tex Café.	$5.00
Fee for cleaning wall, Welcome Tex Café.	.50
Four drinks first-class whiskey at Cowboy Oasis. Not paid for.	.80

Libelous and defamatory statement calling first-class whiskey at Cowboy Oasis epithet approx. "liquid mule waste." Damages.	$2.00
Grabbing money back improperly from Slick Hendricks, sporting man and part owner of Cowboy Oasis.	$7.00
Calling Slick Hendricks "crooked as rail fence" and also "crooked as dog's hind leg" at Cowboy Oasis. Damages to reputation of Slick Hendricks.	$5.00
Referring to occupation of Hog Nose Kate in public and making disparaging remarks about professional competence. Mental anguish and damage to reputation of Hog Nose Kate.	$1.00
One large mirror, Cowboy Oasis. Replacement cost.	$14.00
Failure to halt at first order by officer of law, to wit: City Marshal Owen Sims. Fine.	$3.00
Resisting arrest. Fine.	$3.00
Court costs, if tried, above two counts, $1.00 per count.	$2.00
Damages to Marshal Sims's firearm.	$4.00
Sending Peewee Hawkins down in city well to retrieve firearm. Cost.	$1.00
Striking City Marshal in eye while in performance of his duty. Fine.	$3.00
One pound beefsteak.	.10
Four yards cotton bandage.	.20
Five drinks first-class whiskey, Eddie's Emporium. Not paid for.	$1.00
Insulting and defamatory remarks about Eddie. Damages.	$4.00
Public statement that Mayor J. B. Krenshaw cheats at poker and is bigger crook than Slick Hendricks. Severe mental anguish and damage to reputation, also contempt of elected official.	$7.00
Calling New Orleans Rose epithet while she was verbally defending elected official. Also making lewd and suggestive references. Damage to reputation of New Orleans Rose.	$1.00
Breaking plate glass over large art picture of "Venus Bathing with Maidens," Eddie's Emporium. Cost.	$9.00

Drunk and disorderly, including statement that Turpentine Jackson can whip Mayor and two soldiers. Fine.	$3.00
Making reference to mother of Mayor. Damage to reputation and good name of mother of Mayor Krenshaw.	$7.00
Fighting on public streets, namely Front Street by Cattlemen's Hotel. Fine.	$3.00
One window, Cattlemen's Hotel. Cost.	$1.00
Assault and battery against two soldiers, to wit: one corporal and one private. Fine.	$3.00
Resisting arrest by Deputy Sheriff Perkins. Fine.	$3.00
Calling one corporal and one private "Yankee" plus epithet denying marriage of parents. Damage to reputations.	$2.00
Two gold teeth of Deputy Sheriff Perkins. $4.00 per tooth.	$8.00
Three stitches in nose of aforesaid Perkins, seven stitches in mouth. Doctor's fee.	$2.00
Miscellaneous damage to signs of retail establishments along Front Street, including one barber pole ruined.	$1.50
Refusing to halt at request of three duly constituted officers of the law, to wit: Chief of Police Webbington, Sheriff Trueblood, and Constable Orr. Fine.	$3.00
Continuing to resist arrest, after warning. Fine.	$3.00
False, misleading, and defamatory remarks about aforesaid officers.	$4.50
Sheriff Trueblood's pocket watch. Damages.	$9.00
Constable Orr's spectacles. Damages.	$6.00
Chief Webbington's coat, sleeve torn and pocket ripped out. Damages.	$1.50
Damage to bench in front of City Jail.	$1.25
Miscellaneous derogatory and malicious statements about officials, employees, and citizens of the City of Dodge City, and also the State of Kansas, including U.S. Army personnel stationed therein.	$8.00
Damages inside City Jail, including, but not limited to, one sprung door, one mattress, and toilet facilities.	$24.00

Three counts of Contempt of Court before Justice of the Peace Adcock, $3.00 per count.	$9.00
False and defamatory statement that said Turpentine Jackson can whip Justice of the Peace Adcock.	$2.50
One pound beefsteak.	.10
Six yards cotton bandage.	.30

GRAND TOTAL of damages, fines, costs, unpaid bills $179.35

Minus $4.00 credited to said Jackson for one gold
tooth discovered following morning in chamber pot,
Miller's Boarding House, and returned to owner. $4.00

BALANCE $175.35

Withdrawal of damage claim to reputation of Hog Nose
Kate plus statement that Turpentine Jackson is a good
man at heart. (Opinion only.) Also statement of Civic
Improvement League that said Hog Nose Kate is not
a nice person. (Opinion only.)

WITHDRAWAL OF CLAIM $1.00

FINAL BALANCE $174.35

Now, whereas, the representatives of Turpentine Jackson decline to submit an itemized account of any monies owing to him, the following statement by said Jackson is incorporated as part of the agreement herein: "I know [expletive] I had sixty dollars, two whole months' pay, when I came into this [four expletives] town. I sure didn't spend it, and I got only twenty-five [expletive] cents now."

Further, in answer to the above, Justice of the Peace Adcock swears and affirms that said Jackson had only twenty-five cents on him when he was admitted to the City Jail; and said Adcock says two residents of the City Jail, namely Joe Lefors and Charles Blankenship, saw that the aforesaid Turpentine Jackson had only twenty-five cents, and he can prove it by the said witnesses.

Further, whereas Acting Foreman Elmore McWhirter of the Blackmoor Land and Cattle Company says he only wants to do a good turn and make peace between the parties involved, he, the aforesaid McWhirter, affirms that the Blackmoor Land and Cattle Company takes responsibility for acts of employees only when they are doing assigned duties for the said Company. And further he swears and affirms that he did pay Turpentine Jackson sixty dollars in cash money, and does not know whether Jackson got his money's worth in recreational benefits.

Therefore, whereas no full statement and itemized account is forthcoming from the party of the second part, it is agreed as follows, to wit: The aforesaid Jackson did enter the City Limits of the City of Dodge City with the said sixty dollars; and that subsequent to his entry the money was taken from him, legally or illegally, by person or persons unknown.

Furthermore, whereas various claims are made herein, but not admitted, if one principal condition shall be met, then all debts, damages, fines, and similar charges shall be canceled and forgiven. The principal condition being thus, namely, to wit: that the party of the second part, in particular Acting Foreman McWhirter, but including the owners and operators of the Blackmoor Land and Cattle Company and all persons who may have any control, authority, or influence over the aforesaid Jackson, either now or in the future, shall immediately and forthwith remove the said Jackson from the vicinity of the City of Dodge City. Further, they, the aforesaid party of the second part, shall prevent said Jackson from entering back into said City Limits at any time in the future, either south of the tracks or north of the tracks, nor shall he be allowed to approach the military reservation of Fort Dodge or any personnel stationed thereon. Further they, the aforesaid party of the second party, shall prevent the said Jackson from entering Ford County; and further they shall prevent said Jackson from entering the State of Kansas.

And be it further agreed that Acting Foreman McWhirter and others, should Turpentine Jackson quit the employment of the Blackmoor Land and Cattle Company and thereby come out from under their control, authority, and influence, then Acting Foreman McWhirter and others, if they believe the said Jackson is heading for Kansas, shall notify the proper officials by telegram.

In witness whereof, we, the various parties of the various parts, do affix our signatures in good faith and in the presence of a Notary Public.

END OF AGREEMENT

Well, Mr. Blackmoor, that's the facts as requested, and I admit I signed the agreement for the Company, as I was told and instructed many times when out of contact with my superiors in the Company to use my own judgment, which I did to the best of my ability. I was also asked to make suggestions for the profit and good name of my employers whenever I deemed I ought to, so here goes: We could ship at Denison, Texas, or go plum past Dodge and up to Ogallala, Nebraska, next spring. Sir, there is a rough and rowdy element at Dodge City, which comes from the uneducated buffalo skinners and soldiers and teamsters and such types as gamblers, as well as some that is highly placed officials, and this is a bad influence on cowhands.

I hope this gives to you the explanation in black and white as requested, and respectfully say I don't think you should dock me the sixty dollars.

Yrs. Truly,
ELMORE McWHIRTER
Acting Foreman

Unfinished War

The hotel was not a high-class one. Its red brick walls proclaimed a sturdiness and respectability, but its business would have been poor if rooms were plentiful. It stood on a corner long deserted by the activity which makes a hotel successful. Standing and looking at it, I could not imagine the building as a home or even a shelter for human beings. It seemed, rather, a tall, lonely monument to the past, when this had been an important part of the city, and its four stories of red brick had commanded respect.

I took the three crumbling concrete steps one at a time and opened the heavy door with vague misgivings. The lobby appeared large because of the scarcity of furniture. Opposite the front door was the registration desk, behind which sat a thin-faced man wearing extremely large horn-rim glasses. He didn't look up from his reading until I had crossed the room and stood in front of him.

"Sorry, no vacancy." He said it as though it didn't matter to him, but as if it were part of his duties as clerk to be sorry that there was no vacancies.

"I don't want a room. I want to see Mrs. Georgia Stevens."

The man's face lit up with interest. "Are you a cop?"

"No," I said. "I'm not a cop. Is she in?"

"Not now, she isn't. She'll be back at five. She has to leave word here when she goes anywhere. You know, the police want to keep in touch with her. They told her not to leave town or anything."

"I didn't know that," I said. I turned, wondering what to do. It was only about four o'clock now.

"You can wait here if you want to." The clerk was obviously eager for someone to talk with.

I sat down on an uncomfortable wooden bench which looked as if it might have come out of a church. I didn't care to talk to this character with the glasses, but I wasn't exactly sorry that my meeting with Georgia was to be postponed for an hour. She might take my visit as an intrusion. I had a hard time even convincing myself that I had any good reason for coming to see her.

I hadn't seen her for a year or so, and then our meetings had been lively and interesting only because of the old days back at Junction, which we both took great pleasure in remembering. We had nothing in common now. Maybe the morning newspapers were right about her. Maybe she was the detestable woman described in the account headed in glaring black letters: WIFE DRIVES EX-SERGEANT TO SUICIDE JUMP FROM KELLY BUILDING.

I hadn't wanted to come here. I had told myself all day that it was none of my business. Just one thing had made me decide to come to see her anyway. It was the kind of girl Georgia used to be. We had gone all through grammar school together back at Junction. That kid I had known in school wasn't the same kind of person as the woman who today was smeared over the front pages of all the sensational newspapers in the state.

Georgia had been a likeable kid. She hadn't been much to look at, too chubby, but good natured and loyal, the kind of a girl that a boy can be buddies with. One incident that I remembered was typical of her. We always carried our lunch to school in a brown paper sack. Red Wilson, a big boy about a head taller than I, had taken mine away from me, and was trying to throw it up into a tree and get it to hang up there so I couldn't reach it. Red was bigger even than Georgia, but that didn't bother her when she saw a friend being bullied. While I struggled with him, she came up from behind and jumped on his back. She hooked her arm around his neck and pulled back with all her strength.

I think she would have broken his neck if he hadn't promised not to bother me anymore.

I couldn't picture that girl of our schooldays as the Mrs. Georgia Stevens of today. Of course, people change in fifteen years. I hadn't come to see her because I didn't believe the newspapers; I had come because I knew things were tough, and I wanted to help whether she was in the right or in the wrong.

The thin-faced clerk had pretended to go back to his reading, but I could see his eyes looking me up and down over his ridiculously large spectacles. He raised his head and spoke as if he were just making casual conversation. "You here for an insurance company or something?"

"No." I hoped my brusque answer would discourage his questions, but he came out with another before a minute had passed.

"You a friend of that woman?"

I started to say "yes," but then I realized that I should be trying to get all the facts about the matter that I could. Maybe this guy could tell me some things that weren't in the papers. "No," I said. "She's no friend of mine. I'm here on business." I saw a look of satisfaction in the man's face. "Has she lived here long?" I asked.

"Three months." He came around in front of the desk and slouched against it. "You see a lot of low-down people in this hotel business, but this woman is about the sorriest case I've come across."

"I guess you've found out quite a lot about them, working right here where they lived."

"Yeah, I've seen one or both of them every day. I sure feel sorry for the guy. I knew all the time that he had stood about all he could of her."

"It was all her fault, then, like it said in the papers?"

"Sure it was. She was always arguing with him and making life miserable."

"How do you know the arguments weren't his fault?"

"How do I know? You read the papers, didn't you?" The man went back and rummaged behind the registration desk. "You read the suicide note they found on his body, didn't you?" He discovered a morning paper and after searching through it a moment, started to read with his face close to the print. " 'When I went off to war, I was a hero to my wife. I sent her money and took care of her. Now she doesn't want me. I'm not good enough.' " The clerk looked up at me as though he had proved something that couldn't be disputed.

"I can't see why she would have it in for him so bad when he was just back from overseas," I said.

"Oh, you know how some of these women were while their husbands were gone. She'd probably been having a gay old time and spending his money as fast as it came in. Then he finally got back, things were too dull to suit her."

"You think she was trying to make him commit suicide?"

"Sure, it wouldn't surprise me a bit. I just wish the police could prove it. It would tickle me to see her go to the pen."

"Man, you do have it in for her, don't you?"

His eyes, magnified behind the glasses, searched my face to see how I meant it. "If there's anything I hate to see, it's a woman treating some guy dirty, especially a veteran."

"You must have been in the war, yourself," I said.

"No, I wasn't in, but I know how the guys feel who were. I can understand how it would be to go through a war, and then have to come home to a woman like her." The clerk seemed to be warming up for a long tirade against women in general and Georgia in particular, but he stopped suddenly and looked at the door, listening. "I think that's her," he said.

The door opened then, and Georgia stepped through without even looking in our direction. She was thinner than she had been the last time I saw her, and her face, usually broad and pleasant, was set in hard, tight lines. She headed straight for the stairs in the corner of the lobby.

"Here's a man to see you, Mrs. Stevens," the clerk said.

She stepped at the foot of the steps. "Hello, Georgia," I said. A bit of brightness flashed across her face as she greeted me. The look disappeared at once, but I felt sure that she was pleased at my coming. At the turning of the stairs, I glanced back down at the clerk. He was standing in the middle of the room watching us with an idiotic expression on his face.

"I must apologize for this long climb," Georgia said. "The elevator doesn't work. We're used to it, of course—" She stopped in confusion, and then went on. "Four flights is a long climb when you're not used to it."

She took me into a large room which had a high ceiling. The furniture was plain. Georgia took off her light coat and threw it across a chair. "It's been a long time," she said.

"Yes, it has, over a year, I guess."

"Would you like some coffee? I'm a little chilled." I noticed that her eyes were bloodshot and red around the edges, but the tightness of her face had relaxed a bit.

"Sure," I said. "Coffee would taste good." Georgia went about her coffee making silently. An electric hot plate on a table by the window evidently served as the kitchen. She finally looked up at me and spoke.

"Why did you come?"

"You and I are friends, Georgia. I thought maybe you didn't have many friends now." She sank down on the bed as I talked to her. "I don't care what the papers say. I don't care whether people think you are in the right or in the wrong. You and I are friends."

"That's the kindest thing I've heard for a long time," she said. "I'd like you to understand how it was, though, anyway. It wasn't my fault. He probably didn't even know what he was doing when he wrote the note."

I interrupted her. "Don't tell me about it unless you want to, Georgia. Don't feel that you have to."

"I want to," she said. "I haven't had anyone to tell until now. The way the police have acted and the way people here in the hotel have treated me—it's been pretty hard to take. I keep thinking that everyone I meet on the streets recognizes me from the picture in the papers."

Georgia was trying hard to keep from crying. I would have done anything in the world to comfort her, but I knew she wasn't the kind to cry on a man's shoulders.

"I should have told the police all about it," she said, "but it probably would just have caused more stories in the papers. He was out of his mind. He'd been getting worse all the time. Here in the last few weeks he got the idea that it was my fault, somehow."

"It must have been the war, Georgia."

"It was. I knew it when he first came back. He was changed. There was something brutal and unhuman in him. I couldn't bring myself to leave him, and I couldn't live with him. He couldn't even live with himself."

She was silent for a few minutes. I noticed a picture on the table beside the bed. It was a young man with a pleasant, smiling face. "He was nice-looking," I said.

"It was made before the war."

I thought about how happy they had probably been before the war and how it had been since. "Now that it's all over with, you can be proud of him, Georgia. He died for his country as surely as if he died over there fighting."

She didn't say anything.

"What did he do overseas, Georgia?"

"He—he—" She was crying silently. The coffee boiled over, and she didn't notice it. I walked over and pulled the plug. When I came back to her, she was searching through some magazines on the table beside the bed. She pulled out a thin magazine that looked like the Sunday supplement of a big daily newspaper and flipped through it. When she found what she was looking for, she folded the magazine back at the place and handed it to me.

My eyes lighted first on the title of the article: "He Evened the Score with the Nazis." Half of the page was taken up with a picture. I recognized the man in it at once. It was the same as the picture on the table, except that here he was dressed in army uniform. In his hands he held a rope tied in a familiar knot. Underneath the picture was the caption: "Sergeant Stevens, official war-crimes hangman—he sent nineteen Germans crashing to their death on the gallows."

Leadbelly at the Pearly Gates

All was confusion in the HGK household. It may be called a "household" rather than an "office," for it covered all the floors of the building except the top floor. It was a maze of offices, hallways, stairways, elevators, filing areas, secretaries looking busy. And the senior guards as well as the assistant gatekeepers had living quarters on the premises. Girls in prim suits clicked up and down the halls carrying folders, telephones rang insistently, typewriters clattered. When, frequently, sheaves of documents were dropped to slither along the polished floor, or file drawers came off their rollers to bang and scatter papers, exclamations could be heard: "Good gracious!" "Land sakes!" "Oh, my!" "Ouch!" "Mercy me!"

The HGK himself sat looking at stacks of papers which had been neatly arranged on the glass top of his spacious desk and cursing into his grizzly beard. He was an old-fashioned type with a beard twice as wide as his head, and he could be quite stern when the occasion required it. Also he had the bad habit of muttering curses, which was against his own strict rules. Whenever any subordinate muttered a curse, that one was banished to the Outer Reaches.

The first reason for the hectic atmosphere was a vast renovation project being planned under the supervision of the HGK. The project involved setting extensive specifications and setting up a process for sealed bids. But he had also been aggravated by a phone call this day from Pete the Key. It was well known by his subordinates that the HGK did not like to talk or listen on the telephone, and they always reported to him in person. Of course, Pete the Key was free to operate as he pleased; he ruled over his calm domicile on the top floor, free from the bother of the thousand details of the total operation. His call was for the purpose of giving a little simplistic, gratuitous advice. "We want the finest permanent construction in the renovation. We must be sure to take competitive bids." Such words infuriated the HGK, but there was nothing he could do about it.

However, now the stuff was about to hit the fan. The head guard entered the office and stood quietly until he was noticed by the HGK, who finally stopped muttering and demanded, "What do you want?"

The head guard had a lean and hungry look about him, a certain meekness, together with an air of patient authority. He said, "Your honor, there is a disturbance at the Main gate."

"So?"

"It seems to be a serious disturbance, Sir."

"You idiot! What in the hell is it?"

"I did not hear you say that, Sir."

"Oh, you didn't? Well, would you please be so kind and generous as to tell me why you come in here with these piddling trifles when I am already covered up with important and complicated decisions which demand attention? Would you tell me? Trouble at the Main Gate indeed!"

"Your honor, a black person, a man of dark complexion, is at the Main Gate asking to come in without a pass. He is carrying a twelve-string guitar, which is painted green."

"So?"

"He claims to be the best twelve-string guitar picker in the whole wide world."

"He is not in the world now, you simpleton! Wide or narrow. Can you handle simple problems by yourself? Can you handle the job of head guard? Did it ever occur to you to determine the man's name? Gather a few data on him? Decide whether he is a sinner?"

"Your honor, he gives the name of 'Leadbelly.' I have my men now investigating whether that is his correct and full name."

"Dammit! Is he a sinner?"

"I did not hear you say that, Sir."

"I asked you a question, fellow."

"Your honor, my information at this time indicates that he has sinned in Texas and Louisiana and quite probably in St. Louis, Chicago, Washington, D.C., and other places."

"Then what is the problem? You know the plain regulations. What in the hell do you mean by bringing such issues to me? Can you understand that I am a policy-making authority?" The HGK rolled his eyes up toward the top floor where Pete the Key dwelt in quiet luxury. "The Lord knows that I am left with all policy decisions in addition to a thousand details which incompetent subordinates try to put on me."

For a moment the HGK assumed a position and air of sublime martyrdom; then he abruptly announced, "Dismissed!" and turned his attention to one of the stacks of papers.

The head guard folded his skinny arms to his chest and stood.

Finally the HGK jerked his head up and demanded, "Well?"

"Your honor, some of the people at the gates, including three senior guards, thought Mr. Leadbelly . . ."

"So! You do not intend to follow regulations, nor my direct orders!"

"Your honor . . ."

"Don't you dare interrupt me! Young man, I want to explain to you a few things if your simple mind can grasp them." The beard of the HGK was bristling out so that his lower face looked like an albino porcupine.

"You are a subordinate, fellow! Put that in your pipe and smoke it, but I'd better not catch you smoking on the job. I know that you were interviewed for your present position by Pete the Key. That means nothing! You are thinking you can do as you please. Is that it? Speak up, you meathead!"

"No, your honor, I don't . . ."

"Don't interrupt! I will tell you two or three things. Who took the deathbed confessions of Augustine? Me! Who supervised the construction of seventeen churches and monasteries? Me! Who got Martin Luther into this place on Individual Approval? Me! I have seven hundred years' seniority on you, fellow! If you think you can be insubordinate with me, you will find yourself in the Outer Reaches before you can say Jack Robinson."

The head guard dropped his arms to his side; he was subdued, but still persistent. "Your honor, it was thought that you might want to make this decision yourself since it requires mature wisdom. It is possibly a case of Individual Approval . . ."

"There is no such thing as Individual Approval! Rules are rules! No exceptions!"

"It was thought, your honor, that no one has the authority and judgment but you in the Leadbelly problem. Perhaps . . ."

"All right, fellow. I'm going to explain one more time to you how I function as head gate keeper in regard to subordinates. I make decisions on the basis of details! Facts! Not guesses! You say this person has a dark complexion. Find out! Is he an African, a black, a Negro, a colored person, or a nigger? I want information on whether these people are ruining the neighborhood. I want details on this Leadbelly person's sins. I want to know what is a twelve-string guitar. Why is it painted green? You have investigators! You have researchers! Frankly, you have spies! Now, get me details. What would be Gabe's reaction to this person if he is a musician? Do not—I repeat, do *not*—spread this around so that any information could possibly get back to Higher Headquarters.

"Now go! And don't show your face in this office again to bother me until you are furnished with every possible detail on this impudent Leadbelly person, as well as possible consequences of his admittance."

"In the meantime, your honor, what . . . ?"

"Dammit! Are you going to get out of here and let me work?"

"I didn't hear you say 'dammit,' Sir. I'll go. I was just going."

After he left, the building hummed and buzzed as usual, the prim heels and toes of office girls clicked along the passageways, the mops and electric polishing machines of the janitors swept along the tiled floors. A faint smell of disinfectant permeated the place. The HGK, in an office too big for his stubby form and too small for his frustrated energy, puzzled during the night over the great project, a complete renovation of the Main Gate construction and adjacent fencing.

The HGK did not have a receptionist. He maintained that the constant presence of a female person was a distraction and a temptation of the Devil. It was just as well; none of the office girls wished to be his receptionist. He did have a buzzer button by which he could summon a messenger.

At mid-morning on the following day the head guard appeared again. He stood patiently waiting for recognition. The HGK was working with pencil and paper, trying to add up a column of figures.

He said, "You can stand there until Hell freezes over and I will not notice you."

The head guard folded his skinny arms.

"It wouldn't do any good to notice you. You cannot understand the most simple orders. An idiot could see that you have not brought along the extensive files containing the data I requested on this insolent, itinerant musician, whatever his name is."

"Leadbelly, Sir."

"Don't interrupt! Young fellow, do you have any idea, the slightest idea, what first-grade pearl inlay costs these days? Or even second-grade pearl inlay with a minimum of flaws? Do you know what masonry repair work or original stone and mortar work costs? Do you have the slightest idea of how complicated it is to work out specifications so that the contractors can submit realistic bids? I've asked you a question! Don't stand there like a knot on a limb!"

"Well, no, Sir. I . . ."

"I thought not. Now. I'm going to give you one brief opportunity to offer some pitiful excuse for your insubordination. You know full well that you are in serious danger at this moment of being flayed alive before being banished to the Outer Reaches! Speak up! You idiot! Did I order you not to appear in this office without full details, or did I not? Do you intend to obey orders or do just as you damned well please?"

"I did not hear you . . . I mean, there is an exception, your honor."

"There are *no* exceptions to my orders. You do not need to follow directives from Pete the Key. You understand good and well that he does not know whether his orders are followed."

"There is an exception, your honor."

"What? I am going to have you sprinkled with salt after you are skinned alive! Give me your lame excuse. Right now!"

"Your honor has cautioned me at length many times about . . . Well . . . This is a delicate matter."

"Ha! You say 'delicate.' You will think it is a *sensitive* matter when you are taken to the Outer Reaches without a hide. Give me your sorry excuse; then get down on your bony knees and begin your plea for mercy. Right this instant!"

"Your honor, we find from General Security at Higher Headquarters, through the private information system, that He is missing and undoubtedly out traveling incognito again. For several weeks our operatives have been following leads, and . . ."

The pencil slipped from the hand of the HGK, and he stopped pretending to add up a column of figures. He sat back and stared. "No! Wait a minute! Wait! Tell me you have a tail on Him, and He has gone the other direction."

"Well, Sir, as you know, our activities are covert, and we can only surmise. We have a possible contact only fifty miles away, but . . ."

"Wait! Wait! Don't tell me *but*. He has gone toward another department. Your spies know He is not coming here."

"Your honor, I would like to report the most reliable information we have. Apparently He toured out through the Outer Reaches and then turned down in this direction, following the foot paths. At the Edge of the Reaches, some inhabitants were playing baseball, and a Stranger . . ."

"Playing baseball? What . . . ?"

"Sir, they had nine players on one team and only eight on the other. They needed a center fielder, and none of the spectators would volunteer. The Stranger stepped forward, smiling. He had on brown cotton gloves, and when He took off His glove to put on a fielder's glove, one of our reliable investigators saw that He had a scar from an old wound in his hand."

"What hand? Which hand? Constantine had a war wound in his right . . ."

"This was the left palm, Sir. In the second inning the Stranger got a triple. When He rounded second, He was limping."

"What foot? Which foot?"

"It seemed to be both feet, your honor. He slid into third. He was safe, but when He stood up on the base, He was holding his left side, as if He had some old wound."

"Wait! Wait! After the game, the Stranger walked back in the direction of General Headquarters. Right?"

"I wish I could say that, Sir. Two of our operatives lost Him, but one, who is usually reliable, believes that He is headed this way. The Stranger seems to attract children, and our investigator believes . . ."

"All right! Look! This is an extremely serious matter. Find out about His other hand. Also, it is of utmost importance that all our activities here be beyond any kind of criticism or blame. Unfortunately, this development comes at a time when we are planning the renovation. Everything about the renovation must be beyond reproach. Now, this . . . Led person . . ."

"Leadbelly, your honor."

"All right. Can we send him away quickly? Or can we put off quietly any determination for a few weeks?"

"Sir, Mr. Leadbelly has camped out under that big spreading live oak tree about a hundred yards in front of the Main Gate. It's a very large tree and the limbs spread . . ."

"Stop! Don't tell me things I know better than you! I saw that tree a hundred years before you were born. When it was a sapling."

"Yes, your honor. Anyway, all my guards have waved to him and signaled for him to go away. But he just sits out there grinning and singing and picking his green twelve-string guitar. I have twelve researchers working up complete details on the man—the type of data you requested."

"Don't tell me any more! Leave! I have a thousand things to consider. Leave!"

"Yes, your honor. I will report daily on . . ."

"Leave!"

That afternoon and evening the HGK spent at his polished desk with the neat stack of papers. He ordered a hamburger, cursed the waitress who brought it, ate half of it, threw the rest in the trash basket. Through the night he dozed, waking every two hours to scribble furiously at his figures before dozing off again. The next morning he drank six cups of coffee, black with sugar.

At 1 P.M. that afternoon the head guard ushered into the office twelve young women, each of whom bore a stack of file folders. He lined up the girls and smiled at the HGK. They held the files, some of them a foot high, in front of themselves primly.

"What is this?" the old man demanded. "Get out of here right now!"

"Sir, these are all the details you requested in regard to the admittance of a certain Leadbelly. I have congratulated these ladies on doing such a complete and quick task of research, and I am sure . . ."

"Stop! Look at that shameless hussy on the end! I can see her knees!"

"It's a standard costume, your honor. If one does not bend over to look . . ."

"Don't tell me what is standard! Standard is fifteen inches from the floor. Maximum! That skirt is sixteen or seventeen. What is this place coming to?"

Everyone bent over to look at the young woman's knees. She was blushing.

"Get her out of here! Young woman, go change into decent clothing this minute!"

"I can't . . . I don't have anything else till the laundry comes back tomorrow, and . . ."

"Get out!"

The head guard took her file folders, and she departed sniffing.

"Now, Mister so-called Head Guard! What is the correct and true name of this impudent Leadbelly fellow?"

"His parents had the surname of Ledbetter. He has the given name of Hewdie. But all the records, mostly based on verbal sources, refer to him as Leadbelly."

"Now! These problems may be more simple than your pea brain can conceive. Is Leadbelly a sinner, or not?"

"Your honor, excuse me. I have all the documentation, but would it be permissible for me to state a later development? Last night . . ."

"Dammit! Is he a sinner?"

"We did not hear you say that, your honor. I wish to answer your question, but also to state a pertinent fact."

The HGK had assumed an air of martyrdom, gazing skyward, his arms flung outward.

"Your honor, last night several inhabitants of this area climbed the fence and went out to the spreading oak to listen to Mr. Leadbelly sing and play."

When the information sank in, the HGK asserted, "That's outrageous! Cannot you and your guards maintain the borders? Explain yourself! You are in trouble, fellow!"

"Sir, regulations clearly state that we must completely prevent anyone from climbing the fence *in*, but we have no authority to prevent anyone from climbing the fence *out.*"

"Well, my fine fellow, has it not occurred to your figment of a brain that you might just refuse to let such people back *in* and thus stop such outrageous behavior?"

"Your honor, I've been through all regulations from His Honor Pete the Key and from Higher Headquarters, and they state that anyone with a pass and proper credentials *must* be admitted when he presents himself."

"Stop quibbling! All the more reason to settle the Leadbelly problem. Are you going to stop quibbling and answer my question? Is the man a sinner?"

"Yes, Sir. We have found in the records one thousand, two hundred, and seventeen sins, of which approximately half are sinful thoughts."

"Damn his thoughts! What did he do?"

"We didn't hear you say that, Sir."

"Well, my excellent young fellow, you will find that it is perfectly legitimate to damn evil thoughts. In fact, I order you and these females to damn evil thoughts at every opportunity. Now! What did he do?"

"Your honor, we are prepared to read the complete record. Perhaps . . . well, his most prevalent sin was getting into brawls in honky-tonks. He hit a man over the head with a beer bottle once, and . . ."

"What's a honky-tonk? Ha! You do not know. I told you to get complete data!"

"Your honor, a honky-tonk is a place where low-class persons of both sexes gather, usually at night, to drink beer and gin, to dance, to talk loudly, and to sing sad songs."

"Sing what?"

"Sing sad songs, Sir."

"Why?"

"I don't know, your honor. I consulted an expert who has a degree in Social Psychology, and he did not know."

"Ha! Well, at last you are beginning to admit your ignorance and incompetence. Tell me this little fact: Why is this Leadbelly person's guitar painted green?"

"The best information, Sir, is simply that he did not have any other color of paint."

"All right! All right! Now! I told you to determine his classification, whether African, Negro, Black, and so on."

"Your honor, a complete evaluation indicates that he is halfway between a colored man and a nigger."

"That does it! That rips it! That's all she wrote! He cannot enter! Now, I told you in plain Latin to find out what effect these people are having on the neighborhood. However! You come in here unprepared!"

"Your honor . . ."

"You did not gather the data I asked for, did you? Give your lame excuse. And explain why you have not followed orders."

"Sir, researcher number three, this young lady with the dark hair, has all the available information. I have just completed a survey of the files, and the experts agree that it is a relative matter; much progress has been made toward acceptable integration, but much remains to be accomplished. Statistics indicate . . ."

"Statistics hell! Young man, do you realize that we have musicians up here? Decent, respectable musicians? What would Gabe say? Do you ever use your head for anything but a hat rack? What kind of disruption do you think would result if we admitted this Lead-person? Speak up, you idiot!"

"Your honor, His Honor Gabe is a horn man. Mostly we have horn men and flute blowers and organ players. Most guitar pickers do not come up, and hardly any twelve-stringers. I believe . . ."

"Stop! The answer is *no!* That's my final answer! He may *not* enter! Get these hussies out of my office! Get their prim seductive bodies out of here this instant! I'm trying to plan an important renovation, which involves a thousand details, and you bring me ridiculous problems, and top it off by parading these shameless females."

"There is one more thing, Sir."

"Dismissed! I have work to do."

"I have instructions from your honor to . . ."

"Get out of here! Get these female sex maniacs out of my sight! When I lean over like this I can see half their knees. Look at that shameless floozie in the middle! Trying to look innocent! Are you going to leave my office, Mr. Head Guard, or are you going to suffer the consequences?"

"I am going to follow your standing orders, Sir, about a certain delicate matter. About bringing certain confidential information. About a Person traveling incognito."

"What? What is . . . ?"

"Your honor, our special operatives have kept contact. The Stranger in question stopped in this immediate vicinity where some children were playing mumbly-peg in the dirt. The game is played by sticking one point of a pocketknife in the dirt, then it is flipped."

"I know how to play mumbly-peg."

"Well, Sir, the Stranger removed His brown cotton glove from His right hand in order to take His turn. It was observed by a reliable operative that He has a serious scar in His right palm also. This is now considered positive identification."

"Then He turned and went back toward General Headquarters or another department, didn't He?"

"No, Sir. He seems to be in the immediate vicinity of the Main Gate and Reception Center."

The HGK put his bushy beard on his polished desk and folded his strong arms about his head as if to shut out any more. In a moment, at a quiet signal from the head guard, the young women researchers filed quietly out. The head guard softly pulled the door shut behind him.

Late in the evening the HGK pushed his buzzer and ordered a hamburger with french fries. After insulting and dismissing the waitress, he ate the fries and dropped the hamburger in the trash. During the long hours of the night he paced the office, mumbling to himself, and drank seven cups of black coffee with sugar. Every time he added up a certain column of figures he got a different answer.

It was the middle of the morning when the head guard appeared again. He stood patiently, loudly clearing his throat every sixty seconds.

"I want one thing perfectly clear and understood, you pitiful idiot. I will not accept any more trouble or bad news. If you try to add one iota to my problems I will personally kill you with my bare hands. Is that understood?"

"With all due respect, your honor well knows that I cannot be killed."

"I can damned sure make you wish you were dead! I will have you boiled in oil! How would you enjoy that?"

"I hope your honor will not see fit to do that."

"Well, watch your step! Young fellow, you do not understand. I am a reasonable man. But not one soul knows or appreciates the complications of the renovation. The fencing material, for instance. We have used Damascus sword steel, Toledo blade steel, Samurai steel! And after a few hundred years, what happens? Rust! Plain rust! Now there is alloy: manganese, nickel, chrome, molybdenum. You have to be a metallurgist, along with ninety-seven other things, to do the job of head gatekeeper. Tensile strength! Do you worry about tensile strength in your petty position as head guard? No! What do you care for tensile strength? What do you care for rust? Now you permit inmates to climb the fence! Are you concerned as to what this activity will do to the property in two hundred years? What effect it will have on the fencing?"

"About that, your honor, I have some news . . ."

"Shut up! You pea-brained idiot! I am trying my dead-level best to educate you! In your sublime stupidity you imagine that I will foul up and you will get my job. Alas, you do not know the burdens."

"Your honor, I have some news. We have found out . . ."

"Shut up! You ingrate! You moron! Can you possibly see that I am trying to explain? Do you know what problem transcends all others? Can you possibly conceive of what I am expected to plan and execute and supervise?"

"No, sir, I . . ."

"Shut up! You pipsqueak! Tell me one little, tiny thing. How is it possible to tear down a giant gate structure and build it back at the same time? Would you just explain that? Shut up! How can we replace it right to the foundations, as well as two miles of fence, and at the same sweet time maintain security? You cannot raze a structure and replace it at one time! What happens to security? We can work every guard overtime and they cannot handle it! It's impossible! But who worries about that? Except me? Speak up, you sap head! Do you enjoy just standing in my office with your bare face hanging out?"

"I am trying to report, your honor, that He climbed the fence last night."

"Shut up! Wait . . . What did you say?"

"Sir, He climbed the fence and went out where Mr. Leadbelly plays under the big spreading live oak tree. Just about a hundred yards out there. Where all the No-goods and Rejects sit."

"Who? Who climbed the fence? Stop! Don't tell me!"

They eyed each other for a full minute, the lean and hungry head guard and the stubby, haggard HGK. Finally, the old man asked in an almost civil voice, "What does Leadbelly sing? I mean . . ."

"He sings sad songs, Sir."

"Tell me some of it."

" 'Them Deep Ellum Blues' is one, your honor."

"You mean '*Those* Deep Ellum Blues'?"

"Well, it's not good Latin, Sir, but the title according to the best information is '*Them* Deep Ellum Blues.' "

"What is a Deep Ellum?"

"It's a street in Dallas, your honor, or a community at the far end of the street."

"What's sad about it? What does it say?"

When you go down in Deep Ellum,
Keep yo money in yo shoe
'Cause them Deep Ellum women
They can't get it if you do.
Oh, Mama, Daddy's got them Deep Ellum blues.
Oh, Oh, sweet Mama, Daddy's got them . . .

"Stop! You idiot! Don't try to sing. You will certainly never make the Choir. What I need to know is the meaning. Where does this Leadbelly get his songs?"

"He makes up many of them, your honor. He made up 'Irene, Good Night.' It seems that he got married to a woman named Irene only the previous Saturday night, and they have already split up. For some reason he just keeps telling her 'goodnight' as if it is an obsession."

"So! Ha! That's what I thought! Tell me, does the man sing any song that is *not* about women?"

"Well, Sir, the 'Midnight Special' would be an example. He keeps singing, 'Let that Midnight Special shine his ever-loving light on me.' The experts we have consulted disagree as to the symbolism involved, but it is a very sad song."

"Stop! No more! Get out! I have to do some thinking. Lock the door. Make sure I am not disturbed. If Pete the Key calls, tell him I'm sick. You are not to permit anyone to enter here. Do you hear me?"

"Yes, your honor."

When he was alone, the HGK began to pace the floor, circling his desk. Then he began to listen at the door and at the walls, as if he suspected he might be spied upon. At the long window he peeped through the thin cracks in the venetian blinds. Finally he took from his left shoe a small key, unlocked one bottom drawer of his desk, and took out a half-gallon jug of Kentucky bourbon, ninety proof. He raised the jug and took a big drink, coughed and took another.

So he drank through the night. He paced. Sometimes he pulled with both hands at his frizzly fringe of hair and at his wide beard. He listened for spies at the door and walls and window. And drank.

At nine-fifteen in the morning, when the head guard unlocked the door and entered, the HGK was sitting, half conscious. The jug of bourbon sat in plain sight before him.

"Your honor, I have news."

The HGK grunted.

"Your honor, I have important news."

"I know . . . Yes, I know."

"It's about Him."

"I know. You will be going to the Outer Reaches also. For incompetence, insubordination, and disrespect to superiors."

"No, Sir, it's *good* news. He made a phone call at the public phone booth down on the corner this morning."

"What . . . ? What . . . did He say?"

"We have the phone tapped, of course, your honor. We know that He called General Headquarters, but He spoke in that code which we have never been able to crack. Twenty minutes after His call a Priority Order came into the Communications Center from General Headquarters. The Priority Order may solve the problem of razing the Main Gate structure and rebuilding it back at the same site all at the same time."

"What . . . ?"

"The Main Gate and adjacent fence are to be rebuilt one hundred and twenty yards farther out."

"Beyond . . . ?"

"Yes, Sir, beyond the old spreading live oak tree. The Priority Order is being typed into the proper form for His Honor Pete the Key and for Your Honor the HGK at this time."

The HGK seemed sober. He said, "You are a fine fellow. Have a little drink." He pushed the jug forward on the polished desk.

"Just a sip, your honor, to show my loyalty." Then the head guard took such a big drink that his Adam's apple bobbed four times.

"You are an excellent fellow, Head Guard. Do you think this Mr. Leadbelly with his twelve-string guitar might have any songs relating to the problems of a manager or an administrator or . . . say . . . a bureaucrat."

"I'm not sure, your honor. He has one about 'Them Bushwah Blues.' "

"Do you suppose if I disguised myself that I could climb the fence tonight without being recognized?"

"I will give strict orders that your honor is not to be recognized."

"You are surely a fine officer. Have another little sip."

J.B.'s Ingenious Color-Seater

If I had to describe J.B. in one word, I would call him a genius. I'm glad I don't have to. In the first place I would be crazy to try to describe him at all; in the second place, J.B. is more than a genius in lots of ways, and I never knew him to be much less than a genius in anything he did.

They say genius is the infinite capacity for taking pains. J.B. certainly was never like that. Whenever an idea came into his head, it came all in a flash; but when he started to tell you about it, it came out like something he'd been thinking about for weeks. His mind just completely ran off and left any average mind.

That's the way it was when this bus business started. He began talking about his plan for seating in buses, and I was so far behind him, I couldn't make heads or tails out of what he was talking about. "Wait a minute, J.B.," I had to say. "Start over from the first and explain it all to me."

"What in the world is it that you don't understand?" He was a little disgusted with me, and I couldn't blame him much.

"I don't see the reason behind all this fancy business for making people sit in certain seats," I told him.

"You know that niggers have to sit in the back of buses, don't you? The law makes them."

"Yes, I know that, J.B."

"You know why they have to sit in the back of buses, don't you?"

I nodded vigorously. "Everybody knows that," I said.

"Well, *why?*"

J.B. had me there. All I could do was stammer at him. He sat there looking at me, and I sat there stammering and trying to think up something sensible to say.

"It's because they don't smell good, isn't it?" J.B. said.

"Well, I don't know," I told him. I hated it to seem like I was just agreeing to everything he said. "I think maybe—"

"You think maybe," J.B. mocked. "You don't know. Don't tell me you're another one of those nigger-lovers?"

I changed my way of talking pretty fast then. I certainly didn't want to be known as a nigger-lover. "Of course not, J.B.," I said. "You're right. Niggers do smell. I was just wondering if that was the only reason they have to sit in the back."

"That's one of the main reasons, but it really doesn't matter whether it is or not. I'm just using it to illustrate."

"Oh, I see," I answered, waiting for him to start illustrating.

"Now it's perfectly reasonable to say that some niggers smell worse than others."

I had to admit that it was.

"Then why not let those that smell worst of all sit on the very back seats, and those who don't smell so bad sit between them and the white people."

I nodded but he went right on without paying any attention to whether I agreed with him or not.

"Then take Mexicans. They don't smell too good but at least they don't smell so much like goats. Why not put them between the good-smelling niggers and the white people?"

I nodded some more.

"Even a white man that's been out digging ditches all day may not be too dainty. There's no reason why he shouldn't sit back a few seats from the front."

I began to see what he was driving at. "You mean, J.B., that the smell keeps getting fainter and fainter as you go to the front of the bus?"

"That's the general idea," J.B. said. "You're taking it too literal though. I'm just using smell to illustrate the whole idea. I'm going to use color to actually make the distinction."

I finally caught on. "Oh, I see. That's where that color-seater with the electric eye comes in—the one you were talking about a while ago."

"I knew you'd catch on eventually," J.B. said. "I've got confidence in you, boy."

I grinned at him even though I knew he meant it sarcastically.

"Now here is the way it will work," J.B. went on. "A customer gets on the bus and puts his nickel in the slot. This starts the electric eye to scanning his face. When it gets him classified, it opens the correct door and allows him to go in to the row of seats where he belongs. There can't be any arguments about it, because it's all done mechanically."

J.B. looked at me with a satisfied smile. I knew he had it all figured out but I couldn't help being a little dubious.

"Can an electric eye do all that?" I asked him.

"Sure, an electric eye can do anything. They have them checking tin cans to see if there are any holes in them, and the electric eye finds every hole, no matter how small it is. You've seen these trick drinking fountains with an electric eye to turn them on, haven't you?"

I admitted that an electric eye could probably do the work, all right, but I had another question. "Are you sure you want to divide them up according to color, J.B.? I mean, will it always work out okay that way?"

"That's the beauty of it, lad. You figure it out sometime. Just think about them all: niggers, wops, spicks, Indians, Jews, dagos. Figure out where you think each of them should sit and see where the color-seater will put them. You'll have the white people in the front, the niggers in the back, and all the others strung out in the exact seats where they belong. Figure it out sometime."

Well, I thought he was kind of silly saying that they would all be strung out in the exact seats where they belonged, but I went ahead like he said and tried to figure it out on my way home that night. I began to see that there was going to be considerable lapping over. For instance, some of the light-colored Negroes would be sitting beside some of the darker Mexicans; and the Greeks, Italians, and Jews would be all mixed up. Some of the lighter ones would come up into the edge of the white people. Then's when I began to really appreciate J.B.'s plan. After all, some Negroes deserve to be ahead of some Mexicans; and maybe one Jew should be placed in front of an Italian, while another would belong behind him. By George, I thought, maybe sometime I'll get enough sense not to try to find loopholes in any of J.B.'s brain children.

I slept on the idea that night and dropped in to J.B.'s office the next afternoon when I got off from work. J.B. is the third assistant to the district manager of the Bloomingham City Bus Company, Incorporated, and he has a real nice office down where the car barns are on Twenty-seventh Street. The company's got bus lines in about twenty small cities and a couple of big ones. J.B.'s uncle owns fifty-one percent of all the stock. That's why I've got so much respect for J.B.—because he not only has a very original brain, but holds down a very important job as well.

"Look at this! Look at this," J.B. said when I came in. He was waving a big piece of paper with some drawings on it, but when I tried to get a look, he hunched down over it so low that I could hardly make out what it was.

"What is it, J.B.?"

"It's the plans, of course. This is what it's going to look like." He finished printing "Bloomingham City Bus Company, Incorporated" on it and finally let me get a good look at it.

J.B. doesn't draw well, but I couldn't keep from being impressed with the complicated maze of lines. I noticed that "Bloomingham City Bus Company, Incorporated" was standing up on its end the way I was holding the paper, so I turned it over right. It looked the same as before.

"It looks swell, J.B.," I said. "That ought to do the trick, all right."

"Aw, it's not much of a drawing," J.B. said modestly, "but it'll be good enough to work from. I'm going to start them to fixing up a bus in the morning."

"My gosh, J.B., you're not going to fix up one of the Bloomingham buses, are you?"

"Why not, I'd like to know."

"Why, you might—I mean, somebody might not like it."

"Listen, boy, I'm the assistant district manager around this place." J.B. began to pound on his desk. "I'm one of the bosses. What do you mean 'somebody might not like it'?"

I started to mention that he was only the third assistant to the district manager, but he stopped pounding on the desk so I decided not to bring it up. "I just meant your uncle," I said. "Do you think he would like it?"

"He's not going to know anything about it. No one is going to get any credit for this but me. I'm not saying a thing until I have one bus fixed up and then I'm going to surprise them."

J.B. glared at me like he thought I didn't agree with what he said so I changed the subject.

"I thought over what you said last night about the color-seater putting everybody in the seat where they belong, J.B."

"And what momentous decision did you arrive at?"

"Well, it's going to work better than I thought it was at first. When I thought it all out, I could see that."

"Here's the thing about it," J.B. said. "Before you can appreciate it you've got to be broad-minded. Take a farmer, now—he's just as good as me or you, isn't he?"

"Sure," I said, "there's nothing the matter with being a farmer."

"Well, go back to our illustration about smell. This farmer is used to being around horses and walking around in the cow pen and things like that. Now, you might say that he smells a little bit; at least you can say that he doesn't mind a bad smell too much."

"Yeah, that's reasonable," I said.

"Now, isn't that farmer likely to be sunburned?"

"Sure, most of them are," I said.

"Well, there you are. He can sit between all the foreigners and the white people. You might as well be realistic about it. I try to be broad-minded, but any one has to admit that there are differences even between white people. It's just plain ignorance to recognize only white and black and not any shades in between."

I agreed wholeheartedly with J.B., but there was one little part of the matter that neither of us thought about. It was something important enough that it might have ruined the whole scheme, if we hadn't run onto the idea by accident about a week later.

J.B. and I were walking down East Main Street, and I remember he told me all about how the work was coming on the bus they were fixing up down at the car barns. The electrical stuff had just come in that morning and he thought they would have it all ready to go in three more days. We stopped to wait for a red light before crossing the street. A Bloomingham bus pulled up in front of us. Then was when it happened.

Out of that bus came the most perfect example of class that I have ever seen in any female. She was tall and graceful and had an air about her that made you know she had money or else should have had money. Her long blond hair sparkled like twenty-carat gold in the sunshine.

It was her complexion that attracted our attention. I would bet five to one that she had spent the last two or three months at Miami Beach or in Southern California.

I looked at J.B. to see what he would say about it. She was halfway down the block and he was still following her with his eyes. "There'll have to be a beach-button," he said finally.

"A what, J.B.?"

"A beach-button." He said it like a beach-button was something that you see around all the time and doesn't need any explanation.

"What does it look like?" I asked.

"What does any button look like?" J.B. was slightly peeved. It was several minutes before he finally explained that he was talking about a control button which the driver could push and let any passenger come into the front seat instead of where the color-seater would have put them.

"It won't all be done mechanically then, will it, J.B.?" I said.

"No, but that's the best we can do. I was counting on doing away with the human element altogether, but it won't hurt too much. People like that girl don't ride the buses much."

J.B. and I had planned to drop in at the Kozy Korner for lunch, but he wouldn't consider it now. He said he had to get back to the car barns and start them to working on the beach-button. His uncle would be in town on an inspection tour in four days, and he still hoped to get the bus all finished by then so his uncle could be in at the grand unveiling.

That was one thing I really didn't want to miss and I knew J.B. would let me in on it, me being about the only real good friend he had. I could hardly wait to see the expression on the faces of the district manager and J.B.'s uncle when they saw the color-seater. There was even some vague idea in the back of my mind that maybe they would connect me with the invention some way and give me a job.

J.B. called me up about the middle of the morning on the day when his uncle was supposed to be there. He was all excited. "The bus is finished," he said, "all but just a couple of small details, and my uncle and the district manager are here. Come on over if you want to."

I asked him if he was kidding about me wanting to. Fifteen minutes later I was walking into his office down where the car barns are on Twenty-seventh Street.

J.B.'s uncle was an old man with a fat face and little, suspicious eyes. The district manager was slight of build and I noticed he was careful to look suspiciously at everything which the old man regarded with suspicion. They didn't seem to be overly impressed with me.

No one asked me to sit down, and I was wondering if I ought to when J.B.'s telephone rang. He grabbed it like he was afraid it would get away. "Is it all finished? All ready to go? Well, listen, tell that extra driver down there to jump in and get it up here to the front office right away."

J.B. hung up with a triumphant grin and we all went outside to wait for the bus to come up from the shops.

"Now maybe we'll find out what all this crazy business is about," J.B.'s uncle said.

"I may as well start explaining it," J.B. announced. "You know all the trouble we always have with carrying Negroes and white people on the same buses. Well, my invention, the color-seater, takes care of the whole thing mechanically and, I might add, completely." He went on talking about it without telling exactly how it worked. J.B.'s uncle didn't say anything, so the district manager didn't say anything either.

About ten minutes passed and the bus hadn't come. "For heaven's sake; let's see this idiotic contraption," J.B.'s uncle said.

We walked around the office and down about two hundred yards to the shop where the bus was. It was the first time I had seen the color-seater. It was a big shiny chrome structure sitting just inside the door of the bus. The rest of the doorway was blocked with the small doors that led to the various seats. The bus driver was standing by the door with a puzzled look on his face.

"What's the matter, man?" J.B. asked.

"I can't get in this durned thing," the bus driver told him.

"You go right in through there," J.B. said pointing. "The door that leads to the front seat leads to the driver's seat too."

"I haven't got a nickel change."

"Oh, of all things," J.B. said. He fished a nickel out of his pocket and gave it to the man.

The driver stepped up into the doorway and gingerly inserted the nickel in the slot. There was a slight buzzing noise which slowly increased to a rattle, finishing off with a metallic click; then one of the doors swung slowly open. The driver shrugged his shoulders and stepped inside.

I glanced sideways at J.B.'s uncle to see if he fully appreciated the smooth operation of the color-seater. The old man was looking at J.B. and I couldn't make anything out of his cold, expressionless face.

"Hey," the driver shouted from inside the bus. "I still can't get up where I belong."

The color-seater had put him in the second row of seats.

"Oh, my aching back," J.B. said as he looked in the window. "We'll have to try to reach the beach-button from the outside some way."

"That won't be necessary," J.B.'s uncle said. He was calmer than usual and spoke slowly. "Nephew, you are fired." Then he turned those beady eyes on me. "You also are fired."

I just turned around and walked off without even telling him that I didn't work there. Some people haven't the slightest respect for genius.

Uncle Rufus and the Cat-Scratch

If you want to find out what kind of a man Uncle Rufus is, don't ask Aunt Mamie. You'll get your left ear talked off with a lot of yap-yap, which don't mean anything but the same thing over and over again, which is Aunt Mamie's way. When it comes to Uncle Rufus, she is prejudiced. This is on account of having to live with the, as she says, no-good, worthless hound for thirty years. But if you go over around Red Dog, where there's people that appreciates a man that can drink liquor like an empty barrel and can string out twenty cuss words without getting his breath and can keep up with a pack of coon dogs all night and can outdo any two ordinary men at plain raising cane, there's where to find out about Uncle Rufus. You can get the straight dope on him around Red Dog.

As for drinking liquor, this being a dry county and it being illegal across the river on account of you can't sell it on a Indian reservation, what you drink is cat-scratch. The main expert on it around here is Slim Wiggins. He runs off a batch every week down near . . . but it ain't nobody's business where, it being enough to mention that there is plenty of wooded brakes in the bottomland along Red River where don't anybody ever go except Slim Wiggins's friends.

Some people say cat-scratch will give you a cast-iron stomach, others saying if you don't already have a cast-iron stomach before you take your first drink, it won't give you nothing but delirium tremens besides going blind. You can safely look for anybody that drinks it regular to

also be able to eat devils-head cactus and prickly pears and not notice
the stickers.

The story on Uncle Rufus's drinking is as follows: Aunt Mamie came
out in the backyard one evening and told him she didn't have no coal
oil to cook supper on and he was going to have to take the jug and go
down to the filling station after some, or else get on that woodpile and
cut some wood and fire up the wood stove, them having the two
stoves. Uncle Rufus said he'd go after the coal oil, as he'd been thinking
about going down there anyway and besides he didn't care to be cutting
any wood on such a hot day, it being hot that evening when you got
out of the shade of the cottonwood tree in the backyard where he was.

Uncle Rufus took the jug and went down to the filling station. He
came near to forgetting all about the coal oil, as it wasn't his main idea
for going to the store, no matter what Aunt Mamie thought. And it
wasn't the main business of the feller that run the filling station to sell
coal oil or gasoline either, him being one of Slim Wiggins's dealers.
Him and Uncle Rufus got to dickering over a gallon of cat-scratch. Cat-
scratch hasn't got a set price, which is right, some batches being better
than others and a man wanting it worse sometimes than others and a
man having more money sometimes than others. The filling station
feller didn't have a chance. Uncle Rufus not only talked him down to
dirt cheap, being as good a talker as Aunt Mamie when it came to a
gallon of cat-scratch, but also got him to put it on the bill along with
the coal oil, which Aunt Mamie would pay at the end of the month.

When Uncle Rufus got halfway home, he got tired and hot, it being
uphill all the way from the county road to where he lives. He began to
think it wouldn't hurt to stop and have a little drink, which he did, it
not being the only one, as he stopped and did the same thing every
twenty steps from there on the rest of the way home. It had a good
effect on him being hot and tired, and Uncle Rufus made up his mind
to be sure and tell Slim Wiggins this was the mildest and best-tasting
batch he had run off in a coon's age and not to forget how he did it so
he could do it again.

When he came in, Aunt Mamie began to ask him how come him to
be so long getting the coal oil and how come him to waste his money
on that cat-scratch and she better not find it on the oil bill; but Uncle
Rufus paid no mind to her yap-yap, but went straight on through the
house with his jug and set down under the cottonwood tree. He'd no
sooner uncorked the jug and had a little drink, than Aunt Mamie came
flying out the back door with her hands raised up in front and her hair

knot jiggling on top of her head, and all the time yelling like Gabriel had at last done his duty. "You old fool!" she hollered. "I've filled up my stove with cat-scratch, and you've drank a half gallon of coal oil!"

Uncle Rufus began to look at the jug and he said, "It did taste kind of funny."

Aunt Mamie kept on yelling and calling him an old fool, so Uncle Rufus said, "What's the matter? Ain't a half a gallon of coal oil enough for you to cook supper on?" Then he went inside and drained the cat-scratch out of the stove back into the jug it came in and took it back out to the cottonwood tree shade, which wasn't much of a shade that time of the evening as the sun was getting low.

This may sound like the end of the story on Uncle Rufus's drinking, but it is not, as the end is further on, as well as the best part.

Aunt Mamie stood here, holding the back screen door open and fussing at Uncle Rufus. She said, "Here you have gone and drank all that coal oil, and you'll be sick, and you know good and well tonight is when we've got to go to the meeting."

"What meeting?" Uncle Rufus said.

"What meeting?" she said, saying it the same as he said it, as she thought it would be sarcastic to do that. "Don't act so innocent. You know good and well tonight is when the revival meeting starts over at the schoolhouse. We've got to go, too, even if you get sick as a horse, because anybody that ain't there on the first night, everybody this side of Red River will talk about them."

"Why don't you stop your yapping," Uncle Rufus said, "and go cook supper."

"You ain't going to want any supper when that coal oil hits you," Aunt Mamie said, thinking the coal oil would have some bad effect, as she didn't take any stock in that talk about cat-scratch giving you a cast-iron stomach.

Uncle Rufus had a little drink. "You better go cook supper if you want me to go to meeting with you," he said, "because I sure can't go on a empty stomach."

Then she began to say she would go cook supper, but for him not to drink any more, because it wasn't the thing to do, as the meeting started at eight. But Uncle Rufus argued her out of that, saying he had to have a little drink or two to kill the smell of coal oil on his breath, as someone might notice it and wonder what he'd been drinking.

Uncle Rufus asked her if he had time to have chew of tobacco before supper, and she said "no" so he took him a big chew. Besides being all the other things that he was, Uncle Rufus was quite a tobacco chewer, being able to keep it in his mouth even while drinking cat-scratch. Nobody could find out how he did it, as there is danger in even trying it, as you are liable to get the two mixed. Uncle Rufus doesn't mess with any little wad of tobacco either. He takes a half a plug of Brown's Mule, which is a good-size chew, and having a good bit of strength. As Aunt Mamie says, "When he spits out a chew, it looks like where a mule had passed by," and then says, thinking it's funny, "Maybe it was a mule passed by," it being Aunt Mamie's way to always be casting reflections at Uncle Rufus.

When she finally got supper fixed, there was cabbage, which Uncle Rufus thought was the best thing there was to eat. He always claimed it tasted better than most things, besides being cheap and probably having a bunch of vitamins that nobody knows about. Aunt Mamie kept asking him if he was going to eat the whole pot. Uncle Rufus said, "I don't know but what I might. It's a cinch I don't want to go to no revival meeting on a empty stomach."

After supper, he had two more little drinks before they took off for the schoolhouse. Everybody else was already there, talking and joshing and waiting for Brother Johnson to begin the meeting. One of Uncle Rufus's admirers, him having many admirers on account of being the man he was, offered him a cigar; and Uncle Rufus took it, it not having ever occurred to him to take up cigar smoking along with all the other things he did, but anyhow he thought it was a good idea.

Brother Johnson was a long-winded talker. Once he got lined out, there wasn't no stopping him, as he would say all he knew about one text and then go right into another one, making you wonder if he aimed to go on all night. The people around Red Dog would rather have a little life in their meetings.

Uncle Rufus and Aunt Mamie sat in the back row. Aunt Mamie kept cutting her eyes sideways at him, wondering about him, as he had a strained look on his face and his eyes looked like a dead chicken's eyes. Uncle Rufus had both hands cupped down around his stomach, which was stuck out considerable more than usual, him being a skinny man.

Brother Johnson had run on for two solid hours. He was about to take up a new text, being run out of something to say on the one he was on.

All of a sudden Uncle Rufus stood up. He had taken it into his head to light his cigar, not saying a thing or giving any reason but only standing up and fishing in his pocket for a match. He bit the end of the cigar off. His face was red like a rooster's comb. Aunt Mamie was poking him in the leg and hissing at him, "Set down! You old fool, set down!"

Nobody knowing what goes on in Uncle Rufus's mind, it can't be said why he took it into his head to smoke a cigar at the meeting, it not being considered good manners around Red Dog. Some say he was jealous of Brother Johnson getting so much attention; others say he appeared to be under a strain that night; a few said it was the hand of Providence.

Brother Johnson started reading his new text. "In those days shall appear an angel and out of . . ." He looked up at the disturbance in the last row.

Uncle Rufus was trying to strike a match.

Brother Johnson tried again, louder. "In those days shall appear an angel and out of his mouth . . ."

A sort of rumble came from the last row.

Brother Johnson saw that he was losing the attention of the people in the rear. He shouted in his loudest, most-dignified voice, him being an impressive speaker when he really cut loose. "And out of his mouth shall come a two-edged sword of fire!"

From the last row came a pop like you'd pulled the cork. Uncle Rufus was standing up and all rared back. In his right hand was a match. In his left hand was a cigar. Out of his mouth came a two-edged sword of fire!

Everybody at the meeting began doing things; Brother Johnson taking the window sash with him as he left; his wife yelling, "Hallelujah!" Granny Sykes talking in the unknown tongue; the justice of the peace drawing his guns and trying to shoot the lights out; seven women fainting; and the mayor of Red Dog trampling a widow and two orphans as he tried to get to the door. Everybody did something, if they did it wrong. The meeting was over.

Aunt Mamie didn't say anything to Uncle Rufus on the way home, or the next day, not saying much for several days, only such things as "come to supper" when he lay out under the cottonwood, not giving him any yap-yap at all. She was still so snowed under at the first of the month, it being the date to pay up, that she didn't say a word about the gallon of cat-scratch on the oil bill down at the filling station.

Dear Friends

April 1, 1986

Chlorine, gather all these pieces together, type it up, copy it for my mailing list. Just find as many addresses as you can. But make sure you do not send a copy to Joe Ben Capps. That character will make fun of me and tease me.

Dear Friends:

I write you to ask that if you hear a rumor about my stealing chickens, try to scotch it and tell people I never stole a chicken in my life.

First, the situation here. My cell backs up on the alley, and I have worked loose a small pane of glass. I can push out notes written on toilet paper to my dependable typist, Chlorine Smith. I can get some toilet paper from the cells on both sides, one a young man who was caught rolling a funny cigarette and one an old man who was caught with no visible means of support. The jailer is stingy and says I use too much toilet paper.

Now, recent events. I was strolling along the Brazos River bottoms in Alamo County late at night, meditating and trying to get a good idea to get rich writing. I had my tow sack and flashlight. As you know, fishermen sit on the banks and drink beer and cokes, and when one is empty they fling it back over their shoulder into the brush. But some aluminum can hunter must have beat me to it, for I did not find a single can. I felt sad and hungry. Then I saw up on a rise of land a white-painted modern chicken house, the kind they raise fryers in for the market. It came to me how good it would be to build up a small fire and roast a nice chicken. It was 2 A.M. in the morning, and they would not be awake, but I would leave a dollar bill on the door hasp where they would see it.

To make a long story short, I was caught in a white-painted modern chicken house at 2 A.M. in the morning with a tow sack and a flashlight. By a mad old chicken man with a 12-gauge double-barrel shotgun. He would not listen to reason. The constable would not listen to reason. The Alamo County sheriff would not listen to reason. The jailer will not listen to reason.

My trial comes up August 5.

They give us four pieces of day-old bread and one cup of water each day, but I can dip water out of the top part of the commode when they are not watching.

As you probably know, each spring in the month of May, here at the capital of Alamo County, they hold a grand fiesta for several days. They have a rattlesnake hunt, terrapin race, old-fiddlers' contest, hog calling, husband calling, cockroach race, hat-stomping contest, greased-pig chase for kids under twelve, and many other exciting events. The highlight of the whole celebration is the final event—the public flogging of the inmates of the county jail on the courthouse lawn.

It is considered a great honor to be the Wielder of the Lash, and the County Commissioners by vote selected two finalists they thought are qualified: Mad Dog McGurk and Rowdy Joe Loudermilk. News of the finalists came to us by grapevine, and I'm telling you some colored guy in the cell at the end of the corridor moaned all night. "Oh, Lawd! Not Mad Dog McGurk! No! No! Anybody but Mad Dog! Please, Lawd! No! No!" You couldn't hardly sleep.

Well, we got lucky. They flipped a coin and Rowdy Joe Loudermilk won. As you may know, he was a bear trainer before he went into wrestling. I guess he did bite one of his opponents' ears off in a match, but they say he's cheerful. I'm one of the lucky ones. Horse stealing and insulting county officials is thirty lashes, but spitting on the sidewalk and chicken stealing is only fifteen. Besides, they say Rowdy Joe yells and laughs and jumps around so much he uses up a lot of his energy that way. Furthermore, the county medical officer, a certified veterinarian, stands by with a swab and a bucket of saltwater in case of excessive bleeding.

Anyway, just wanted you all to know the facts. My dependable typist, Chlorine Smith, will relay this on to you. Remember to scotch any rumors about my stealing chickens.

Am doing fine and hope you are the same.

Just sign it Ben, Chlorine.

Dear Sir or Madam as the case may be:

This is a note to explain. If you have ever tried to type something up off of wadded-up toilet paper written on with a pencil, then you will excuse my efforts.

It is difficult to keep Mr. Capps's office running properly on account of the expenses. I cash his royalty checks but they hardly cover all that should be covered. I have had to cut down on office parties because of lack of funds.

As you may know, Mr. Capps has stated that he would try to improve my character. He has advised that I stop reading romance novels and drinking gin and start reading westerns and drinking bourbon. I have already read *Riders of the Purple Sage* and drank seven gallons of bourbon. With every gallon I feel that my character is improving.

As for the rumor about chicken stealing, please put your mind at rest. I have a lot of friends and kin who are connected with the media. I called my cousin in Bangor, Maine, who works on a newspaper, and told her about it, and she did not think it is a serious problem. Same with my niece, who is society editor of the *Atlanta Constitution.* Same with my second cousin, who writes a gossip column for the *Denver Post.* Same with my sister-in-law, who works for a magazine in San Francisco. So I do not believe the story will spread around the country very much.

Must close this letter, as I have to go to the liquor store and get office supplies.

Very Truly Yours,
Y'r Ob'd'n't S'r'v'n't,
CHLORINE SMITH, Office Manager

April 1, 1987

Dear Friends of the Capps-Smith Writing Service:
Knowing that you would want to know how the business is doing since Mr. Capps escaped from jail, I drop you this line to let you know the facts.

Well, he moped around all the time and frowned, and he was trying to think of some good things to write about to get rich. I realized that his brain was tired, so fortunately I worked up a good plan. I took seventeen multivitamin capsules and dissolved them in a cup of sulfuric acid. When Mr. Capps was sleeping on his side, I poured two tablespoonfuls in his ear. He twitched a good bit, then got still, so, seeing that it was all right, I poured the whole cupful in his ear. He stayed still a long time, so I tried to awaken him, but could not. I had to call the ambulance.

Fortunately, the office is only two miles from a big modern hospital where they do organ transplants and everything. In fact they have been doing experimental transplants of simian brains, whatever that is.

The nurse let me go to the operating room with her and gave me a white smock to put on. When the surgeon put down the saws and knives and took out Mr. Capps's green-looking brain, the nurse passed out. Fortunately, I had taken a few drinks that day or I might have passed out too. The surgeon put the brain in a white dish, gave it to me, and said, "Here, take this down to the basement lab and ask them to clean it good."

Well, that was on the seventh floor and I didn't trust the elevator, so I took the stairs. The dish was slick and the brain was slimy. A little ways down it slipped out of the dish and went tumbling down. Then a gray tom cat came from somewhere and started chasing it. I thought he might help me with the brain, help catch it, but he didn't. He would bat it back and forth with his paws and shake it back and forth with his teeth. When I would come close, the cat would bat it tumbling down the next flight of steps. By the time we got down to the basement, Mr. Capps's brain was so dirty and strung out from being shook back and forth that I didn't even try to stop the tom cat when he ran out the back door with it.

Fortunately I saw a laboratory door open, and a shelf had a row of nice clean brains in big clear jars. I took a big pink one that looked nice and put it in my white dish. This time I took the elevator to go back up to the operating room. The surgeon seemed pleased that it was clean.

To make a long story short, Mr. Capps recovered very nice, and I took him home in three weeks. But he seemed changed. He was so filthy in his habits that I had to chain him to a tree in the backyard. His legs are kind of bowed for some reason. But he seems happy. When I take him a banana, he jumps up and down and says, "Chee! Chee!" and scratches himself on both sides. Mr. Capps is a very proud person, and I know he doesn't wish to smell bad, so I hose him down once a week with the garden hose.

As you know, office expenses are very high, and royalty checks are no bigger, so I have had to economize and cut down on office parties. All of Mr. Capps's lifetime savings were taken up in hospital bills and transplant services. Also, I had to make an out-of-court settlement with the hospital director, who claimed I had poisoned his tom cat. Then, thinking we might increase the income by selling writing, I gave Mr. Capps a pencil and piece of paper. He ate the paper and stuck the pencil in his ear.

Fortunately, my Uncle Lige passed away just in time. He was famous in the Ozarks, of course, for making the best refreshing drink for miles around, and he had been wounded by the revenoors five times. Anyway, he left some of his best equipment to me, mash barrel, boiler, copper tubing, and all. I have set it up in the Smith-Capps Writing Service offices.

Uncle Lige used wood to burn under the boiler, and my biggest problem was to find something good to burn. Fortunately, I had a great idea . . . books. Mr. Capps had got hold of many books, thousands, the bookshelves full and stacked around on the floor in three rooms. I found out that they will burn good and a long time. Most of them have already been read at least once, and some are quite worn, just sitting around in the way, taking up space.

Mr. Capps's chain is long enough for him to come up to the window. He acts funny when I stoke the boiler. He did not do a thing when I burned Plato, but started moaning when I burned Homer and Aristotle. Same moans with Chaucer and Cervantes, which is some kind of foreign language nobody can read. Same with Gibbon and Shakespeare and H. G. Wells and Durant and Prescott and those kind nobody ever heard of. And a bunch of Russians. Well, I buy a few romances to read between office parties and waiting on customers in the alley, and when he sees me putting romances under the boiler, that's the only time he laughs. He moans most from Melville and Mark Twain and Faulkner and Steinbeck, and a big tear will run down his cheek when he's looking in the window. I think Mr. Capps acts funny that way because he wants to come inside and help with the increased business, but he has such nasty habits that it is not best to unchain him.

I run off about two gallons a day for office use and three or four more for sale in order to meet rising office costs. As receptionist as well as office manager, I have to dress well and now am able to add nice suits, shoes, coats, and other apparel to my wardrobe.

We are all doing well and hope you are the same.

Sincerely your ob'd-'nt servant.

CHLORINE SMITH
President and Manager
Smith-Capps Writing Service